"Don't worry," Reed assured her

"Despite your anxiety, you're perfectly safe with me."

Helen took a deep breath. "I'm not anxious," she declared, and although the words sounded defensive, it was true. No matter how unlikely it might seem in the circumstances, she did trust him.

"No?" Reed questioned now, regarding her with some skepticism. "Forgive me if I find that hard to believe."

Helen bent her head. "That's your problem," she said tautly.

"Yes, it is." Reed's fingers drummed on the table for a moment. "Or rather, you are," he added cryptically. He paused, and then continued softly, "Because we have met before, haven't we, Helen? As soon as I touched you, it all fell into place."

ANNE MATHER began her career by writing the kind of book she likes to read—romance. Married, with two teenage children, this northern England author has become a favorite with readers of romance fiction the world over—her books have been translated into many languages and are read in countless countries. Since her first novel was published in 1970, Anne Mather has written more than eighty romances, with over ninety million copies sold!

Books by Anne Mather

STORMSPELL
WILD CONCERTO
HIDDEN IN THE FLAME
THE LONGEST PLEASURE

HARLEQUIN PRESENTS
1044—BURNING INHERITANCE
1122—TRIAL OF INNOCENCE
1210—DARK MOSAIC
1251—A FEVER IN THE BLOOD
1315—A RELATIVE BETRAYAL
1354—INDISCRETION

HARLEQUIN ROMANCE
1631—MASQUERADE
1656—AUTUMN OF THE WITCH

ANNE MATHER

blind passion

Harlequin Books

TORONTO • NEW YORK • LONDON
AMSTERDAM • PARIS • SYDNEY • HAMBURG
STOCKHOLM • ATHENS • TOKYO • MILAN

Harlequin Presents first edition March 1992
ISBN 0-373-11444-3

Original hardcover edition published in 1991
by Mills & Boon Limited

BLIND PASSION

CHAPTER ONE

'BUT why does Jonathan have to come *this* weekend?'

Ignoring the sunlight streaming on to the terrace, and the blue-green waters of the Sound creaming on to the rocks below the balcony, Victoria Wyatt regarded her brother's bent head across the breakfast table with an unconcealed air of frustration. It wasn't as if it was the first time she had asked the question, since her nephew had phoned to say he was coming home for a couple of weeks at the beginning of July and bringing a guest. But either Reed wasn't listening, or he refused to give her a straight answer, and the time was fast approaching when it would be too late to make alternative arrangements.

'Reed!' she said again, sharply and impatiently, and, as if her shrill use of his name had at last got through to him, her brother lifted his eyes from the air-mailed copy of the *Financial Times* that had arrived from London the previous afternoon.

'This is his home, too, Tori,' he remarked mildly, though his expression was not entirely serene. 'It's not as if he spends a lot of time on the island, is it? What do you want me to do? Tell him he can't come?'

'No. No, of course not.' Victoria plucked irritably at her napkin, her long nails scarlet slashes against the crisp white linen. 'It's just that I've made all the arrangements for the party, and I don't want Jonathan, or one of his awful girlfriends, fouling things up. This is an important occasion, Reed. The opening of a new gallery is always a media event, and with Luther Styles making his debut it promises to be a huge success.' She pursed her lips. 'Or it did.'

Reed sighed, and put his paper aside, realising he was not going to be allowed a moment's peace until this matter was settled, one way or the other. 'So,' he said evenly, 'what do you want me to do?'

His sister lifted her rather well-padded shoulders and then, as she met Reed's cool grey gaze, her resentment subsided. 'I don't know, do I?'

'Don't you?' Reed contained his own impatience with an effort. 'I thought that was what this was all about. I thought you had a solution to the problem.'

'Not exactly.' Victoria's shoulders hunched. 'I only asked why it had to be this weekend that Jon came home. After all, as you said a few moments ago, it's not as if he treats this place as his home. More like a hotel, actually. Somewhere he comes when he's out of work, or out of cash!'

'I don't know any hotels, even here in Bermuda, that provide quite that service,' responded Reed drily. 'Nor do I remember saying that Jon didn't regard this place as his home. On the contrary, it's because this is his home that he expects to be able to invite himself here any time he chooses. And if he brings along a girlfriend, why should we object?'

'Because of the type of girls Jon is attracted to,' retorted Victoria shortly. 'Surely you haven't forgotten that awful hippy type he brought here two summers ago? The one who insisted she was "into" painting, and didn't know a Monet from a Matisse!'

'I know a lot of people who wouldn't know a Monet from a Matisse,' observed Reed flatly, but Victoria just ignored him, and continued her tirade.

'What about that dancer he brought last year?' she insisted. 'She said she performed body sculptures, and it wasn't until she had had too much to drink and started taking her clothes off that we discovered she was really a *stripper*!' She snorted. 'I was never so embarrassed in my life!'

'Oh, God!'

Reed breathed a sigh of resignation as Victoria wrapped the folds of her pure silk wrapper about her generous curves, and started to get up from the table. It was obvious his sister was not going to let the subject drop, and her sulky expression boded ill for family unity.

'Very well,' she said now, pausing by his chair. 'As usual, you refuse to listen to reason. So be it. Just don't blame me if the opening is a complete fiasco. It's not my money you're wasting.'

Reed groaned then, and, pushing back from the table, he got to his feet. 'You're seriously telling me that Jon's arrival could jeopardise the whole affair?'

'I'm saying that we don't want any adverse publicity, that's all. And after all, Jon is something of a—minor celebrity on the island.' She said this grudgingly. 'If he appears at the opening with some totally unsuitable female in tow, you can imagine what will be said. The tabloid Press would much rather print some gossipy piece about Jon and his latest conquest than concentrate on the *real* reason they've been invited.'

'Which is?'

'To give Luther Styles and the other painters the publicity they deserve,' exclaimed Victoria impatiently. 'Oh, really, Reed, you know that as well as I do. You just don't seem to care about the work I've put in.'

Reed shook his head. 'That's not true. I know you've worked hard to get the support, and the backing, to open the gallery.' He hesitated. 'How would it be if I expressly asked Jon not to attend the opening party? It's not as if it's his kind of thing anyway. And if he's bringing a— guest—with him, I doubt if he'll care about missing your "media event".'

Victoria sniffed and looked up at him a little mistily. At a fraction over six feet, Reed was considerably taller than she was, and despite her ample girth he always made her feel small, and feminine. Indeed, only Reed had ever been able to make her feel that way, and, knowing she owed her position in Bermudian society to the fact that her brother was one of the most influential men on the island, she never failed to thank providence that Reed's marriage had floundered. Of course, it had been a most unsuitable alliance, right from the start. Although Diana had had the right background, she had been far too flighty to settle down to marriage. She had needed constant amusement, and attention, and if Reed didn't give it to her she had sought it elsewhere. That was why Jon had turned out as he had, Victoria thought now. What else could you expect, when his parents had spent the first twelve years of his existence fighting a war of attrition? Nevertheless, it had made her life considerably easier, and, as marriage for its own sake had never appealed to her, she had happily returned from exile to pick up the pieces.

Now, she summoned up a beguiling smile, and lifted her hand to touch Reed's cheek. 'Will you do that, darling?' she exclaimed. 'Oh, I'd be so grateful. And relieved. You've no idea how important this is to me. To actually open a gallery here, in Hamilton. Well, it's like a dream come true!'

Reed wouldn't have put it in quite those terms, but he was quite prepared to believe that, to his sister, it was a momentous occasion. It was what she had been working towards ever since she returned to the island ten years ago. Oh, allegedly she had come back to take charge of his household, to take over the role Diana had never really played, and to look after Jonathan. But it was obvious, from the beginning, that Victoria had ideas of her own.

Until then, she had had to content herself with working in someone else's gallery, with discovering new talent for someone else to reap the kudos from. That was what she had been doing in New York, during the latter years of his marriage to Diana, but it was apparent that this didn't satisfy her—didn't fulfil her, as Victoria herself had put it.

Of course, it had been her choice to go and live in the United States after his marriage. Until then, she had been quite content to stay on the island, and ambition, in a woman, had been quite a dirty word. But, not surprisingly, she and Diana had never got on. Because Victoria had always been overweight, her size had never been a problem, but after his marriage to Diana it had suddenly become an issue. And Diana could be quite a bitch, when it suited her. Reed grimaced. Didn't he know it!

Anyway, Victoria had eventually decided to go and stay with some friends on Long Island, and from there she had graduated, with Reed's assistance, to her own apartment on the Upper East Side. That was when she had got her first job in a gallery, and from then on she had devoted herself to learning all she could.

Even so, it was quite a step from working in someone else's gallery to establishing a gallery of one's own, so perhaps it was not so surprising that she should be touchy about the opening, Reed reflected, as he lifted his jacket from the back of his chair and slid his arms into the sleeves. And because she had been there when he needed her, and because she was so intensely loyal, he felt he owed it to her to do what he could to make the occasion a success. Which probably meant playing the heavy father with Jon, he conceded, without much enthusiasm. But his son was inclined to mock what he called 'the establishment'.

He left for his office a few minutes later. His house, which was set on a promontory, overlooked the bay, with the white roofs of the island's capital, Hamilton, visible across the clear blue waters. Like other houses around it, it sprawled over half an acre, with extensive grounds. Their privacy was protected by thick screens of flowering shrubs. A private unpaved track gave access to the Harbour Road, and Reed negotiated the dusty Mercedes out of his driveway for the fifteen-minute drive to the city.

It was a beautiful morning, but then, most mornings on Bermuda were beautiful, he reflected drily. It had an almost ideal climate, and although he had been tempted many times to move nearer one of the financial capitals of the world, Bermuda was his home and he loved it.

His father had brought his family here thirty-five years ago. Robert Wyatt had unexpectedly inherited half a million pounds from a distant relative, and, although he might have been more sensible to invest the money in Britain, he had chosen to give up his job as a teacher and move to Bermuda.

With hindsight, of course, he had realised his mistake. Without a job, without roots, without any of the friends he had had in England, Reed's father had found that the idle life of a rich man soon began to pall. Reed supposed they could have moved back to England then, but his father had been a proud man, and giving up what he had seen as an impossible dream would have smacked too much of failure to Robert Wyatt. Instead, he had started to drink, and gamble, and by the time Reed was eighteen his parents' marriage was veering towards the rocks.

Even so, no one could have foreseen the tragic sequence of events that had happened during Reed's first term at university. Driving home from a drinks party one evening, his father had crashed his car, killing himself and a woman who had been with him. The shock had been too much for Reed's mother. The day after her husband's funeral, she had had a stroke from which she never recovered, and Reed had abandoned his studies to come home and be with his sixteen-year-old sister.

Of course, that had all happened many moons ago, thought Reed ruefully, braking for the lights at the entrance to Front Street. It was twenty-five years since his parents had died, and what to his father had never been a real home had become for him the place where he had put down roots. It had never occurred to him to pack up and go back to England when he and Victoria were orphaned. There had been enough money left for him to employ a housekeeper to take care of the house, and he, and Victoria, had completed their education on the island.

He had been lucky, he knew that. In his public life, at least. It was as if his father's lack of success with money had given him the will to succeed, and his ability to predict trends was quickly recognised. Banking had always fascinated him, and he had been fortunate enough, upon leaving college, to join a firm of merchant bankers with worldwide connections.

Unfortunately, he had not been so successful in his private life. His precipitate marriage to Diana Charters, soon after leaving college, had been a big mistake. They had both been too young to make such a binding commitment, and, unlike Victoria, he didn't blame Diana for what had happened. During the early years of their relationship he had spent a lot of time travelling, visiting and working in the various branches of Jensen Lockwood, and learning the international money markets inside out. It hadn't made for a strong personal relationship and, not unnaturally, Diana had resented what she saw as the exciting life he was leading. She, meanwhile, had been closeted at home, knowing her sister-in-law resented her, and with a baby she had never wanted.

Yet, if it hadn't been for Jonathan, Reed knew the split would have come sooner. As it was, he had done his best to keep the marriage together for Jon's sake, even though common sense had told him that the boy would suffer either way. Eventually, when Diana deserted him for an American football player she had met during one of her frequent visits to the States, he had felt a sense of relief, a relief which was compounded when Jon decided he wanted to stay with his father.

Reed sighed now, manoeuvring the car through the stream of tourists disembarking from one of the cruise ships berthed at the quay. Hamilton was lucky enough to have a deep-water harbour, so that cruise ships could actually tie up in the heart of town, and during the summer months it was rare if one or more vessels were not tied up along Front Street.

Thinking of tourists, and Jon, brought his mind back to his son's projected visit, and his arrival the following afternoon. It was six months since he had seen his son, and while Victoria might consider that of little importance, Reed still felt a reluctant responsibility for the boy. Only he wasn't a boy any more, he reminded himself. Jon was twenty-two now, a year older than Reed had been when he married his mother. And for the past four years he had been making a creditable living in England, as lead guitarist with a marginally successful rock group called Cookie Fortune.

Victoria had been worried when Jon left school at sixteen, and announced his intention of trying to make a living in popular music. The years since Reed had joined the firm of Jensen Lockwood had seen many changes in their lives, not least her brother's rise from a very junior actuary to the bank's senior partner, and the idea of his son, and her nephew, making his name as a rock musician had filled her with dismay.

Actually, Jon had proved to be a good musician, and although he didn't make enough to keep him in the life-style to which he was accustomed, he preferred to live in England, where the action was, as he put it—which suited Victoria admirably. He saw his father as often as was necessary to ensure that the generous allowance Reed paid him didn't dry up, and although this horrified his sister Reed rarely took offence. As far as he was concerned, he was at least in part to blame for Jon's cavalier outlook on life, and as he had nothing—and no one—else to spend his money on, why not?

It was only when Jon came back to the island that the even tenor of his days was disrupted. Like his mother before him, Jon was apt to scrape nerves otherwise left untarnished. He was brash, and he was careless, and he could be an absolute pain on occasion, but equally he could be charming, and Reed preferred to be tolerant.

The British Airways flight from London had left at eleven-fifteen but, after six and a half hours of flying, it was still early afternoon in mid-Atlantic. Below the huge jet, the vast panorama of blue, blue sea was just occasionally being marred now by tiny specks of darkness, which Jon had told her were part of the hundred and fifty islands that made up the Bermuda archipelago. Although the seven principal islands of the group were linked together to form the main land mass, there were over a hundred uninhabited atolls, and Helen thought how amazing it was that they existed at all.

She had had plenty of time during the journey to think about this and other matters. After lunch had been served, and the shutters in the first-class cabin had been closed to allow the in-flight movie to be shown, Jon had fallen asleep. And, as she wasn't interested in the film, Helen had hoped that she might sleep, too. But she hadn't. Her mind was too active to allow her to relax, and she had spent the time worrying about their arrival.

After all, this was a mildly traumatic experience for her. Apart from the fact that she had never flown so far before, she had never been invited home to meet a boy-friend's parents. Or rather one parent, his father, a rather serious-sounding individual who was something of a financial wizard. She hoped he would like her. Jon was such a frenetic kind of person, it was difficult to imagine what his father might be like.

And then there was Alexa. She had left her daughter with her mother and father in the past, but it was the

first time she had left her for so long. Her job, as
personal assistant to the managing director of an engineering company, often entailed her being away over-
night in Paris, or Munich, or Brussels, and Alexa was
used to staying with her grandparents in Chiswick. But
that didn't stop Helen from worrying about her, or
wondering if she had done the right thing.

Not that Alexa seemed to mind. She was a happy child,
bright and well-balanced, and the fact that she had never
known her father didn't seem to trouble her. There were
several children from one-parent families in Alexa's
school, so perhaps that was why she took the situation
so philosophically.

Even so, Helen knew that *she* would miss her daughter.
They had always been very close, despite the fact that
Helen had always had to go out to work, and at the end
of the day she enjoyed the time they spent together.
Which was probably why there had been so few men in
her life, she acknowledged wryly. Those who were
prepared to tolerate a lively nine-year-old were usually
very boring.

Jon, however, had proved the exception, which was
remarkable really, considering he was four years younger
than she was, and a musician into the bargain. Helen
still found it incredibly difficult to assimilate the Jon
Roberts she knew with the public's image of a rock star.
Not that Jon was really a rock *star*. The group with
whom he played had never quite achieved that status.
But nevertheless he did have his own following of loyal
fans, and, until she had actually got to know him, she
would have put him down as just another wild performer.
Certainly, that was the image the newspapers chose to
promote. But then, who wanted to read about a talented
but law-abiding instrumentalist?

Helen supposed she might have got a different
impression if she had attended one of the group's con-
certs before meeting Jon. But she hadn't. She had been
sitting in the bar of a hotel in Munich, waiting for her
boss to come back from a meeting, when a dark, good-
looking young man, wearing jeans and a leather jacket,
had edged on to the stool beside her.

Even then, they might never have struck up a conversation. Helen was wary of speaking to strangers, particularly in foreign bars. But when she'd got up to leave she dropped her handbag, and Jon's head had bumped hers when they both bent to pick it up together.

'God, I'm sorry,' Jon had begun, and then, as if suspecting she didn't understand him, he'd added in hesitant German, *'Es tut mir leid——'*

'It's all right. I'm English,' Helen had interrupted him quickly, and the resulting laughter they had shared had broken the ice between them.

Surprisingly, for Helen, she had found Jon amazingly easy to talk to, and by the time her boss had come to join them the attraction between them had already taken root. In some ways he seemed a lot older than she was, but in others his youth and immaturity complemented her tendency to be too serious. He reminded her of someone, although she had never been able to decide who, but it had been obvious from the beginning that they intended to see one another again.

And they had. In spite of the demands of Cookie Fortune's German tour and Helen's own job in London, they had managed to see one another at least once a week for the next couple of months, and eventually Helen had invited him home to meet Alexa.

He had known about her daughter, of course. At the beginning of their relationship, Helen had told him she was a single parent, and that she and Alexa were very close. But Jon hadn't seemed to mind. Unlike some of the other men she had dated from time to time, he had shown no hesitation in being presented to an inquisitive nine-year-old, and, from the first, he and Alexa had become firm friends. It helped, naturally, that his image as a pop star raised Alexa's kudos among her schoolfriends, but, that aside, they shared an easy camaraderie. They liked many of the same things; they had a similar sense of humour; and, when they were together, Helen often thought that Alexa treated Jon like a favourite older brother.

Which was good for her association with Jon, too. It meant there was no tension when they were together, no incipient jealousy to spoil their growing affection for one

another. Indeed, if Helen had any doubts at all about
Jon, they were that she might be confusing the relief she
felt that Alexa didn't feel threatened with her own uncertain emotions. For the first time in her life, she had
found a man who could deal positively with her daughter.
But was that a significant part of their relationship, or
did she genuinely care for Jon?

It was a problem that she had yet to resolve, and this
holiday—this visit to Jon's home in Bermuda—was in
the nature of a sabbatical for both of them. She knew
Jon had spent very little time at home during the past
four years. She had wondered if his relationship with
his father was not all it should be, but when she asked
him Jon had denied any rift between them. Nevertheless, he had admitted that in recent years his vagrant
lifestyle had caused some friction in the household, not
least because his aunt, who lived with his father and acted
as his housekeeper, looked upon his occupation as a
blatant corruption of his musical talent.

'Aunt Vee would like me to play classical guitar,' Jon
had told Helen once, when they were discussing his aunt's
artistic leanings. 'Or Gilbert and Sullivan, at the very
least,' he added, his blue eyes sparkling roguishly. And
Helen, who suspected she knew him rather better than
his aunt, guessed that he was not averse to being deliberately provocative when it suited him.

Even so, it was not his aunt—however daunting she
might be—who caused Helen the most trepidation, as
the aircraft that had brought them from London began
its descent towards the islands. It was Jon's father who
presented the most immediate problem, and whether he
would consider that the fact that, as well as being four
years older than Jon, she had a nine-year-old daughter
created an insurmountable barrier to any serious
relationship with his son.

CHAPTER TWO

HELEN didn't quite know what she had expected Jon's
Aunt Vee to look like, but certainly any preconceptions
she had had were far from the truth. In all honesty, she
hadn't known what to expect of a middle-aged lady who
had devoted the latter half of her adult years to caring
for her brother and her nephew. She supposed the twin
ideas of an angular harridan or an apple-cheeked
motherly individual had been closest to any estimate she
had made, but Victoria Roberts defied description.

For one thing, she looked anything but angular, or
middle-aged. On the contrary, in spite of being at least
forty pounds overweight, Jon's aunt looked as exotic as
her surroundings. She wobbled into the reception area,
as they were clearing their luggage through Customs, on
heels at least four inches in height. Helen doubted she
could have stood up in the shoes, let alone walked in
them, but Jon's aunt was not very tall, and she evidently
felt she needed the extra inches. To add to this incon-
gruity, she was wearing a flowing gown in colours of
sun-streaked chiffon, and a wide-brimmed straw hat with
matching ribbons that floated behind her like a flag.

Helen didn't immediately know who she was, of
course. But her attention was caught, like that of the
other disembarking travellers. However, it was Jon who
swiftly enlightened her, his disrespectful wolf-whistle
causing an irritated blush to colour the lady's cheeks.

'Hey—Queen Vee!' he greeted her wickedly, abandoning their suitcases to a grinning porter and sweeping
his aunt into an all-enveloping hug that took her off her
feet. 'You came to meet us. Isn't that nice? I didn't realise you'd be so keen to see me.'

'I'm not,' retorted the fat little woman shortly, and
Helen knew a moment's anxiety until she met Jon's
laughing eyes. 'Oh, let go of me, Jonathan, do. You're
messing up my hair. Your father asked me to come and
meet you, if you must know. He's tied up in a business
meeting until later, and, unlike me, he felt one of the

family ought to be here to welcome you and your—
friend.'

The way she said the word 'friend' caused another
frisson of alarm to slide along Helen's spine, but Jon
appeared to have no such misgivings. 'If I didn't know
I was your favourite nephew, I'd take that to heart,
Auntie Vee,' he declared, setting her on her feet again.
'But as I know you're only teasing, let me introduce you
to Helen.'

'Don't call me Auntie *Vee*,' Victoria fussed unneces-
sarily, as Jon drew Helen forward. Then using one hand
to straighten the wide-brimmed straw on outrageously
yellow curls, Victoria extended a white-gloved hand in
Helen's direction.

Feeling a little as if she were in the presence of royalty,
Helen shook hands politely. 'Miss Roberts,' she murmured, hoping there were no threads of lint on her rather
crumpled navy trousers. 'Thank you for inviting me.'

'Roberts?' echoed Victoria, frowning. 'My name's not
Roberts, Miss—er—Helen.'

Helen was momentarily nonplussed. 'Oh—but I
thought——' Had Jon only been teasing when he said
his aunt had never married?

'It's my fault,' Jon broke in now, grimacing at both
of them. 'I should have told you, Helen. Roberts is only
a stage name. My real name is Jonathan Robert Wyatt.
I'm sorry. I should have explained.'

'Wyatt!' Helen had to concentrate hard to prevent her
voice from betraying her. But whenever she heard that
name, a wave of panic swept over her. No matter how
many years it was since that night, she still felt the same
thrill of apprehension when she heard it.

'Yes, Wyatt,' said Jon, looking at her strangely. 'Are
you all right? You look a little pale.'

'I expect it's the heat. It affects people like that sometimes,' declared Victoria Wyatt crisply. She looked
around. 'Is this all your luggage? Have the porter fetch
it out to the car.'

The 'car' turned out to be an air-conditioned limou-
sine, hired from a livery service in the capital. Victoria
ensconced herself in the front seat of the car, beside the

elderly driver, while Helen and Jon got into the back
for the journey from St George's to Hamilton.

Helen was relieved that in the bustle of hiring a porter,
and getting their bags installed in the boot of the car,
her own momentary start of agitation had been forgotten. Besides which, it had given her time to recover
her equilibrium, and by the time Victoria turned to ask
her what she thought of the island she could answer quite
truthfully that she found it enchanting.

And it was. As they bumped over the causeway that
linked the airport with the North Shore Road, she had
her first glimpse of Castle Harbour, the blue-green waters
quite transparent as they lapped against the rocks.
Beyond, the road climbed between clusters of flowering
shrubs, bending and twisting to accommodate the
shoreline. There were houses and churches that reminded her of England, and tiny piers and inlets, where
sailing boats and other pleasure craft bobbed at anchor.

'You live in London, I believe,' Victoria added now
and Jon pulled a wry face at his aunt's obvious attempt
to categorise her visitor. 'Are—er—are you in the music
business too, Miss—er—Helen?'

'Her name's Helen Caldwell, and she's not in the music
business,' he replied smoothly, taking a pack of ciga-
rettes out of his pocket. 'At least, not directly,' he added,
to Helen's surprise, shaking a cigarette out of the packet
and catching it expertly between his teeth. 'She's a go-
go dancer in a strip club actually.' He paused, allowing
this to sink in, and then went on, 'Say, do you have a
match? I never use lighters. They say they're awfully
bad for your health.'

His aunt's face was the picture of outrage, and while
she guessed there was more to this than simply Jon's
perverted sense of humour, Helen could not allow it to
continue.

'Actually,' she said, using his word, 'I work with the
managing director of an engineering company, Miss—
Wyatt.' She forced herself to use the name without
flinching. She gave Jon a reproving look, and ignored
a latent desire to share his shameless grin. 'And, yes, I
do live in London. In Hammersmith. Not far from Earl's
Court, if you've heard of it.'

'Oh, yes, I've heard of it,' replied Victoria, rather stiffly. 'I know London very well, as a matter of fact. I have excellent contacts with galleries there.'

'Really?' For a moment Helen was nonplussed, and Jon chose once again to intervene.

'My aunt is an angel, aren't you, Auntie Vee?' he asked mockingly. And then, to Helen, 'She plays fairy godmother to struggling artists, both here and in the States.'

'They're painters, Jonathan,' his aunt corrected him irritably. 'And I'm not an angel. I just do what I can to see that the island's talent is recognised.'

'And you do it so well,' Jon assured her, though his eyes were dancing, and Victoria turned away with a not inaudible snort of disapproval.

'You're very lucky to live here,' Helen put in quickly, realising that antagonising Jon's aunt was hardly the best way to begin her holiday, but she had obviously said the wrong thing because the look Victoria turned on her then was far from friendly.

'What do you mean?' she demanded, swinging round so swiftly that the ribbons of her hat caught the chauffeur a stinging swipe across his cheek. 'Why shouldn't I live here? This is my home.'

'Well, of course——' began Helen helplessly, turning to Jon now for assistance, and for a moment he met her imploring gaze with the same indifference he had shown to his aunt.

But then, as if relenting, he took pity on her, and, shifting his arm so that it lay possessively across her shoulders, he said, 'Helen didn't mean anything, Vee. She just thinks you're lucky to live in such idyllic surroundings. And you are. Surely you'd be the first to agree?'

'Oh—well, yes. If you put it like that...' Victoria's animosity drained away. 'It's just that—well, let's say I'm a little tired, hmm? I've been working very hard recently. What with the opening of the—gallery and everything. Not to mention caring for your father...'

'Oh, yeah.' Jon's fingers moved from Helen's shoulder to toy with the short, chunky braid she had made of her hair. 'How is Dad? Is he OK? He said something about you opening your own gallery here in Hamilton in his last letter. I guess he's had a hand in it, right? Whatever Tori wants, Tori gets, hmm?'

For a moment Helen didn't understand who he was talking about, but then she put two and two together. Vee; Victoria; Tori; they were all one and the same person. And that person was sitting in front of her looking decidedly put out once again.

'I don't think there's any reason for you to say a thing like that, Jonathan,' she declared shortly. 'I'm sure your father has always given you everything you ever wanted, not least a career in London you must know was not his choice for you.' She sniffed. 'However, that's by the by. As it happens, your father is well. Working hard, as usual. Something you know very little about.'

'Making money, you mean,' Jon observed, his finger-tips massaging the nerve that throbbed in Helen's nape. 'And isn't that lucky for all of us? You, me, and the new gallery.'

Helen sighed, and shrugged his fingers away. This was a side of Jon she hadn't seen before, and she didn't much like it. Teasing was one thing; being insolent was another. And taking a deep breath she made another attempt to cool the situation.

'I can't get over the colour of the water,' she said, leaning forward to peer through the car window. And it was true. The clear, translucent shading of blue through to palest turquoise was quite indescribable, with dark rocks and pink-tinged beaches forming a picture of unspoilt beauty.

'Yes. It is quite lovely, isn't it?' Victoria agreed after a moment, hopefully deciding that her nephew's views weren't shared by his companion. 'We like it, naturally. I can't imagine living anywhere else now.'

'And—have you always lived here?' Helen asked, praying it wasn't a loaded question, and Victoria nodded.

'Except for a few years, when Jonathan was little,' she replied, ignoring his expression. 'When—when my brother's marriage broke up ten years ago, I came home to—well, to pick up the pieces, I suppose. My brother needed somebody to look after things, and—I was happy to do it.'

Ten years ago! Helen hid a rueful grimace. That had been a traumatic time for her, too, she thought wryly. Ten years ago, she had met Alexa's father. Perhaps she and Jon's father would have something in common, after all. Ten years ago they had both been victims of one kind or another.

They were nearing Hamilton now. Road signs indicated that the island's capital was only a few kilometres away, but before they reached the city they turned on to the Harbour Road. Now Helen could see the buildings of Front Street just across a narrow expanse of water, and a huge cruising liner tied up at the quay.

'Oh, isn't it pretty?' she exclaimed, admiring the pink and white roofs of the city, and the sun-splashed marina that lay between. She had expected it to be different, and exotic, but not as beautiful as it was. No wonder Victoria had wanted to come back here, she thought. It was the kind of place that could get into your blood.

'Like it?' Jon asked, speaking to her for the first time since she had pulled away from his playful fingers, and Helen nodded vigorously.

'Who wouldn't?' she exclaimed, assuring herself that Jon's arm was where it belonged before relaxing back against the leather upholstery. 'Alexa would love it here,' she added dreamily, and then kicked herself anew when Victoria picked up on the name.

'Alexa?' she enquired politely, adjusting the brim of her hat. 'Who is Alexa? Your sister?'

'Alexa is Helen's daughter,' Jon informed his aunt coolly, and Helen saw the calculating gleam that came into Victoria's eye. Perhaps she was wondering if Alexa was Jon's daughter, too, Helen reflected ruefully, wishing she had not been so careless. Alexa's existence was something she had hoped to keep to herself. At least initially. Now she was going to have to explain, and she didn't think Victoria Wyatt would approve.

'You have a daughter, Miss—er—Caldwell?' she asked now, her tongue circling her lips with obvious anticipation, and Jon sighed.

'Call her Helen, for God's sake,' he exclaimed, giving his aunt a scathing look. 'And, yes, she has daughter. A *nine-year-old* daughter, as it happens. So I couldn't

possibly be the father, no matter how disappointing that
might be!'

Victoria's plump cheeks flamed. 'Really, Jonathan, I
don't think that was called for——'

'Don't you?' Jon was unrepentant. 'Well, at least it's
cleared the air, don't you think? Now you won't have
to worry about how you're going to tell Dad. Alexa's
Helen's responsibility, not ours. Although I have to
admit, I wouldn't mind if she were mine.'

Helen supposed she should be grateful to Jon for
making this observation, but she couldn't help wishing
he had not chosen such a provocative way of saying it.
It was obvious that Victoria was now employed in doing
her sums, and it wouldn't take a great mathematician to
calculate that, unless Helen had had Alexa when she was
barely thirteen years old, she had to be older than
Jonathan.

But, as luck would have it, it seemed their journey
was at last drawing to a close, and Helen couldn't deny
a sigh of anticipation at the prospect of escaping from
Victoria's speculative gaze. As the car turned off the main
highway on to a much narrower side road, she was able
to catch glimpses of the water ahead of them, which
surely meant they were nearing their destination. She
told herself she was looking forward to seeing where Jon
had been born, to staying on this beautiful island. But
something, some instinct, was warning her that it wasn't
going to be as straightforward as she had thought, and
it was difficult to sustain her enthusiasm.

In spite of the way Jon treated his aunt, Helen guessed
that Victoria Wyatt's personality did not match her
appearance. She might look frivolous, and a little silly,
but Helen thought she was also fairly shrewd. After all,
for the past ten years she had succeeded in running her
brother's household, without any apparent interference,
and that in itself was an achievement. Considering that
when Jon's parents' marriage broke up his father must
have been a comparatively young man, and with a child
of Jon's age, he might conceivably have married again.
But he hadn't. Of course, Helen didn't know the circumstances of the break-up of the marriage. All Jon had
told her was that he had continued to live with his father,

which Helen had taken to mean that his mother had been the guilty party. Maybe the circumstances of that break-up had been so painful that Jon's father had never wanted to marry again. But Helen suspected that Victoria Wyatt would not make it easy to bring another woman into the house.

The car was turning between stone gateposts now, and Helen determinedly put such thoughts aside. She had no real reason for making these assumptions about Jon's family, and she was impatient with herself for allowing such ideas to take root. Just because Jon's aunt had asked some perfectly reasonable questions on the journey from the airport, she was allowing her imagination to create situations that had no basis in fact. All right, so Jon's aunt was inquisitive, and a little arrogant at times. So what? Jon had done his utmost to rub her up the wrong way, after all. And she, Helen, wasn't here to make speculative judgements about either Jon's aunt or his father. Her most immediate problem was to decide whether the feelings she had for Jon were strong enough to sustain a closer relationship. Whether the relief she felt at his acceptance of Alexa, and her fondness for him, were clouding her emotions. She didn't think so. She really cared for Jon. And as the concept of some blind passion coming along at this late stage in her life was one she no longer subscribed to, surely genuine friendship and affection were more than she could have hoped?

The drive curved, and the thickly flowering bushes which had hidden the house from view gave way to sloping lawns and a flagged terrace. A cluster of exotic poinsettia partly concealed the stone walls of the veranda, but white-painted roofs rose above the scarlet blossoms, arching away in all directions, and revealing the generous dimensions of the house.

Helen was at once impressed, and daunted. Although Victoria Wyatt's manner had warned her that Jon must have been a little economical with the truth when he had described his home, she hadn't honestly expected a millionaire's mansion. Even the many beautiful homes she had seen dotting the hillside as they drove from the airport hadn't disturbed her. Jon had always seemed so—

ordinary. He had always fitted into her life without any obvious adaptation on his part at all. But now she suspected he had been playing a role, and the idea of herself fitting into these surroundings was infinitely less believable.

'Welcome to Palmer's Sound,' he was saying now, but he seemed to sense her instinctive withdrawal. 'Hey—don't you like it?'

'Did you expect I would?' she countered tautly, her voice low and cool, and Jon heaved a heavy sigh.

'I guess that means you don't,' he observed, looking not a little discomfited. 'Well, don't blame me. This is where I was born. And, you know, I like your flat much better than here. At least it's a home, not a showcase.'

'Don't patronise me, Jon.' Helen turned away from his troubled expression and stared tensely towards a pink-painted cupola, arching above a cluster of date palms. No wonder Victoria Wyatt guarded her position here, she thought wryly. She must resent any intrusion that might threaten her domain.

'You don't like the house, Miss Caldwell?' she was asking now, with what Helen recognised as a mixture of gratification and disbelief, and Helen knew she had to be honest.

'On the contrary,' she said, understanding a little of the impatience Jon felt when dealing with his aunt. 'From what I can see, I'm sure it's quite beautiful. Is that the Atlantic? It's so blue! I simply can't understand how Jon can bear to live anywhere else.'

Victoria's lips tightened, but the car had drawn to a halt beneath an arched colonnade, and already Jon was opening his door and uncoiling his long length from the back.

'It's the Sound,' Victoria replied offhandedly, indicating the sweep of blue-green water that lapped a stone jetty below the house. 'You do know what the Sound is, I suppose?'

'I think so.' But Helen forbore to offer an explanation. To detail her understanding that the sound in question was the channel of water between Hamilton harbour and the outlying islands would have sounded very much like a catechism, and she was too tense as it was. Jon should have warned her, she thought frustratedly. It wasn't going to be much of a holiday if she couldn't even relax.

All the same, she couldn't help a ripple of excitement as Jon helped her from the car. Through open double doors, she could see the cool, shadowed hall of the house, and an enormous cream Chinese carpet laid upon the wood-blocked floor. Tall glazed vases contained sprays of the flowering shrubs that she had seen growing wild about the island, and a huge-leaved fan turned constantly, creating a pleasing draught of air.

'OK?' Jon asked now, the question only audible to her and, after a moment's hesitation, she nodded.

'I suppose so,' she agreed, allowing him to pull her close to his lean frame, and it was as they were in this briefly intimate position that a man appeared within the shadows of the hall and came towards them.

Helen thought at first he must be a servant. She had become so sensitive to the fact that she was going to have to get used to these luxurious surroundings that she had already steeled herself for whatever form that affluence might take. After all, she had told herself, she was here as Jon's guest, not as an interloper. And, whatever attitude his aunt might adopt, this was Jon's home as well as hers.

But the man was not a servant. Helen sensed that, even before he stepped out on to the porch. Even though he was wearing knee-length shorts, and a white shirt and formal tie, he had an air of authority, and although his skin appeared to be darkly tanned his ancestry was not in question.

Even so, it was not until he emerged into the sunlight, slanting down through the leaves of the bougainvillaea, that Helen was able to see his face. Until then, her impression was of a tall man, who moved with a lithe athleticism; a powerful man, whose balance was perfectly co-ordinated.

Jon, who had sensed that her attention had been diverted, supplied an identification. 'Dad!' he exclaimed in an unmistakably delighted tone, and, after squeezing Helen's arm, he left her to greet the other man. 'Hey, it's good to see you,' he added, as his father stepped across the threshold to grasp his hand. 'Vee said you were in a meeting.'

'I was,' said his father, but Helen barely heard his explanation. She was too busy holding on to the roof of the car, telling herself desperately that she had to be mistaken. But it wasn't Jon's father's unexpected appearance that had shocked her so badly she was in danger of losing control. Nor was it her embarrassment that he should have interrupted their embrace. In spite of Victoria Wyatt's hostility, and Jon's reticence about his background, she could have coped. After all, she had coped with being pregnant when she was only sixteen. She had coped with being an unmarried mother. She had even coped with attending evening classes, when Alexa was just a baby, so that she could hold down a job during the day. She had needed those classes, to finish the secretarial course she had had to give up when she'd become pregnant. Otherwise, she would never have had the qualifications necessary to become Alan Wright's assistant.

No. In spite of any anxiety she might have felt at meeting Jon's father for the first time, she was sure she could have handled it. He was just a man, like any other, and she was used to dealing with men. But what she was not used to—and what was in danger of sweeping the legs from under her—was coming face to face with a man she had not seen for over ten years. *Reed Wyatt*, she thought disbelievingly, striving to recover her equilibrium. She had been right to feel apprehensive when she heard that surname. Dear God, what would happen when he recognised her? How on earth was she going to get out of this?

CHAPTER THREE

A COUPLE of hours later, Helen stepped out on to the balcony of her room and took a deep breath. The balcony itself was made private on two sides by the walls of the rooms adjoining, and a white-painted iron handrail fenced the fourth. Above her head, the slatted roof would give protection from the heat, but right now it wasn't needed. With the sun sinking into the waters of the bay, a golden glow engulfed the islands of the Sound, its warmth all-embracing, but in no way threatening.

Resting her hands on the rail, Helen looked down at the garden of the house two floors below. Her room was on the first floor, and immediately below her windows a flowering casuarina spread its branches. Beyond, the lawns sloped away to the jetty, where the shifting waters of the bay lapped against its stone walls. Out in the bay, yachts and smaller craft lay at anchor, their lights becoming visible as the sky darkened. And, in the distance, she could see the rapidly increasing cluster of lights that must be Hamilton, and the looped decoration of a cruise liner as it slowly made its way into port.

It was all very beautiful, incredibly so, but Helen was not in the mood to appreciate it. On the contrary, she still felt numb, and although her eyes registered the beauty of her surroundings the message was incapable of reaching her brain.

Not that she truly wished for anything else, she thought, with a fleeting trace of humour. So long as she remained numb, maybe she could still handle the situation. It was only when the sharp edge of reality pierced her paralysis that she felt her balance slipping. But so long as she could sustain her insentience, she had a chance. So long as she could control her hysteria, surely she had nothing to fear.

Because Reed Wyatt hadn't recognised her!

Incredible as it seemed, he hadn't batted an eyelid when Jon had introduced her to him. Instead, he had been disarmingly kind and friendly, his concern for her apparent unsteadiness in sharp contrast to his sister's impatience.

Helen tipped her head back on her shoulders, and felt the muscles bunch with tension. How had she managed it? she wondered now. How had she succeeded in shaking Reed Wyatt's hand, without screaming her accusations from the rooftops? When Jon had turned and drawn her forward, what she had really wanted to do was run, but instead she had swallowed her panic and waited for the fire to engulf her.

But it hadn't happened. Nothing untoward had happened—except that she had been shaking like a jellyfish, and her skin had been damp with sweat. When Reed had taken her hand, she had half expected him to cringe at its clammy feel, but he hadn't. He had simply asked her if she wasn't feeling well, and she had found herself stammering out some tale about having a migraine, which had caused both Jon and his father to show concern.

Which really was the last thing she should have said, she acknowledged now. Instead of keeping cool, and pretending she was as ignorant of Reed's identity as he was of hers, she had drawn everyone's attention to herself, and only Victoria's barbed comments had diverted them.

'She's not pregnant, is she?' Helen had heard her hiss in her nephew's ear, as Reed was suggesting they went into the house, but she hadn't heard Jon's reply. Only the coldness of his father's tone, as he silenced his sister, rang in her ears, harsh with warning. And in that instant Helen had realised that, no matter how secure Victoria might consider her position, it was only as secure as her brother chose to make it.

Which was all par for the course, she thought bitterly. Reed Wyatt was a man who liked his own way, and usually got it. She knew that, to her cost. Was that why his wife had left him? Not through any fault of her own, but because there had been one too many other beds?

Helen groaned. What did that matter now? Reed Wyatt's past relationship with his wife was not her concern. What did concern her was that she had been put in an impossible position. And no matter which way she turned she couldn't see any way out.

And yet, ironically, it had been Reed who had made it easier for her to escape the immediate consequences of her situation. After escorting her into the blessedly cool environs of the entrance hall, he had summoned a servant to take her up to her room, and ordered tea and aspirin to ease her headache.

'I suggest you try and sleep for a while,' he said, while Jon stood helplessly beside him. 'We eat fairly late here, so you've plenty of time to rest. And if you don't feel well enough to join us for supper, don't worry about it. We'll quite understand.'

Of course, Jon had gone up with her, to show her to her room, and he had been embarrassingly sympathetic. 'Why didn't you tell me you had a migraine coming on?' he asked, as she stood guiltily in the middle of the floor of her bedroom. 'I'd have stopped Vee from asking you all those questions. Nosy old bat! Just because Dad lets her have her own way most of the time, she thinks she can say what she likes.'

'It's all right.'

Helen had been embarrassed enough as it was, and she was glad when a young black man had arrived with her luggage, followed almost immediately by an olive-skinned Asian girl with a tray of tea. It meant Jon's presence was becoming an intrusion, and, endorsing his father's suggestion that she should try and sleep, he had followed the servants out.

Of course, she hadn't slept. Not surprisingly, she had found it almost impossible to relax, and she still hadn't decided what she was going to do. How could she stay here, forced to accept the hospitality of a man she had hoped never to see again? And yet, conversely, how could she go—without arousing questions she had no wish to answer?

But—dear God!—what was she supposed to do, when the man who had fathered her child hadn't even recognised her? Of course, it had been ten years, and no doubt she had changed. But not that much! Surely! She knew she would never forget his face.

But then, it had obviously meant more to her than it had to him. After all, she had lost more than her innocence that night. She had conceived the seed of another human being, her daughter, born nine months later without Reed Wyatt's either knowing or caring. That Jon's father should be Alexa's father, too, was unbelievable. No wonder she had thought Jon reminded her of somebody. It was Alexa. They were half-brother and -sister.

Tipping her head forward again, Helen heaved a sigh. Then, tightening the ends of the bath towel she had wrapped sarong-wise about her slim body after her shower, she gazed once more at the view. It was almost dark now. The sun sank faster here, and already stars were appearing on the silver-streaked horizon. It wasn't cold, however. The air was soft and seductive, stroking her skin like velvet, and inviting her to enjoy it. This was supposed to be a holiday, after all. An exotic vacation. To help her relax.

But how could she? she asked herself helplessly. So far she had been spared any conversation with the man, but that was not going to last. Reed would want to know the girl his son had brought to stay in his house. He would want to know everything about her, and because she had inadvertently blurted Alexa's name to Victoria there was no way she could prevent his learning about her daughter, too.

Her skin cooled with sudden anguish. What if he heard about Alexa's existence and put two and two together? Might he want to take her daughter—*his daughter*—from her? Oh, God, she shouldn't have come here. She had made a terrible mistake.

She tried to calm herself, but it wasn't easy. She had had no idea when she met Reed in London that he was a man of such affluence, and the realisation that he could turn those resources against her, and Alexa, was terrifying.

Panic flared, but she determinedly tamped it down. She was being foolish, creating problems where none existed. The likelihood of his remembering her now was totally unrealistic. And for him to claim some kind of association with her would arouse the kind of questions he wouldn't want to answer. No. She, *herself*, was her own greatest danger. So long as she was able to keep her head, she would have nothing to fear.

Realising it was getting late, Helen turned and walked back into the bedroom behind her. Switching on the bronze-shaded lamps beside the bed, she gazed gratefully at their warm illumination. For all her bravado, the encroaching darkness outside had become vaguely hostile. She needed light, and reassurance, and the familiarity of her own things around her.

She wished she could ring Alexa, but it was long past her bedtime in England, and besides, until she knew what she was going to do, it would be difficult talking to her daughter. Alexa would be sure to ask questions, interested, as any little girl would be, in her mother's whereabouts. And what could Helen say to her? Oh, by the way, Alexa, I met your father today, quite unexpectedly. We're staying with him actually. Isn't that nice?

A glance at the watch, which she had left on the table beside the bed when she went to take her shower, warned her she had less than thirty minutes before she might be expected to join the others downstairs. Jon had told her to come down at about half-past eight, if she felt like it, and while it would have been easier to pretend that her headache was no better, she knew that putting off the evil day was not going to make it any easier. Quite the reverse.

Until she had gone to take her shower, she had been lying on the wide, queen-sized bed that would have dominated her room at home. However, it fitted perfectly in these surroundings, and she had to admit the rooms she had been given were extremely comfortable. The bedroom alone would have impressed her, but adjoining its undisguised luxury was a small sitting-room, with soft-cushioned easy chairs in an island print, and a polished-wood writing desk, with stationery provided. There was a cream carpet, into which her toes curled appreciatively, that spread throughout the suite; except in the bathroom where cream-veined marble tiles took over. It was all very beautiful, of course, but it was not the kind of accommodation Helen had expected when Jon had invited her to his home. Still, she reflected wryly, it was just another obstacle to surmount. Compared to the shock she had had, she felt she could have handled all the rest standing on her head.

So, now she had to open her suitcase, and choose something suitable to wear. Fortunately, she had taken her mother's advice and packed several uncrushable dresses, which were adaptable to day or evening wear. Her own taste was more towards casual clothes; vests and trousers in silky synthetic fabrics, or loose-fitting shirts and sweaters worn over leggings. Of course, leggings wouldn't have been practical in this climate, anyway, but she had brought shorts and skirts, and lightweight cotton trousers.

However, for this evening pride dictated that she wear something rather special. She needed all the confidence she could muster. And, if somewhere in that resolution was an insidious desire to make Reed Wyatt envy his son's good fortune, then so be it. She was not ashamed of feeling vengeful. It would serve him right if she exposed him for what he was.

But, of course, she knew she wouldn't do that. Pride again, she thought bitterly. And fear, of what he might do to Alexa. And consideration for Jon. He didn't deserve that kind of back-stabbing.

A navy blue and white silk dress seemed an admirable choice. It was one she had not yet worn, and its wrap-around style was both cool and sexy. The bodice's cleavage drew attention to the dusky hollow between her breasts, and because the skirt was draped it exposed a healthy expanse of bare leg above the knee as well as below. Belled, elbow-length sleeves complimented her slim arms, and a handful of narrow bangles was all the jewellery she needed.

Her hair provided the biggest problem. She had washed it when she took her shower, and dried it with the hand-drier that had naturally been provided. But she had been in no mood to take a lot of care with it, and now it was rioting wildly. Having naturally curly hair could be an advantage, but not when she had no means of taming it. She should have had it cut before she left England, she thought impatiently. As it was, only the stumpy pigtail seemed a realistic option.

But she couldn't go down to dinner with her hair in a pigtail, she concluded grimly. It took a little longer, but she managed to coil its fiery strands into a modest chignon. It made her look older, but she couldn't help it. And on the one occasion Jon had seen it that way, he had approved. He was the only person she wanted to please, after all.

Her hair was done, unknowingly exposing the pure lines of her profile, and she was dressed and almost ready when someone tapped at her door. Giving one final sweep of bronze mascara to her lashes, Helen put down the brush and surveyed her appearance. On with the motley, she thought unsteadily, her hand shaking as she touched the red-gold tendrils that had escaped the hairpins. It was a pity she wasn't an actress. Then she might have appreciated the chance to give the performance of her life.

Crossing the sitting-room, on legs which were not entirely reliable, she opened the door to the Asian maid who had brought her tea earlier.

'Mr Wyatt sent me to ask if you are well enough to join the family for supper,' she said, her sloe-black eyes widening appreciatively. 'But you are obviously feeling much better,' she added, with a friendly smile. 'Are you ready to come down?'

Helen took a deep breath. 'I think so,' she said, and then caught her breath on a gasp as the man whose identity she had been trying so hard to deal with came walking along the gallery towards them. In a loose-fitting white shirt and narrow black trousers, the belted waistband hanging low on his hips, Reed Wyatt looked even more attractive this evening than he had done that afternoon. Of course, then Helen had been more concerned with who he was than what he looked like, and although her brain had subconsciously registered his appearance, the fact that the last ten years had had little effect on him had not been of paramount importance.

But now, with at least a part of her functioning as a sane and rational human being, she couldn't help noticing how kind the years had been to him. He must be how old now? she wondered. Forty-two? Forty-three? He looked years younger. And only the sun-streaked lines around his eyes betrayed a greater experience.

All the same, it was easy to see why she had been attracted to him all those years ago. Tall, lean-limbed, but with a muscled hardness to his body that belied his executive status. He looked more like a yachtsman than a banker, his healthy tan an indication that he enjoyed the outdoor life. He wasn't a particularly handsome man, she acknowledged, trying to be objective. His eyes were too deeply set, his nose was too long, and his mouth was too thin for beauty. Yet those same eyes were fringed with long, thick lashes; the angular planes of his face

exposed a hard intelligence; and the mouth—which had
once explored every inch of her body—had a warmth
and sensuality that she had found it impossible to resist.
Oh, yes, she thought uneasily, he had lost none of his
sexuality. He might have a few grey strands in the silvery
light hair that brushed his collar, but it was still as thick
and vital as ever. The wonder was that he had never
married again. He must have had plenty of opportunity.

'Ah—Helen,' he said now, and although he smiled as
he said the words she sensed he was surprised to see her.
But whether that surprise was because he had not
expected her to recover so quickly, or because of her
appearance, she couldn't be certain. After all, she must
look a lot different from the way she had looked this
afternoon. At least she wasn't shaking now—not visibly
at least—and her skin was faintly flushed, not pallid as
a ghost's. However, he swiftly controlled whatever
emotion her appearance inspired, and as the maid
nodded politely and walked away he halted in front of
her. 'I see your headache's much improved.'

'Yes.' Helen tried to speak casually, but in spite of
her best efforts she could hear the edge to her voice.
Even being civil to this man was going to be difficult,
and she wished Jon were around to make it easier for
her.

'Good.' His tone was noticeably warmer than hers,
and if he sensed her animosity, he didn't show it. 'I was
just coming to tell Laura——' he flicked a hand after
the maid '—not to disturb you. But I'm glad you're
feeling so much better.'

'Oh—I am,' said Helen stiffly, wishing he would just
go and leave her to make her own way down.

'I'm delighted.' Reed's mouth revealed a momentary
wryness. 'So—if you're ready? My sister's waiting for
us in the library.'

Hoping Jon wasn't skipping supper because he thought
she was, Helen closed her door. Then, praying Reed
wouldn't touch her, she started off after the maid. And
he didn't; he merely fell into step beside her, adjusting
his pace to hers.

Supremely conscious of his arm only inches from her
own as they walked, Helen endeavoured to focus her

attention on her surroundings. That afternoon, she had paid little heed to where they were taking her. She had followed Jon up the stairs, without even noticing that the entrance hall was a huge atrium, arcing three floors above her head. She hadn't cared that each level had its own galleried landing, or that the stairs themselves were a free-standing loop of mahogany that formed a square central column.

Helen looked about her as they went down the carpeted stairs, which were wide enough for them to walk side by side with ease, feigning an interest in her surroundings. But after a while her interest didn't have to be feigned, and her head was tilted back, to allow her to study the huge chandelier that was suspended overhead, when Reed put his hand beneath her elbow.

She jerked away, as if he had made a pass at her, her momentary lapse of awareness instantly dispelled. Just for a moment, she had forgotten where she was and who she was, but the touch of his hard fingers was a shuddering reminder. Putting the width of the stairs between them, she allowed her hand to move over the bone where his fingers had rested, resisting the impulse to scrub at the skin. There were dangers here, she thought, that she hadn't even anticipated. Not least, her own inability to deal with her emotions.

'I'm sorry if I startled you,' Reed said now, his eyes narrowed, but not unfriendly. 'Only you weren't looking where you were going, and I'd hate you to fall and add concussion to your other doubts about this place.'

Helen was startled. 'My—other doubts,' she echoed uneasily and Reed nodded.

'Well, correct me if I'm wrong, but I get the impression you're not exactly—overjoyed to be here,' he remarked. He pushed his hands into his trouser pockets, and looked at her sideways. 'Jon tells me his aunt asked a lot of personal questions on the way from the airport. Is that right?'

Helen swallowed, not knowing whether to be anxious, or relieved. 'Um—some,' she conceded warily.

Reed sighed. 'I see. Well, I hope you won't let Victoria upset you again. She can be rather—insensitive, I know.'

Helen allowed her breath to escape, albeit unevenly, and dragged her features into a tight smile. But it wasn't easy, not easy at all, when Reed was looking at her in that disturbingly sympathetic way. In spite of all she knew about him, she could feel herself wanting to respond to his charm, and she took another gulp of air to try and restore her balance.

'Jon is partly to blame for his aunt's attitude,' Reed remarked now, as they continued down the stairs—this time with Helen's hand resting securely on the banister rail at her side. 'Occasionally, he has brought some rather—odd people home.' The corners of his attractive mouth lifted humorously. 'Not that I'm suggesting you're in any way odd,' he added quickly. 'Far from it. But the fact remains—well, my sister is very conservative.'

'And—you're not, Mr Wyatt?'

Helen couldn't prevent the automatic rejoinder, but Reed did not seem offended by her candour. 'Oh, yes, I am,' he admitted ruefully. 'I'm just as conservative as Victoria, though I try not to be. I guess that's what happens when you get older, Helen. And your calling me *Mr* Wyatt just accentuates how much older I am!'

His smile was disarming, but Helen wouldn't allow herself to be fooled by it. Just who did he think he was kidding? she thought bitterly. What would he say if she asked him how conservatively he had behaved after a party in London, ten years ago?

'Anyway,' he appended, as they reached the ground floor, 'I hope we can convince you that our island is well worth a visit. It's a pity you couldn't bring your daughter with you. Our beaches and rock pools are ideal for young children.'

Helen caught her breath. 'You know about Alexa?' she got out in a strangled voice, and Reed frowned.

'Is that your daughter's name? Alexa? Yes, I'm afraid Victoria told me about her. Lord, wasn't she supposed to? Well, I'm sorry, but she did.'

Helen struggled to recover her composure. For a minute there, she had been in danger of betraying everything. When Reed had mentioned Alexa she had thought, for one agonising moment, that he was telling her he knew all about her, that he knew who she really was. She had forgotten—*how had she?*—that she had inadvertently mentioned her daughter in Victoria's hearing. But talking to Reed tended to scramble her brain cells and she couldn't always think coherently.

'I—I don't mind,' she said now, wishing he would indicate which way they had to go. Long corridors led off the hall in several directions, and she had no idea where the library was.

'It's this way,' Reed said then, as if aware of what she had been thinking, and she hoped all her thoughts weren't so open to interpretation. 'We call this the gallery, for obvious reasons. My sister is a patron of the arts, and this is the work of some of her protégés.'

'They're very nice,' said Helen inadequately, looking at the paintings that were hung between the long windows of the gallery without really seeing them. She realised he probably thought she was ignorant now, as well as stupid, but she couldn't help it. And besides, what did it matter what he thought of her? He was the last person she wanted to impress. Nevertheless, if she intended to go through with this—and she still couldn't see any alternative, without arousing a lot of awkward questions—she would have to get her act together. Having discovered she had nothing to fear from his father, it would be ironic if Jon was the one to become suspicious about her. Yet, was there really any point in continuing their relationship? No matter how she might feel about Jon, nothing could alter the fact that he was Reed Wyatt's son. And the idea of becoming part of *his* family was something she couldn't handle.

Beyond the windows, lights winked in the darkness, and the unmistakable scent of oleander was sweet and subtle. There was music, too, a rhythmic calypso drifting over the water, that stirred her blood in spite of herself. Tropical surroundings, tropical music—she should have been ecstatic. But, as Reed opened the double panelled doors at the end of the gallery, and invited her to precede him into the library, all Helen could think about was how to escape.

CHAPTER FOUR

THE party following the opening of the gallery seemed to be proving as successful as the opening itself. Standing on the sidelines, drinking his third glass of vintage champagne, Reed cast a faintly cynical eye over the proceedings, but he had to admit Victoria's skill in public relations had to be admired. She had organised the event perfectly; and although Luther Styles was undeniably the most successful painter present, none of the lesser-known contributors to the exhibition had been neglected. On the contrary, already many of the paintings that adorned the walls of the gallery bore the satisfying little red spot, which indicated that they had been sold. And there was the steady hum of conversation in the room as dealers and collectors exchanged their views.

It was obvious his sister was enjoying her achievement. He could see her now in the middle of the room, surrounded by a group of newspaper columnists and admirers, holding forth about the difficulties faced by craftsmen in all fields of the arts. Luther Styles was beside her, and Reed observed that his sister's arm was very firmly linked with that of her most noteworthy discovery. He frowned, wondering if Victoria really thought that Styles was interested in her. For himself, he had his doubts. In his opinion, the man was both arrogant and sycophantic, two adjectives which, in Styles' case, were not mutually exclusive. Even as he watched, he saw the other man's eyes straying to female forms of less generous proportions, but whenever Victoria spoke to him he was quick to hide his interest. Reed suspected he was only using Victoria, and he was very much afraid his sister was going to be hurt.

Still, he reflected wryly, surveying his empty glass with some resignation, it was really nothing to do with him. It wasn't as if Victoria was a girl any more. She was a grown woman, only a couple of years younger than himself, and surely capable of making her own mistakes. He couldn't be expected to watch out for her interests, as he had used to do when they were younger. He wasn't her father, even though sometimes it had felt like it.

The trouble was, Victoria was totally inexperienced when it came to men. Because she had been only sixteen when their father and mother had died, and because of the circumstances of their parents' deaths, he supposed, she had never had a normal adolescence. When she should have been having fun, making friends and going out to parties, she had spent her time at home, sewing and reading, and looking after the house. She had, in effect, taken over their mother's role, and it was only when he'd married Diana that she had realised it couldn't go on.

Reed sighed. Perhaps it was his fault, too. If he'd married someone who would have taken the trouble to make a friend of Victoria, things might have turned out differently. As it was, the two women had hated one another on sight, and, until Victoria had accepted defeat and moved away, the atmosphere in his home had been almost tangible.

Of course, she had spent several years working in the United States, travelling back and forth to London and Paris, and generally behaving as any young, liberated woman should. But when Diana walked out she hadn't needed an invitation to pack up and come home, and Reed was very much afraid he had taken advantage of her good nature.

Even so, that was then, and this was now, and the last ten years had given her the confidence she had been lacking. And, he knew, Victoria herself would not welcome his interference in her affairs at this stage. So far as she was concerned, Luther Styles could do no wrong, and the idea that once he had achieved his ambitions he would drop her like the proverbial hot potato was not what she wanted to hear. She was totally convinced of the man's integrity, and therefore anything Reed said was suspect.

In that respect, her attitude was much like that of their visitor's, thought Reed now, exchanging his empty glass for a full one from a passing waiter. Jon's latest girl-friend was definitely a prickly young creature, and it was becoming embarrassingly obvious that she had no time

for him. He wondered why. Clearly, Jon hadn't told her
much about his background before bringing her here,
and perhaps she resented the fact. But was that really
any reason for her to treat him as if he were entirely to
blame for her misconceptions? After all, he had done
his utmost to make her feel at home, even if Victoria
still regarded her in much the same light as she had regarded all of Jon's previous girlfriends. But then,
Victoria was biased. She still hadn't got over the fact
that Helen had a daughter—an *illegitimate* daughter, as
she insisted on putting it.

However, the fact remained that Helen was not like
any of the other females Jon had brought home. For
one thing, it was obvious that he cared about her, more
than he had cared for any of the others; and if nothing
came of their relationship Reed suspected it would not
be for want of effort on his son's part.

Which made her attitude towards him all the more
difficult to understand. Surely, if she did care about Jon
she would try to cement her relationship with his family,
not sabotage it. And yet, whenever Reed tried to initiate
a conversation with her, she froze him off. It wasn't so
much anything she said as the way that she said it,
showing him, in no uncertain manner, that she had no
wish to be sociable with him.

Reed was puzzled. He couldn't deny it. And in-
trigued. He was not a conceited man by any means, but
he had not reached his present age without having been
made aware that generally women enjoyed his company,
and Helen's behaviour was so uncharacteristic. He had
watched her with Jon; he had seen how relaxed and
enchanting she could be in his son's company; and he
was convinced that it was not natural for her to be
brusque and stand-offish. No, that particular side of her
character was reserved for him, and it was an unpal-
atable truth that the knowledge disturbed him.

He swallowed a mouthful of vintage champagne
without really tasting it, and expelled his breath on an
impatient sigh. The trouble was, there was something
about her that was vaguely familiar. Not that he imagined
they had ever met before. He was too old to play with
that particular line. But, nevertheless, the more she

goaded him, the more compelling the feeling became, and sometimes it was difficult to sustain a calm indifference.

Of course, her association with Victoria was little better—but Reed knew that was more Victoria's fault than hers. His sister was still smarting over the way he had spoken to her the night Jon and Helen arrived, and consequently she was in no mood to make things easier, for any of them. Besides, she had been involved in finalising the arrangements for the opening of the gallery, and her main concern had been in ensuring that Reed kept his promise about asking Jon not to attend.

And he had, Reed acknowledged now, remembering that conversation with his son without enthusiasm. Reed had never considered it to be a particularly good idea, and Jon's attitude had endorsed that opinion.

'What's the matter?' Jon had asked sarcastically. 'Is the V.W. afraid I'll steal her thunder? Isn't she—*big* enough to stand the competition?'

'In a manner of speaking,' Reed had said, realising there was little point in denying the truth. 'And when you speak of your aunt in that derogatory manner, can you wonder?'

Jon had sighed. 'Well—she makes me so mad! I get the feeling sometimes that I'm a visitor in my own home. It's only because you never do anything to oppose her that she doesn't do the same to you.'

'That's enough.' Reed could only let his son go so far. 'If you're regarded as a visitor here, it's your own fault. We only see you when you want something, be it cash, a new car, or accommodation for your girlfriends. Can you wonder your aunt gets impatient with you? She cares about you, Jon, but you don't even notice.'

'Well, OK.' For once, Jon had been prepared to concede the truth of this statement, and his father had scarcely recovered from this anomaly when he added, 'Maybe you have a point. Maybe I have treated this place like a hotel in recent years, but maybe that's going to change.'

'To change?' Reed's response had been wary.

'Yes.' Jon seemed to consider his words. 'I'm thinking of leaving the group, as a matter of fact. I've had it with living my life out of suitcases, playing gigs in places you'd rather not know. Since—well, since I met Helen, I've been thinking of spending more time writing music, rather than performing it. Getting a permanent base. Maybe settling down.'

'Here?' Reed had enquired faintly, strangely reluctant to voice the question, but Jon had not been reluctant to answer.

'Could be,' he had replied, without any hesitation. 'So maybe Aunt Vee ought to get used to me being around. And if she has a problem with that, then maybe *she* ought to make other arrangements.'

Still, so far Jon had respected his wishes, Reed reflected wryly. His own fears that Jon might gatecrash the party had not been realised, and Victoria should have nothing to complain about. And as for Helen——

'Now, Reed, what are you doing hiding yourself away over here?'

Reed's reverie was abruptly severed by the teasing voice of a brittle, pretty woman in her thirties whose startling cleavage revealed a generous display of white flesh. Sliding possessive fingers over his sleeve, she allowed her hip to brush against his, her scarlet lips parting to expose a seductive tip of tongue.

Reed straightened from the lounging position he had been adopting, and in so doing put what he hoped looked like an inadvertent amount of space between them. 'Hello, Amanda,' he responded pleasantly, making a conscious effort to be sociable. 'Where's Harry? Don't tell me he's let you out of his sight.'

Amanda Austin's expression momentarily faltered. 'As if you cared,' she retorted, barely audibly, revealing she had not been unaware of his discreet withdrawal. And then, 'Oh—Harry's about somewhere. Isn't he always? But tell me, where's that sexy son of yours? I hear he's back on the island.'

'Yes, Jon's back,' Reed conceded, welcoming the diversion. 'But he's not here tonight. He—er—this isn't exactly his sort of thing.'

'No, I heard he'd brought a rather juicy female with him,' responded Amanda drily. 'Is she really that bad?'

Reed sighed. 'I don't know what you mean.'

'Sure you do.' Amanda gazed up at him challengingly. 'I guess old Victoria refused to let him show her up again. So—what's this woman like? Is she loud—or wall-eyed—or what?'

Reed turned his head aside, wishing Amanda would find someone else to talk to. In spite of her antipathy towards him, he had no desire to discuss Helen with Amanda or anyone else, and he was thinking of making some wholly unforgivable remark, which would sever their connection—for this evening at least—when his eyes were drawn to a small disturbance that was taking place by the door. There seemed to be an argument going on between the security men Victoria had hired for the evening and someone else who was trying to gain entrance, and even as he hazarded a guess at what it might be his companion uttered a gurgling laugh.

'Oh, darling,' she exclaimed, grabbing his arm. 'Do you see what I see? It looks like I'm going to find out for myself.'

Reed shook off her restraining hold without really being aware of it, covering the crowded space between where he had been standing and the door without a second thought. *Jon*, he thought frustratedly, handing his empty glass to a curious waiter. He should have known better than to be smug. When had his son ever taken his advice?

By the time he arrived at the door, Jon, and the young woman who was with him, had already been admitted. Clearly someone else had recognised him, and who was going to prevent the owner of the gallery's nephew from attending its opening?

'Hi, Dad!'

Jon's greeting was only faintly defensive, and, as there were plenty of people milling around to hear their conversation, Reed had, perforce, to be civil.

'Jon,' he acknowledged, his eyes meeting those of his son with rather less civility. 'Helen.' His gaze moved to the young woman at his son's side with only slightly more warmth. 'What made you decide to come? I thought this wasn't quite your scene.'

'It was Helen's idea,' replied Jon carelessly, and although Helen looked a little shocked at this

announcement she didn't contradict him. 'She used to
work in a gallery in London, didn't you, love? And when
I told her about this bash, she couldn't wait to see it.'

Reed was aware that Victoria had now noticed what
was going on, and he didn't need to see her furious face
to know that she would blame him for letting it happen.
Already, one or two of the newspaper people were
drifting over to hear what was happening, and it wouldn't
be long before they, too, realised who Jon was.

Forcing back a desire to leave them all to fight it out
between them, Reed turned to Helen. 'You—worked in
a gallery?' he echoed absently, while his mind laboured
furiously, trying to find some way of salvaging the situation. 'Um—Victoria worked in London for a time.
Perhaps she would know of it.'

'I shouldn't think so.' As usual, Helen's voice was stiff
when she spoke to him. 'I—er—I only worked there a
couple of evenings, to—to help a friend out.' She licked
her lips, and avoiding his gaze she looked beyond him
to the paintings that lined the walls of the gallery. 'Jon—
shall we look around? I—I'm sure your father is too
busy to chat to us right now.'

Reed's brow creased. If it hadn't been for the fact that
Helen always treated him like a leper, he would have
suspected she was nervous. Perhaps that was it. Perhaps
he made her nervous. It would be reassuring to think it
was something as innocent as that, and not just his own
personality.

'Hey, aren't you Jon Roberts?'

A girl who didn't look much older than Jon himself,
and who reputedly wrote for one of the fringe maga-
zines, was staring at him now, and Reed groaned as the
inevitable happened. One by one, the journalists,
scenting a controversial twist to their stories, left Victoria
talking to herself and surrounded her nephew instead.

'How long are you staying on the island, Jon?' one
of the men asked.

'I hear there's a new album,' someone else intervened.

'Do you want to give us a quote about the latest drug-
abuse figures?' added another. 'Is it true that your
drummer, Ricky Ellis, was arrested in Denmark for
smuggling cocaine?'

'Oh, *God*!'

With a gesture of frustration at his sister, Reed drew back from the group of reporters around his son. There was nothing he could do now, he realised, lifting his shoulders at Victoria's expression. But, later on, Jon was going to feel the sharp edge of his tongue. For heaven's sake, he had asked him to stay away. What the hell was Jon playing at? Pretending it was all Helen's fault just wasn't going to do it.

'It's my fault really.' As Reed was raking weary fingers through his hair, he became aware that the young woman in question was not sharing Jon's limelight. Instead, she was standing beside him, and looking decidedly anxious. 'It is my fault,' she insisted, as her words captured his attention. 'But I didn't realise what was going on. I thought it was just another exhibition. But it's not, is it? Your sister—that is, Victoria—she's involved, isn't she?'

It was the first time she had spoken to him without any obvious animosity, thought Reed objectively, looking at her with faintly guarded eyes. So, nervousness was not her problem, he deduced with a frown. Whatever, the present situation had evidently aroused some latent sense of responsibility.

'You mean, it was your idea to come here, but you didn't know it was the opening night?' he enquired evenly, and Helen nodded. A becoming trace of colour had entered her cheeks as he spoke, and Reed found himself thinking what an attractive girl she was. Until then, he realised, he had never really looked into her eyes, her usual attitude towards him not encouraging him to show an overt interest in her. Before this evening, he had regarded her with a certain amount of impatience, but now he noticed that her hair, which was loose for once, had a natural curl, and the artificial light caught streaks of red-gold in its thick strands and turned them to flame. She was wearing red, a colour which should have clashed badly with her hair, but somehow didn't. She had worn red before, he thought, though when that occasion had been he couldn't quite remember. Nevertheless, the silkily draped bodice and matching wide-legged trousers were undeniably controversial for someone of her colouring, and because the outfit emphasised the rounded swell of her breasts and the flattering length of her legs, Victoria would definitely not approve.

But he approved, Reed acknowledged to himself, half irritably, realising he was giving her far too much attention. If he wasn't careful, some other shrewd eye would notice it, too, and he had no wish to be accused of ogling his son's girlfriend. All the same, he was beginning to understand why Jon was so fascinated by her. She was a very feminine individual. And, although he had no way of knowing it, he was sure there were layers to this young woman that he was scarcely aware of.

'This opening—it has something to do with your sister, hasn't it?' Helen was venturing now, and Reed had to concentrate to comprehend what she was saying. 'Jon—well, Jon just said there was an exhibition in town.' Her tongue circled her lips, and Reed felt a prickling of heat around his collar. 'I had no idea what was involved, or that there'd be reporters, and—and everything.'

'Didn't you?' Reed found he believed her. 'Well—as you've guessed, this is Victoria's big night. This is her baby, you see. This gallery—it's hers. She wanted the opening to be a big success, and, to be honest, I asked Jon not to come.'

'Oh, lord!'

Helen looked even more embarrassed at this, and to his astonishment Reed found himself making excuses for her. 'It's not your fault,' he declared, deliberately ignoring Victoria's frantic attempts to attract his attention. 'You weren't to know what was happening. Come on. I'll buy you a drink and show you around, if you like. You might enjoy it.'

In the event, Reed suspected he enjoyed it as much, if not more, than Helen. Surprisingly, she proved to be quite knowledgeable about art, and artists, and her comments about the painters represented in the exhibition were both intelligent and constructive. They even found they had the same sense of humour, sharing a covert amusement over some painter's interpretation of the human form. But when Reed remembered what Jon had said, and mentioned the London gallery where she had worked, Helen quickly clammed up. It was as if she had some reason to hide the fact that she had ever been involved in the art world, and Reed wondered if it was conceivable that she had known Victoria before she came to Bermuda.

But that didn't make sense, he argued silently. If Victoria had done something to warrant Helen's attitude towards the family, surely she would know about it. Nevertheless, Victoria did have a habit sometimes of rubbing people up the wrong way. Particularly junior members of staff, as Helen must have been when she was moonlighting.

It was frustrating not to know, but for the present he had to contain his curiosity. Besides, he did have other problems to contend with. Not least the fact that other eyes were following their progress around the room, with varying degrees of speculation; particularly those of his sister, who could scarcely contain her indignation.

When she could eventually stand it no longer, and came stomping across the room to join them, Luther Styles at her heels, Reed steeled himself for the worst. 'I knew this would happen,' she exclaimed, dismissing Helen's presence with a contemptuous glance. 'But you wouldn't listen. You let him come here, when I expressly asked you to forbid it. And now look what's happened! It's a total fiasco!'

'Not entirely, Vicki,' drawled Luther Styles, apparently seeking to pour oil on troubled waters, though Reed noticed his eyes lingered longest on Helen. 'Is this your son's young lady, Wyatt? I bet you wish you were twenty years younger.'

Reed controlled his temper with an effort and introduced them, but Victoria was fidgeting beside him, and he had to placate her. 'Jon is over twenty-one, Tori,' he essayed tautly, wishing he could hear what Luther was saying to Helen. 'I can't ban him from his own home, as I've said before.'

'But this is not his own home,' hissed Victoria violently, so angry about what had happened that she was not keeping her usual eye on her protégé. 'Reed, I don't ask much of you in the normal course of events, but I did ask you to speak to him——'

'I did speak to him,' said Reed heavily, his voice growing increasingly devoid of expression. 'Tori, this is neither the time nor the place to conduct an inquest. I agree, it would have been better if Jon hadn't come. But he's here now, so why don't you make the best of it? He's your nephew, isn't he? Doesn't it occur to you that some of his publicity could rub off on you?'

Victoria blinked, opened her mouth as if she was going to say something, and then closed it again. He could see she was thinking about what he had just said, and mentally arguing the pros and cons of it. And why not? he thought grimly. It was not a half-bad suggestion. It was amazing what the brain could come up with in moments of extreme aggravation.

'You know,' she said, after a moment, 'you could have a point. I mean, I was quite prepared for some of these Press people to scarcely give us a mention, but now that Jon's here...'

Reed sighed. 'Precisely.'

'All the same...' Victoria's fluttering gaze suddenly took in the fact that Luther and the young woman her nephew had brought to the party were having what appeared to be an intimate conversation, and her expression hardened. 'All the same,' she repeated, revealing her annoyance, 'it might be a good idea if you were the one to suggest the idea to Jon, Reed.' She determinedly took Luther's arm. 'Come along, my dear,' she added, ignoring Helen completely, 'I want to introduce you to my nephew. He's quite a celebrity, you know. Well, here on the island, at least,' she finished damningly.

Reed expelled a weary breath. He had to go with them. Having set the wheels in motion, he had to make sure it didn't end in another unholy pile-up. 'Will you excuse me?' he said, turning to Helen, with a rueful grimace. 'I think it will be safer if I speak to Jon.'

Helen was looking anxious again. 'There won't be a row, will there?' she asked, her eyes following Victoria's progress, and Reed hoped he was not being too optimistic when he shook his head.

'I think Jon's too much of a professional for that,' he remarked, realising he was delaying the moment when he would have to leave her. 'Anyway, thanks for showing *me* round the exhibition. I did enjoy it.'

She seemed to hesitate, and he guessed she was debating whether to say she had enjoyed it, too. But why the hesitation? He could have sworn that for a few minutes there she had actually dropped her guard with him, and there was no doubt she had spoken more freely than she had ever done with him before. For God's sake, what had Jon told her about him? he wondered. He was beginning to think he must have been painted as some kind of middle-aged lecher of the first order. What other reason could she have for looking at him that way?

'I—enjoyed it, too,' she admitted at last, and Reed knew how it felt to be damned with faint praise. 'Um— I think your sister's waiting for you,' she added. 'Perhaps you'd better go, before something awful happens.'

'You mean it hasn't?' Reed remarked drily, and saw the faint colour that rose in her cheeks at his words. What on earth was she thinking? He shrugged. 'Oh, well,' he declared, glancing ruefully across the room, 'I suppose you're right. Sorry about Victoria. You'll just have to accept that we're not your conventional sort of family!'

CHAPTER FIVE

WHICH was something of an understatement, thought Helen the next morning, as she showered before joining Jon and his family for breakfast. There was nothing remotely conventional about Reed's fathering a child he didn't even know existed, or in not remembering the girl he had once been so intimate with.

Helen sighed. The memories just went round and round in her brain, in a never-ending spiral. And, in spite of the fact that she had decided she couldn't hold Jon responsible for his father's actions, the situation hadn't improved. Oh, she had considered all the alternatives, before deciding she had to stay here. She had thought of pretending that Alexa was ill and asking for her, but in those circumstances, she knew, Jon would have insisted on accompanying her back to England, and what would she say then, when he discovered it was all made up? Besides, it wasn't wise to invent an excuse like that. Lies of that sort had a habit of coming true, and Alexa was far too dear to her to risk wishing an illness on her.

Another idea she had considered had been to pretend that Alan Wright had sent a message, via her parents, asking if she could come back right away. As she had phoned her parents, and Alexa, the day after their arrival, it had been a viable proposition. But Jon knew Alan, too, and if she made up some story that he had sent for her, she would have to invent another set of lies for Alan, to induce his assistance.

And then, there was Alexa herself. How could she explain to her daughter why she didn't want to stay with Jon's family? Apart from a natural reluctance to be separated from her mother for a fairly long period of time, Alexa had been quite excited about the trip, particularly as Jon had told her that maybe one day she could visit the island, too. When Helen spoke to her on the phone, the little girl had been full of questions about what it was like, and where they were going, and Helen would have had to have had a heart of stone not to respond enthusiastically.

So, here she was, she thought wryly, preparing to face her fourth day at Palmer's Sound. And after last night's little altercation, she was not exactly looking forward to seeing Victoria again. In spite of the fact that Jon's intervention at the exhibition had been turned to her advantage, Victoria had still been less than friendly when they arrived home. So far as she was concerned, Jon's motives in attending the party had not been excusable, and she had lost no time in telling him so, once the *paparazzi* were not around to report on the event.

For her part, Helen had wished she had never heard of the exhibition. No matter how she might argue that Jon had used her to annoy his aunt, the fact remained that she had been the one to show interest in the exhibition. And it wasn't until she had come face to face with Reed that she had realised that history could repeat itself.

Dear God, she should have known better. The idea of entering any art gallery where Reed Wyatt might be present should have made her run a mile. But, the truth was, she had seen the exhibition as a way of avoiding Jon's father. She had had no way of knowing that he would be in attendance. So far as she had been concerned, it was an opportunity for her and Jon to spend the evening alone together, visiting the exhibition first, and then dining at one of the many restaurants that were available in the city.

Of course, she might have suspected Jon had an ulterior motive. He had certainly been in good spirits as they were chauffeured into town, and although he was usually cheerful he had been exceptionally so. It was obvious he would jump at any chance to irritate Victoria, and the opening of her gallery was too good an occasion to miss.

All the same, if she was honest, Helen had to admit it was not Jon's, or Victoria's, behaviour which was troubling her now. It was her own. Meeting Reed like that, allowing history to repeat at least a part of that night in London, had left her feeling unnerved, and strangely disorientated. She hadn't wanted to spend any time with him, but she had; and, what was worse, there had been times when she had actually *enjoyed* his company.

Lord!

Stepping out of the shower now, Helen took one of the fluffy cream bath-sheets from the rail. Then, towelling herself vigorously, she made a determined effort to dispel the sense of panic her thoughts had incited. For heaven's sake, she told herself fiercely, what was so dreadful about admitting that Reed Wyatt was still an attractive man? Attractive physically, that was, she amended. His character wouldn't bear such close examination. Nevertheless, if a man like him set about to be charming, she would have had to be less than human not to respond to it. And she had found herself only too human once, where he was concerned. So why

assume that he must suddenly have grown horns and a
tail?

Because of what he had done! Because of the callous
way he had done it! her emotions argued desperately.
All right, objectively Reed was a physically good
specimen—for his age, she appended maliciously. And
it was obvious she wasn't the only woman to think so.
That blonde he had been standing with, when they
arrived at the party, for instance—oh, yes, she acknowledged bitterly. She had noticed him as soon as she had
stepped into the room. But, anyway, *she*, the blonde,
had been gazing at him as if he were the most tasty item
on the menu, and Helen's jaw tightened at the thought
that she might be his current mistress. For she was sure
Reed would have a mistress. A man like him—a man as
sexual as him—was bound to have some woman, somewhere. Just because he had never married again was no
reason to assume he was celibate. No. There had to be
someone, and it was probably someone like her.

She was dry now, Helen discovered, the heat of her
body obviously assisting in the process, and she dropped
the towel disgustedly. And, as she did so, she caught a
glimpse of her reflection in the long mirrors that lined
the wall above the bath. She looked pale and tight-lipped,
she fretted impatiently, the brightness of her hair only
accentuating the whiteness of her skin. Even two days
on the island had added little to her colouring, the
faintest trace of redness over her shoulders and forearms,
and on the upper half of her thighs, the only indication
she had spent any time in the sun. Of course, she had
to be careful. Her skin was very sensitive—
unfortunately—and she had to apply a liberal amount
of screening lotion to prevent herself from burning. But
even so she and Jon had spent most of their time out-
doors, and he was already looking as if the holiday was
doing him good.

But it wasn't doing her much good, she thought frustratedly. At least, it didn't feel as if it was. She was
constantly on edge; constantly at the mercy of her nerves;
and increasingly aware that she was not as invulnerable
as she had thought.

Endeavouring to put her fears about the night before aside, Helen opened the walk-in wardrobe, and put her mind to deciding what she was going to wear. It would have to be shorts, of course. Everyone wore shorts, of one sort or another, and she was grateful that her legs could stand the exposure. For the rest, she had found T-shirts or cotton tops were the regular accompaniment, with usually a bathing-suit worn underneath, to cover all eventualities.

Forcing any negative thoughts aside, Helen admitted, on reflection, that there had been times during the past couple of days when she had been able to forget her circumstances. For instance, Jon owned a motorbike, and he had taken great pains to show her the rest of the island. Although cars were limited to one per family, to avoid the obvious congestion that unlimited motoring would bring to the narrow roads, tourists were able to hire motorbikes and scooters, too, and, riding pillion behind Jon, Helen had felt just like a tourist.

And she had seen a lot. Somerset Bridge—which was quite a beauty spot; the little town of St George's—with its ritual enactment of the ceremony of the ducking stool; and Gibbs Hill Lighthouse—from where it was possible to see the individual islands that made up Bermuda, with their linking causeways and sun-splashed coves. They had swum in Warwick Bay, and Horseshoe Bay, and visited the underground caverns at Leamington. Jon had even taught her how to go snorkelling, and, although she wasn't too keen on the rubber mouthpiece, she had to admit she had seen a lot of colourful fish.

So, she chided herself firmly, as she plaited her hair into a single braid, there was no real reason why she shouldn't relax and enjoy herself. In fact, if you looked at the situation from another angle, it was Reed, not herself, who was the unlucky one. After all, he had forfeited any rights to a little girl any parent would be proud of, and she was enjoying his hospitality. Whereas when—if he realised who she was, he would probably die of shock.

Or would he? Once again, Helen's doubts resurfaced. If he ever did remember who she was, how would she explain the situation to Jon? But equally how could she

confide in him, when it was his father who had robbed
her of her youth? There was no doubt it was an impossible dilemma, and there was little wonder that when she
was in Reed's company she found it difficult to behave
naturally. And yet, yesterday evening...

Determinedly putting that particular incident aside,
she thought instead about the exhibition. Looking at it
objectively—if that was possible—she had enjoyed seeing
the paintings, and there was little doubt in her mind that
Luther Styles was going to be very successful. His work,
particularly his portraits, had a depth of feeling not often
found in someone so inexperienced. Reed—Reed? Well,
dammit, she had to acknowledge his existence, didn't
she? So—Reed—had said that Victoria had found him
by the harbour in St George's, sketching portraits for
the tourists. But she had recognised his talent, and with
her help and encouragement he had been able to set up
his own studio.

Even so, despite the evidence to the contrary, Helen
sensed that Victoria's interest in Luther extended far
beyond that of a philanthropic patron. Indeed, it was
possible she had opened the gallery because of him, and
although she was inadvertently helping other painters,
no one could deny that he was her favourite.

For her part, Helen had found him amusing, but
arrogant. She didn't like people who were so full of their
own importance, and there was no question about the
fact that Luther was vain. She was so much more used
to Jon, who took his success as a pop musician very
casually, that she had found the other man lacking in
humility, and she wondered if Victoria really knew what
he was thinking.

Deciding she had spent enough time worrying about
someone who evidently didn't care for her, Helen took
a last look at her appearance before leaving the room.
Navy shorts, and a navy and white striped midi top,
looked reasonably attractive, she thought, and at least
the conservative colours helped to minimise the paleness
of her skin. Some bright colours, she had found,
accentuated the fact that she didn't tan.

Leaving her suite of rooms, she hesitated a moment
before walking along the landing towards the stairs. Jon's

room, she knew, was several doors away from her own, down a couple of stairs, and along a narrow passage. It was actually in a round tower that formed one corner of the house, and although Helen had seen it she was loath to venture there uninvited. Besides he might get the wrong impression, and the last thing she needed was a complication of that sort.

Nevertheless, she wished she knew if he was up. This was the time of day she liked least, when there was always the possibility of facing Reed alone. So far, she had been lucky. Because of the time change, Jon had been up early both mornings they had been here, and, although Reed and his sister had been present at the breakfast table, Reed had tactfully read his newspaper and Victoria had buried her nose in a pile of correspondence. No doubt finalising her plans for opening the gallery, Helen thought now, with hindsight. Which was another reason why she hoped that Jon was up.

She went lightly down the stairs, her rubber-soled boots making no sound on the carpeted treads. It was easy to think she was alone in the house, she reflected fancifully. It was so big for two people—or four, now that she and Jon were here.

In the hall below, streaks of sunlight from the vaulted dome above her head cast bars of sunlight over the marble. *Bars* of sunlight! Helen grimaced. They weren't *bars*, they were simply shafts of brightness. No doubt a psychologist would have a field day with *that* particular interpretation.

The morning-room where they usually ate breakfast was situated at the back of the house, overlooking the blue-green waters of the Sound. And, although Helen had gradually become accustomed to the fantastic view from the morning-room's windows, the colour of the sea was something she found continually enchanting. And this morning was no exception. Which was just as well, as it provided the only distraction from the start-ling realisation that only Reed Wyatt was seated in his usual place at the table.

'Good morning,' he said, putting his paper and his napkin aside, and getting to his feet as she came unwillingly into the room. 'Did you sleep well?'

'Er—fine,' she muttered, after acknowledging his greeting. She glanced awkwardly over her shoulder. 'Um—where is everybody?'

Reed shrugged, his shoulder muscles moving easily beneath the apricot knitted silk of his polo shirt. The shirt, beige shorts and scuffed trainers were all he was wearing, and for a moment Helen could only stare at him in confusion. She was so used to seeing him in the dress shirts and ties he wore to his office that his casual gear caught her unawares, and it took her several seconds to comprehend that it was Sunday.

'At a guess, I'd say Victoria was sleeping off the effects of too much champagne,' he replied wryly, as she suddenly realised she was staring and switched her attention elsewhere. He paused, and then went on quietly, 'As for Jon—don't you know?'

Helen caught her breath. 'We don't sleep together, if that's what you're implying,' she flashed back at him angrily, and Reed held up an apologetic hand, as if regretting his words. But Helen was too incensed to think clearly, and before she could stop herself she had added, 'I don't sleep around, Mr Wyatt. Whatever you may have assumed to the contrary!'

Reed was momentarily lost for words. She could see that—just as she could see that she had been unforgivably rude. And, even though she told herself she was glad she had embarrassed him for a change, it would be awful if her reckless tongue caused him to have second thoughts about her. What if he *did* remember who she was? Dear God, how could she have been so stupid?

'I'm sorry,' Reed said now, and for once his tone was lacking the warmth she had become used to. 'I guess I spoke without thinking. Young people today——' He lifted his shoulders in a deprecating gesture. 'As you say, one should never assume anything.'

Helen bent her head, looking down at the toes of her boots with a feeling of total humiliation. So much for embarrassing him, she thought tensely. All she had succeeded in doing was making a complete fool of herself.

'I'm sorry, too,' she mumbled, lifting her head to meet his cool gaze with wary green eyes. 'I didn't mean to—to be rude.'

'Didn't you?' To her dismay, Reed didn't take her apology at face value. 'Forgive me, but I think you did. In fact, I'd go so far as to say that you've been looking for an opportunity like that ever since you got here.'

Helen's face blazed with unwelcome colour, and she was sure she must look as guilty as she felt. 'I—I beg your pardon?' she got out at last, but now it was Reed's turn to ignore her excuses.

'I think you heard what I said,' he replied evenly. 'You haven't exactly hidden your feelings, have you? For some reason, you resent us. *Me!* I'm not sure which. But I'd sure as hell like to find out why!'

Helen swallowed. This was dreadful. 'You're wrong——!'

'Am I?'

'Yes.'

'Convince me.'

'What?' Helen stared at him with disbelieving eyes.

'I said—convince me,' Reed repeated, stepping round the table, and resting his hips against the rim. He folded his arms and regarded her steadily. 'Tell me that you haven't avoided speaking to me, whenever it was possible to do so. Tell me that you haven't treated me like some particularly objectionable form of life.'

Helen shook her head. 'You're mistaken——'

'I don't think so.' Reed was disturbingly close, and she could feel tiny rivulets of sweat trickling down her spine, as he continued to stare at her. His eyes were grey, she knew. As grey as Alexa's, in fact. But right now they looked almost black, and her mouth dried as she realised what a dangerous situation she had created.

'I'm sorry if you think I've been ungrateful,' she ventured at last, but Reed's expression didn't alter.

'Who said anything about ingratitude?' he countered drily. 'I want to know what it is about me that bugs you. What did I say, for heaven's sake? What did I do?'

That was too close for comfort, and no matter how she might despise herself later Helen knew she had to distract him. Plastering a weak smile to her lips, she gave what she hoped sounded like a gurgle of laughter. 'Honestly, Mr Wyatt,' she exclaimed, moving round him to take her place at the breakfast table, 'I don't know how you've got that impression. Why, last night I thought we were getting on together rather well. I really appreciated you showing me round the gallery, and I did apologise for giving Jon an excuse to gatecrash his aunt's party.'

Reed expelled his breath on a long sigh, turning his head so that he could look at her over his shoulder. 'Last night was an exception,' he declared flatly. 'And you know it.'

'Was it?' Helen forced herself to look up at him with innocent eyes, and Reed's brow furrowed.

'You know,' he said, pushing himself away from the table, 'you remind me of someone.' He shook his head. 'But I can't remember who it is.'

Helen could feel the colour draining out of her face, but she managed not to flinch. 'Do I?' she countered, keeping the tremor out of her voice with a supreme effort. 'Someone nice, I hope.'

'I can't remember that either,' he declared, resuming his seat with a resigned expression. 'That's what comes of getting old. The memory is the first indication.'

Helen moistened her lips. 'You're not old,' she said, still trying to divert him, and Reed looked across the table at her, his eyes intent.

'You don't have to lie to make a point,' he told her gently, and Helen hated the way her stomach muscles melted at his words. Just the sound of his voice was like a rough hand scraping across her emotions, and her own vulnerability had never been more apparent.

'I'm not lying,' she said, as much to convince herself that she could handle the situation as anything else, and Reed lifted his shoulders in a dismissing gesture.

'OK,' he conceded, his lean mouth turning up slightly at the corners. 'So—let's talk about something else, hmm? Like—what are you and Jon planning to do today? And does the idea of spending a few hours on the yacht appeal to you?'

As it happened, one of the Asian maids appeared at that moment to ask Helen what she would like for breakfast, but the breathing-space she might have had was swallowed up with her insistence on having toast and nothing else. And, by the time the maid departed, she was still at a loss for words.

'The yacht?' she said at last, pouring herself a glass of orange juice, holding the jug with both hands to prevent it from clattering against the rim of the glass. 'You—you have a yacht?'

'Didn't Jon tell you?' Reed's eyes were disturbingly perceptive. 'Well, no. Perhaps he wouldn't,' he added humorously. 'The last time he took the yacht out, it capsized.'

Helen concentrated on her orange juice to avoid looking at him, and made a suitable sound of distress. 'No, he never mentioned it,' she admitted, licking a speck of zest from her lip. 'Are—are you a keen sailor, Mr Wyatt?'

'I like to take the yacht out occasionally,' he responded, and she was aware of him helping himself to another cup of coffee. 'And I think I asked you to call me Reed,' he added. 'Or is that something else I'm mistaken about?'

Her head jerked up unwarily, and she met his intent gaze with unguarded eyes. She had thought she had averted a crisis, but she found at once she hadn't. 'I—no—that is, I didn't like to,' she stammered, furious that she had let him disconcert her once again. 'I mean—you are Jon's father. And—and we hardly know one another.'

'True.' Reed was reluctantly prepared to be benevolent, and she breathed a little more easily. 'Nevertheless, I think I'd feel better if you could dispense with the formality. If we're going to be friends, it seems unnecessary.'

Helen forced another smile, and then the maid came back with her toast and some fresh coffee, and for several minutes she was able to divert herself by dealing with her breakfast. But she wasn't hungry. Indeed, it took an immense amount of will-power even to lift the buttered toast to her lips. Perhaps she should have ordered scrambled eggs, she thought uneasily. Maybe she could have swallowed them without such an effort.

'Tell me about your daughter,' said Reed suddenly, and she was forced to acknowledge him again. He had

finished his breakfast now, and instead of resuming his
appraisal of the previous day's *Financial Times*, as he
usually did, he was lying back in his chair, watching her
with unnerving speculation. God, where was Jon? she
fretted desperately. The last thing she wanted to do was
discuss Alexa with him.

'Um—there's not a lot to tell,' she mumbled, her
mouth full of the toast she was trying unsuccessfully to
swallow. She turned her head deliberately and looked at
the Sound. 'You are lucky living here. Imagine seeing
this view every morning.'

Reed barely cast a glance at the dark blue waters of
the bay. His interest was still trained on herself, and she
realised that by being evasive she was only deepening his
curiosity.

'She's called Alexa, isn't that right?' he remarked,
almost as if Helen hadn't said anything, and she was
just arming herself for another bout of verbal fencing
when Jon came slouching into the room.

Her relief was almost palpable, and it took an
enormous effort not to get up from her chair and throw
her arms around him. However, almost immediately she
realised that something was wrong, and Jon confirmed
this opinion by throwing himself into the chair opposite
and propping his head in his hands.

'Do you have any aspirin, Dad?' he asked thickly. 'I've
got the most God-awful headache!'

Reed pushed back his chair and got to his feet. 'I'm
sure we'll have some about here somewhere,' he said,
and although he exchanged another look with Helen his
attention was distracted. 'Just a minute. I'll have a word
with Laura.'

He left the room and Helen, who had been gazing at
Jon with anxious eyes, left her seat and went round the
table to him. 'What's caused this?' she asked softly,
massaging his neck muscles. 'Too much champagne?'

'Hardly,' responded Jon drily, lifting his hand to cover
one of hers. 'It feels like a migraine. I guess riding the
bike without any shades could have done it.'

'What a shame!' Helen squeezed his shoulders. 'Is
there anything I can do?'

'Well, I have heard that sex can help,' he answered teasingly, looking up at her with an obvious effort, and Helen pressed her finger gently down upon his nose.

'You're incorrigible, do you know that?' she exclaimed, making a face at him, and Jon was just reaching up to pull her head down to his when Reed came back into the room. Immediately, Helen jerked back, and Jon gave a grunt of protest as his father came towards them.

If Reed had noticed the little tableau that was being enacted in his absence, he gave no sign of it. Instead, as Helen withdrew to her own side of the table, he poured some of the orange juice into a glass, and set it down, together with a couple of tablets, in front of his son.

'Take them,' he said, standing over Jon as he did so. 'Laura says her mother swears by them.'

'Laura's mother's a witch,' declared Jon grumpily, but he took the tablets anyway, grimacing as he did so.

'Whatever, she's usually right,' Reed responded evenly. 'She also said you should rest for a while, to give them time to work.'

Jon groaned. 'I can't do that.'

'Do what?'

'Rest.' He sighed. 'What about Helen?'

'Oh, honestly——' Helen began to protest that she was perfectly capable of entertaining herself, when once more Reed intervened.

'I'll take care of Helen,' he assured his son firmly. 'It will give us a chance to get to know one another better. Isn't that right, Helen?'

'Oh—right,' murmured Helen unwillingly, and then forced a smile to her lips as Jon looked at her for confirmation. 'Really. You go and get some rest.'

Jon pushed himself to his feet again with an effort. 'Well, OK,' he said. 'If you're sure you don't mind——'

'She'll be fine.' Reed gave his son a gentle push towards the door. 'Go on. We'll see you later.'

Jon gave Helen one last rueful grimace before leaving the room. But it was obvious he was relieved to be going back to bed. Which was great for Jon, but not so great for her, thought Helen, trying not to feel envious. Now all she had to do was convince Reed that she could take care of herself for the next few hours. The last thing she wanted was for him to feel he had to entertain her. The less time they spent alone together, the better.

Resuming her seat at the table, she lifted her coffee-cup to her lips, hoping Reed would get the message and leave her alone. But she was wrong on two counts. One, her coffee was cold, and two, Reed exploded any hopes she might have had about escaping to her own room by saying casually, 'It looks as if I'll have to take you sailing myself. When you're finished there, join me down at the dock.'

CHAPTER SIX

OF COURSE, Helen protested. She said there was no need for Reed to feel responsible for her, that she couldn't possibly take up his time, and that, in any case, she had things she wanted to do—but it didn't do any good. Reed insisted he had promised Jon he would look after her, and besides, he was looking forward to taking the yacht out.

'You can crew,' he said, pausing in the doorway, and, when she objected that she had never done any sailing before, he assured her that it was a piece of cake.

'I suppose that's why Jon capsized, the last time he went out,' she retorted, stung into instinctive retaliation, but Reed only smiled.

'It wasn't this yacht he capsized,' he told her toler-antly. 'And in any case I'll be with you.' He paused. 'Bring your swimsuit. And don't be long.'

His arrogance infuriated her, but there was nothing she could do. And, when she eventually made her way down to the jetty, she found Reed loading a can of petrol into what appeared to be a launch with an outboard motor. With his hair rumpled by the breeze off the water, and a smear of oil on his cheek, he looked little older than his son, and she realised unwillingly how easy it must have been for the sixteen-year-old Helen to be attracted to him. Compared to the boys she had known at that time, he must have seemed so cool and sophisticated—only she hadn't used words like sophisticated in those days. To her, he had been exciting, and sexy, and the dangers he represented had only added to his appeal.

He looked up then, and saw her, and his lips twisted as he misinterpreted her troubled expression. 'This is *not* it,' he declared drily, straightening and holding out a hand to help her aboard. 'She's anchored out there,' he added, indicating the yachts moored some distance from the shore. 'These waters are too shallow, and too rocky.'

'I see.'

Helen accepted his assistance to climb into the launch, but she extracted her hand from his as soon as it was humanly possible, and bumped down on to the plank seat at the far end of the boat. But her hand was still tingling, even after she had stowed the canvas bag containing a second swimsuit and her protective cream down at her feet.

If Reed noticed her withdrawal, however, he gave no sign of it. Hauling a wicker basket into the launch after him, he cast off the line and started the motor. Then, seating himself beside the tiller, he guided the fast-moving little boat out to where a cluster of masts bobbed on the tide.

Helen spent the time it took to reach the yacht reading the names of the craft that were moored offshore. She saw lots of female names, like *Felicity*, and *Aurora*, as well as cuter appellations such as *Stingray*, *Dream Trader*, and *Sea Fever*. She wondered what Reed's yacht would be called. Something classy, she expected. She couldn't imagine him calling a boat *Sassy Alice*, or *Match O'Man*. No, she speculated wisely, more like *Ariadne*, or *Desdemona*. Something with a classical connotation.

She was wrong—which was only to be expected, she thought crossly, as the launch nudged the hull of a vessel with *Ocean Tramp* painted on its side. She should have known that one thing Reed Wyatt was *not* was predictable, and she sighed a little heavily as he stood up to toss both the basket and the can of oil on to the larger vessel. And it was *much* larger, Helen saw, with some anxiety. At least forty feet in length, with sleek, racing lines. How on earth were the two of them going to handle it?

Reed noticed her look of trepidation then, and grinned. 'What's the matter?' he said. 'Are you wondering how you're going to get aboard?'

In fact, that particular obstacle hadn't occurred to her, and she shook her head. 'It seems so—big,' she murmured, making no attempt to get up from her seat. 'Don't—don't we need Jon, too?'

'To sail it, you mean?' suggested Reed, securing the launch to the mooring mast. 'No. It's possible to sail it single-handed, actually. What's wrong? Aren't you a good sailor?'

'I don't know,' replied Helen honestly. 'I've never tried.'

'But you can swim.'

It was a statement, more than a question, but Helen nodded indignantly. 'Of course.'

'OK, then.' He regarded her tolerantly. 'Let's go.'

She stood up unwillingly, the misgivings she had about being alone with Reed combining with a sense of unease about this whole expedition to turn her legs to jelly. Stepping clumsily over the centre seat, she made it to the end of the boat where he was standing, trying not to notice the fact that their combined weight caused the side of the boat to dip perilously close to the water. It was funny, she thought; she could swim in these waters without turning a hair, but the idea of falling out of a boat seemed intrinsically dangerous.

'Now,' said Reed, taking her hand again, 'step on to the gunwale, can you? That's the side of the boat,' he added, for her benefit. 'Then, you'll be able to climb aboard.'

'Will I?'

Helen couldn't prevent the doubtful rejoinder, and Reed chuckled. 'Don't worry,' he said. 'I won't let you fall. I'll be right behind you.'

That's what worries me, thought Helen uneasily, but this time she made sure the words didn't pass her lips. Instead, she concentrated on following his instructions, trying not to remember the last time she had felt his strong lean body close to her own.

In the event, it proved easier than she had anticipated. Or perhaps she had wanted to prolong those moments when his arms had been reaching past her on to the deck, Helen acknowledged unsteadily. Whatever, in a short space of time she was standing on board the *Ocean Tramp*, and the fascinating sights all around her were a welcome compensation.

Until then, she had not realised how interesting it would be. She had watched the craft using the Sound from her bedroom window, of course, and envied their owners' skills in avoiding one another. But now, she was actually part of the activity, and it was infinitely more exciting to be out here on the water. She almost felt a sense of gratitude to Reed for bringing her. Except that gratitude was something she reserved for people she could respect.

'All right?' asked Reed casually, going forward to cast off the lines, and Helen came abruptly down to earth.

'Fine,' she agreed, glancing nervously about her. Now they were completely alone, and that realisation robbed the scene of much of its previous glamour.

Yet, in spite of her misgivings, Helen couldn't deny a sense of well-being as the elegant vessel moved slowly away from her mooring. With Reed at the wheel, and the twin engines providing power until they were clear of the other craft moored off Palmer's Sound, *Ocean Tramp* truly belied her name. She wasn't a tramp at all, thought Helen, gazing about her. She was a lady; a beautiful, graceful lady, whose sleek lines and polished paintwork gleamed brilliantly in the sun.

Beyond the dozens of small islands that littered the gateway to the Great Sound, Reed switched off the engines, and the yacht drifted on the tide while he hoisted the sails. Helen, who still had images of round-the-world yachtsmen and women in her mind, had expected this to be a rather arduous operation, but once again she was wrong. All the deck winches were hydraulically powered, and only the touch of a button was needed to accomplish the task successfully. She understood now why Reed had been so confident of handling the yacht single-handed. There was no hauling on ropes—or *sheets*, she amended ruefully. She had to get the jargon right, if she was going to tell Alexa all about it when she got home. Everything was automated, and technically advanced.

But what was she going to tell Alexa? she wondered, momentarily distracted by the prospect. She could hardly say, 'Your Daddy took me sailing,' could she? Apart from anything else, so far as Alexa was concerned her father was dead.

The yacht was picking up speed now, and Helen was obliged to abandon her anxieties in favour of keeping her balance. Not that the boat was tipping over on to its side, or anything revolutionary like that. But it was catching the wind, and pitching a little on the waves, and every time the yacht lunged her stomach lunged accordingly.

She hoped she was a good sailor. It would be too embarrassing to be ill in front of Reed. But her knowledge of boats was limited to rowing craft and pleasure steamers. Which was hardly the best experience for someone in her present situation.

Abandoning her stance by the rail, she felt her way aft to the cockpit. Reed had a chart spread over the wheel, and didn't look up when she reached him. But he had evidently heard her approach, and, tipping his head towards the stairway that led down below decks, he said, 'Do you want to make us some coffee? The galley's forward of the main cabin. You'll find what you need down there.'

The idea of leaving the heaving deck to grope about below did not appeal to Helen at all, and she gripped the roof of the wheelhouse with desperate fingers. What was it her father used to tell her? Watch the horizon, was that it? When everything else was rising and falling, the horizon was always blessedly steady.

'Hey—are you all right?'

Reed had realised she was not moving, and now he was looking at her with some concern. She was probably as white as the chart in front of him, Helen thought impatiently. Was she forever doomed to be humiliated in front of this man?

'I—I just feel a bit unsteady, that's all.' It was a modest distortion of the truth, but she couldn't admit to feeling seasick. Goodness, they were hardly any distance away from land.

'I see.' Although she hadn't been entirely honest with him, Helen had the depressing feeling that Reed knew exactly how she was feeling. 'Well, don't worry,' he told her reassuringly, 'this rough patch won't last. Once we've cleared Spanish Point, it gets smoother. Believe me. This is just the turbulence caused by the Sound, which is fairly land-locked, meeting the open sea.'

Helen nodded, understanding, but not wholly convinced of his logic. And where was Spanish Point, for heaven's sake? she wondered. How much longer would this choppiness go on?

'Come here,' he said, after a moment, stretching out his arm towards her, as if he had sensed her trepidation. And, although she was sure it was not the wisest thing to do, she took his hand and allowed him to draw her into the cockpit. 'Now,' he said, bracing himself behind her, 'take the wheel. That's right. Hold it gently, but firmly. Give a little, but don't let it spin out of your hands. OK. Have you got it? Right. Now, you're in control.'

'I am?' Helen was so intent on holding on to the wheel that she forgot about her queasiness. There was something so exhilarating about actually having control of a boat of this size, and as the hull sliced cleanly through the water she began to understand the fascination people acquired for sailing.

'I guess you like it,' remarked Reed over her shoulder, and Helen was so excited by the sense of power she was experiencing that she forgot to be offhand.

'Oh, yes!' she exclaimed, turning her head, and then wished she hadn't when she realised how close he was. Although he wasn't exactly touching her, she could feel the heat of his body at her back, and when she turned her head his face was only inches from hers.

Helen was mesmerised, her green eyes caught and held by his amused gaze in a moment of shared communion. She wanted to look away—she knew she *ought* to look away—but she couldn't. For that fateful second, she was totally helpless, in the grip of emotions too basic to be controlled by conscious thought. Instead of twisting

round again, and giving her attention to steering the
vessel, she continued to stare at Reed instead, and his
teasing, humorous expression gave way to a questioning
awareness.

The ground seemed to be tilting beneath her feet.
Suddenly, it was impossible to keep her balance, and she
knew a fleeting sense of incredulity. What was happening
to her? To both of them? she wondered wildly, half prepared to believe it was all in her mind. And then Reed
lunged past her and grabbed the wheel.

Immediately, the world righted itself, although the
deck heaved a little as Reed fought to bring the yacht
back under control. And, as Helen struggled to keep her
balance, she realised, with some dismay, that she had
been responsible for what had happened. In her stupid
fascination for Reed, she had allowed the wheel to spin,
and without his swift reaction the vessel could have
turned over.

'I'm sorry,' she said miserably, as Reed anchored the
wheel and went forward to secure the boom, and he lifted
his head to give her a wry smile.

'It was my fault,' he said, checking the sails with a
practised eye. 'I should have realised sooner what was
happening.'

'You can't blame yourself,' she exclaimed, and he
straightened to come back to her.

'Oh, I can,' he assured her drily. 'It was your first
time at the wheel, and I should have known better than
to distract you.'

Helen lifted her shoulders helplessly, feeling the colour
invading her cheeks at his words, but Reed seemed indifferent to her discomfort. Was it possible he hadn't
been conscious of her reaction to him? she wondered
unsteadily. Had she only imagined his awareness?

'Well—I was stupid, anyway,' she muttered, pushing
her hands into the pockets of her shorts. 'Um—shall I
make that coffee now?'

Reed shrugged. 'If you think you can?'

'It is calmer now,' Helen explained, indicating the
smoother waters around them. She licked her lips.
'Sugar, but no cream, is that right?'

Reed's lips twitched. 'You noticed.'

'Hmm.'

Helen didn't stay to debate yet another example of her own weakness, and, going forward again, she carefully descended the companionway. She found herself in a teak-lined cabin, with areas set apart for both dining and sitting. Comfortably cushioned banquettes flanked an oblong table at one side, while soft leather armchairs provided a luxurious living area at the other.

The galley was beyond the main cabin, as Reed had said, and it was provided with every conceivable appliance. There was a microwave, and a dishwasher, as well as a fridge-freezer and a regular oven. When she checked inside the cupboards that lined the walls, she found china, and glassware, and canned and freeze-dried foods of all kinds. Like the rest of the boat, it was lavishly equipped, with no expense spared to make it more efficient.

A chrome-plated tap ran fresh water into the electric kettle, and all she had to do was sit back and wait for it to boil. While it did so, she took the opportunity to explore a little further, and beyond the engine-room she found two more cabins—one a double, and the other fitted with twin bunks—and two bathrooms, or heads, as she knew they were properly called.

It was certainly a beautiful boat, she admitted, running her fingers over the rich Sanderson fabric that had been used to quilt the luxurious duvet in the double cabin. No minor detail had been omitted, and even the showers in the bathrooms had gold-plated taps.

The kettle was boiling when she got back to the galley, and in her absence the wicker basket Reed had hauled aboard the yacht had been set on the marble console. It meant he had brought it down while she was exploring the sleeping cabins, and she sighed impatiently at the thought that he might think she was nosing into his private apartments. Which she was, she acknowledged ruefully. She had just hoped he wouldn't find out.

Deciding there was no point now in wishing for the impossible, she took two ceramic mugs from one cupboard, and spooned instant coffee from a jar she found in another. The coffee smelt delicious, and after adding sugar to Reed's she looked for some milk for her own.

She found tiny pots of long-life cream in the fridge, and, determinedly ignoring the wicker basket and its possible contents, she put the two mugs on a small silver tray and carried them up the stairs to the deck.

'Mmm, great,' said Reed, taking his mug and swallowing a mouthful of the steaming liquid. 'Just what I needed.'

Helen half smiled, and propped her hips on the raised roof of the cabin as she drank hers. In spite of her misgivings, there was something companionable about sharing a cup of coffee, and she was beginning to feel almost relaxed. But she had to mention something about what she had been doing below-decks, and licking her lips she said awkwardly, 'By the way, I hope you don't think I was being nosy just now. I mean—when you brought the basket down. I—er—I was just curious about—about the layout of the rest of the boat.'

Reed regarded her steadily. 'I know.'

'I wasn't looking into drawers, or opening cupboards, or anything like that,' she added, feeling compelled to expound on her explanation. 'At least, I was in the kitchen—I mean, the galley—but I had to find the cups and the coffee.'

'I'm not complaining, am I?' Reed shrugged. 'In any case, you're welcome to look around as much as you want. Apart from the leather handcuffs and whips under the bunk in the spare cabin, I've got nothing to hide.'

Helen's jaw dropped, and then, as she realised he was teasing her, a smile spread over her face. But their shared amusement was too disturbing to sustain, and, looking down into her cup of coffee she murmured, 'I just didn't want you to feel that—well, that I was one of those awful people who can't help poking their noses into other people's affairs.'

'I never thought that for a moment,' replied Reed softly, finishing his coffee, and setting the mug aside. He paused. 'Did you open the basket?'

'No!'

Helen's denial was instinctively defensive, and he grinned. 'OK, OK,' he said placatingly. 'I just wondered. You could have, anyway. It contains our lunch.'

'Our lunch?' Helen stared at him now, and Reed inclined his head. 'But—what about Jon?'

'Jon will sleep for at least four hours,' replied Reed evenly. 'Those tablets Laura gave him weren't just pain-killers. They contain a sedative, too.'

'But——' Helen was aghast. 'Does he know that?'

'I guess so. He has taken them before.'

'Oh.' Helen took another sip of her own coffee, and considered what this meant. Not just a morning spent in Reed's company, but the better part of a whole day.

'Is the prospect so daunting?' Reed enquired now, and Helen lifted her head.

'I beg your pardon?'

'The idea of spending the day with only Jon's old man for company,' declared Reed drily, and Helen shook her head.

'I—I just thought—we were going out for—for a couple of hours,' she admitted, her slim fingers massaging her coffee-cup.

'Well, we can do that,' said Reed, indicating the coastline that paralleled their course. 'That's Pembroke over there. We can turn back, and be home in less than an hour.'

Helen hesitated. 'Where—where were we going?'

Reed bit down on his lower lip. 'A bay I know, a few miles out of St George's,' he replied at last. 'But—no sweat. I'll turn this thing around.'

'No.' The word was out before she could prevent it, and although Helen could hardly believe she had been so reckless, it was too late to retract it.

'No?' Reed, who had been looking up at the mast-head and measuring the force of the wind, now looked at her instead, and Helen felt the spread of heat all over her body.

'Well, it seems—ungrateful,' she said uncomfortably, not knowing how to answer him, and Reed groaned.

'Hey, changing your mind I can take,' he exclaimed ruefully. 'But—*ungrateful*! I'm not a charity case, you know.'

'That's not what I meant,' Helen was getting more and more embarrassed. 'I mean—I am enjoying myself.'

'Oh, thanks.' Reed grimaced. 'You have the perfect knack of putting me down.'

'No.' But Helen could feel a smile tugging at her own lips now, and Reed compounded her self-betrayal by grinning at her.

'How about if I say, you're making an old man very happy?' he suggested irrepressibly. 'It's not every day I get a chance to take a beautiful girl out on my boat.'

But Helen sobered now. The connotations of this statement were too painful to ignore. 'I'm sure that's not true,' she said, meeting his teasing gaze with suddenly guarded scepticism. 'Don't underestimate yourself, Mr Wyatt. I don't think that's your style.'

CHAPTER SEVEN

THE bay where Reed anchored the *Tramp* was small and deserted. Which was remarkable, considering this was the height of the holiday season. But, he told Helen, it was usually possible to find solitude somewhere on these islands. The whole coastline was scattered with secluded bays and coves.

An attractive proposition, if you wanted seclusion, thought Helen wryly, still not convinced she had made the wisest decision in agreeing to spend the whole day with Reed. But, so far as Reed was concerned, she was Jon's girlfriend, and despite what had happened earlier she didn't think he would do anything to betray his son. As to what had happened ten years ago—well, she supposed that had been at least partially her own fault. She was not excusing him, she reminded herself tautly, but nothing could alter the fact that she had been attracted to him, and let him know it. And, although he had taken advantage of her, she had not been an unwilling accomplice.

The trouble was, Reed was an attractive man, and the longer she spent in his company the more she became aware of it. Which was probably why she was making excuses for him now, she thought impatiently. But, she argued, if she really thought about what she was doing,

she wouldn't be able to go through with it, and putting
the fact that Reed was the father of her child out of her
mind was the only way she could function normally.

But was she functioning normally? the insistent voice
inside her protested. What on earth was normal about
treating Reed like a decent, caring human being, when
he had played such a destructive role in her life? She
should have told him who she was as soon as she got
here. She should have confronted him with the consequences of his behaviour. She wondered how he would
have reacted then, if she had accused him of seducing
her. She doubted she would be here now, pretending to
enjoy his company.

She sighed. The trouble was, she wasn't pretending,
not completely, she admitted unwillingly. And she
couldn't have told the truth—not when she arrived; *not
ever*. She had too much to lose; more than he would ever
know. She could not run the risk of losing Alexa,
however unfair to her daughter that might be.

The bay Reed had chosen shelved steeply away from
a sickle-shaped wedge of coral sand. It meant he could
anchor the yacht within swimming distance of the beach.
And, because the bay was small, they were not far from
one of the rocky headlands that jutted out into the water.
Helen knew, from past experience with Jon, that the
waters around the rocks teemed with fish, and she
wondered if Reed had snorkelling equipment on board.
Not that she wanted to go snorkelling with him, she
reminded herself severely. So far and no further, she
thought, tipping her face up to the sun. She'd be civil
to Reed, but that was all. Anything else was pure insanity.

Thinking of Reed, she looked around, and found he
was tugging his polo shirt over his head. It left his silvery
blonde hair standing on end, and he raked lazy fingers
over his scalp to straighten it. It also exposed the muscled
expanse of his chest, with its slight covering of sun-
bleached hair, which arrowed down into the waistband
of his shorts. Revealed, too, the fact that it was not only
his face, arms and legs that were lean and sun-tanned.
His body was, too, his shorts hanging low on sharply
angled hips.

'So,' he said, tossing his shirt aside, and Helen quickly averted her eyes, 'Do you want to come swimming before lunch?'

Helen took a steadying breath. 'Um—I don't know,' she murmured, wishing she could be as unselfconscious as he was. 'I think I'd rather sunbathe.'

'If that's what you want to do,' he remarked flatly, pulling off his trainers, and then going forward to squat down beside a locker set into the polished deck. Opening it, he unravelled the rope-ladder that was stored inside, and dropped the end of it over the side. 'OK,' he said, straightening and looking at her again. 'I'll see you later.' And, stepping over the rail, he dived into the water.

Helen stepped forward at once, ridiculously anxious to assure herself that he had surfaced, but when his sleek wet head appeared above the water she quickly stepped back again.

What now? she wondered, feeling the sun hot on her shoulders, even through the cotton of her top. Now that the boat had stopped moving, the heat was quite intense, and she knew if she intended to stay on deck she would have to put some cream on her skin. But, at the same time, she knew it was pretty pointless to put cream on her shoulders if she did intend to go swimming. It would be more sensible to swim first, and put the cream on later.

A glance across the water ascertained the fact that Reed had swum ashore, and watching him wade out of the shallows and walk up the white sandy beach she felt a sense of envy. She could be doing that, she thought frustratedly, pressing her lips together. And why not? What was she afraid of? Only herself!

With a clenching of her teeth, she unbuttoned the midi top and dropped it on the deck. Her shorts soon followed, and she perched on the edge of the roof to unlace her boots and take them off, too. Then, pulling the hem of the panties of the swimsuit down over her buttocks, she walked to the side of the boat.

As she dived into the water, she couldn't help a sense of relief that she had chosen to wear a fairly modest *maillot*, instead of one of the bikinis she had brought on holiday with her. At least it could be relied on to stay in place. And, when they came back to the boat and she had to change into her dry swimsuit, which was a bikini, she would simply put on her clothes as well.

The water was cool at first, but deliciously soft on her heated shoulders. It was the first time she had ever swum in really deep water, her outings with Jon always starting from the beach and seldom venturing far from the shore. In consequence, it was a whole new experience, and she ducked and dived delightedly, revelling in the new-found freedom.

It was a pity Reed wasn't with her, she reluctantly acknowledged. It would have been fun to have someone to share it with, but she knew it was just as well. It was hard enough to hang on to the past. She didn't want to think how she would react if he ever chose to test her hollow resentment.

She surfaced again, and looked towards the beach. Reed appeared to be stretched out on the sand, and she watched him for a few moments before kicking her legs and swimming into shallower water. She told herself she just wanted to find out where the shallower water began, but even after she was able to touch bottom with her toes she kept on going.

And, because the only sound was the sound of the ocean, she wasn't really surprised when Reed heard her splashing about, and sat up. 'So, you decided to swim, after all,' he commented, drawing up one leg and resting his elbow on it. 'What are you waiting for? Aren't you coming ashore?'

Helen splashed her feet in the shallows. 'It's too hot,' she said obliquely, lifting her shoulders. 'It's all right for you, but my skin burns.'

'Yes.' Reed picked up a handful of sand, and let it drift through his fingers, before saying thoughtfully, 'You do have very fair skin, don't you? I once knew a girl who had skin like yours.' He frowned. 'She was English, too.'

Helen's knees trembled, and she wished now she had never left the boat. Surely there was nothing about her that was familiar in a swimsuit. He had only seen her naked once.

Thankfully, Reed seemed not to have noticed her consternation. He appeared to be deep in thought, and realising she had to distract him Helen uttered a sudden cry, and kicked at the water as if something had startled her.

Immediately, Reed sprang to his feet, but her forced laughter caused him to halt, uncertainly. 'Crabs,' she exclaimed, hurrying to explain herself before he jumped into the water to help her. 'Ugh!' She gave a realistic shake of her shoulders. 'I don't like crabs anywhere near me.' She paused, to allow her words to sink in, and then added firmly, 'I think I'll go back to the boat. It's really too hot to sunbathe.'

'If that's what you want.' Reed's eyes dropped swiftly down the whole length of her body, and then, as if he suddenly didn't like what he was thinking, he turned away. 'I may do the same.'

It wasn't exactly what Helen had had in mind, but she could hardly forbid him from boarding his own yacht. Still, she did have a few yards' advantage, and turning she plunged back into deeper water.

He overtook her long before they reached the boat, and Helen's legs lost all co-ordination when he slowed to adjust his pace to hers. In consequence, she took an unwary breath and filled her lungs with salt water, and she added coughing and spluttering to her other humiliations.

'Come on—I'll help you,' Reed said, hiding his amusement with difficulty. But Helen spurned his offer of assistance.

'I can manage,' she choked, testily, catching hold of the ladder hanging over the side of the yacht, and forcing her feet on to the bottom rung. Then, ignoring the pain in her chest, she made a wobbly ascent to the deck, her legs as weak as water as she climbed over the rail.

Reed followed her up the rope-ladder, and as he was able to move rather more agilely than she was he reached the deck only seconds after her. And, although Helen would have preferred to escape to one of the heads to get changed, his presence made that impossible. It was his boat, after all, and as she realised belatedly that she hadn't even brought a towel with her she knew she had to ask before taking anything for granted. But he beat her to it.

'I'm sorry,' he said, as she struggled to compose herself, and for a moment she could only stare at him, uncomprehending. 'For laughing at you,' he explained, squeezing the moisture out of his hair. 'But you did look funny, floundering about like that. I thought you were kidding, at first, but then I realised you were in real trouble.'

'I was not in *real trouble*,' retorted Helen shortly, pulling the securing band from her braid, and tugging angry fingers through her own hair. 'I just swallowed some water, that's all. Haven't you ever done that?'

'Of course I have,' said Reed soothingly. 'Everyone has. I just don't want you to think I was making fun of you.'

'Weren't you?' demanded Helen tautly, forgetting, in her anger, that she was supposed to be avoiding any controversial arguments, and Reed sighed.

'No,' he said flatly. 'No, I wasn't.'

'Like hell,' retorted Helen rudely, turning away, but Reed's hand on her arm prevented her escape.

'I've said I'm sorry,' he reminded her tersely, his fingers around her quivering biceps both firm and cold, and Helen shivered.

'All right,' she said, realising she had gone too far, but although she tried to twist her arm free he didn't let her go.

'It's not all right,' he contradicted, looking down at her reddening flesh between his fingers. 'What is it with you? Why is it that I have to be so careful not to offend you? For God's sake, I'm not unreasonable. Why can't you act like a normal woman?'

Helen took a deep breath. 'And how would a *normal* woman act?' she retorted, not knowing how else to answer him, and Reed's eyes darkened until they were almost black.

'Well, perhaps like this,' he said, jerking her towards him, and she sensed that in that second they had crossed an invisible line. Until then, he had been in command of the situation, and, although she had been the one who had started the argument, Reed had always been in control. But suddenly the tenor of their exchange had altered. In that fateful moment, the realities of their situation ceased to exist. They were just a man and a woman, and when Reed's mouth came down on hers Helen was incapable of preventing it.

His arms went around her, hauling her close against his wet body. And, in spite of the fact that his skin was cold to her touch, heat was pulsing from him. She knew she ought to protest, to stop him, to prevent what was happening from going any further, but she didn't. Not then. As his mouth moved hungrily over hers, she felt herself responding, a blind, instinctive reaction to forces that were stronger than she knew.

It was strange, she thought unsteadily, as her hands spread helplessly against his damp chest, how the sub-conscious refused to follow the dictates of the conscious mind. She was sure she had stifled the feelings Reed had once aroused inside her, but she was wrong. With his arms around her, with the lean strength of his thighs pressed against hers, the memories were inescapable— and almost as seductive as they had been so long ago.

Only she wasn't a naïve teenager now. She was a woman, who was not unaware of the demands of a man's body. Particularly this man's body. And, when the moist pressure of his tongue sought entry to her mouth, she forced herself to press her lips together and turn her head away.

He let her go at once. It was as if her enforced refusal had brought him to his senses. Wiping the back of his hand across his mouth, he put some distance between them, making an effort to calm himself before looking at her again.

'*Hell,*' he said at last, smoothing both hands over his head as he spoke, plastering his hair to his scalp. '*That* was not meant to happen.'

Helen, who was not half as controlled as he apparently assumed, managed a slight shrug. 'These things happen,' she murmured unsteadily, desperate to regain some sense of balance, but Reed's angry expression decried her attempt to escape the consequences.

'Not to me,' he contradicted harshly, his mouth a forbidding line. 'For God's sake, Helen, what kind of man do you think I am?'

Helen could have told him, but she kept her mouth shut, not least because she was devastated by the realisation that she was still so vulnerable to him. She had to remember that, as far as he was concerned, they hardly knew one another. If she started acting as if something terrible had happened, he was bound to get suspicious.

'It doesn't matter,' she said at last, when it became apparent that something was required of her. 'Look, we—I—provoked you. Can't we just forget it? It isn't that important.'

'Can you?'

Reed's face was half contemptuous now, but whether that contempt was for her, or himself, she couldn't be certain.

'Please,' she said, realising she had to defuse this situation before it got totally out of hand, 'it was just a—a momentary aberration. On my part, as well as yours. All—all we can do, is—put it out of our minds.'

Reed regarded her with a speculative gaze. 'And will you tell Jon what happened?' he enquired flatly.

'No!' Helen's response was rather more forceful than she could have wished, but she couldn't help it. 'What—what would be the point of that?' she asked, less aggressively. 'I mean—it's nothing to do with Jon, is it?'

'Isn't it!' Reed arched one cynical brow. 'Oh—what the hell!' He turned away. 'How did we get into this situation?'

Helen took a steadying breath. 'I'm cold,' she said, and although she knew the shivery feeling she had was coming from inside rather than outside her body, she effected a convincing shudder. 'Could I take a shower?'

Reed looked at her over his shoulder. 'Of course,' he conceded, with an indifferent gesture. 'You do know where the bathrooms are, don't you?'

'Yes.' Helen bit her lip. 'I won't be long.'

Amazingly, the water in the shower was hot. In fact, she could have had it scalding hot, if she'd wanted. And she was tempted. Indeed, if she had thought it was possible to burn the memory of Reed's touch from her skin,

she would have done it. But, of course, it wasn't possible. Instead, she adjusted the heat to a temperate forty
degrees, and allowed the pulsing jets to rain down upon
her body.

And there was something infinitely soothing about
standing there, letting the water stream unheeded over
her head and shoulders. She tipped her head back, and
let the spray beat against her closed eyelids. Even so,
she couldn't wash her thoughts away, and the unbelievable awareness of what had just happened was always
present.

But how had it happened? she asked herself bleakly.
How had she let herself respond to him, however fleet-
ingly? She hated him, didn't she? She despised him for
what he had done to her, and to Alexa.

She opened her eyes again, and tried to re-evaluate
the situation. At least she had stopped him before anything irrevocable happened, she thought with some relief.
And he had only kissed her, for goodness' sake. She was
over-reacting like mad, to what had been—in actuality—
a simple mistake.

A *mistake*!

She reached for the plastic container of shower gel
that was suspended from the wall of the cubicle with
shaking hands. Opening it, she discovered it had a
distinctly masculine fragrance, and she guessed it was
Reed's. But, although the idea of using his soap was not
appealing, she decided she didn't care what it smelled
of. So long as it did the job, she thought grimly, scooping
a handful into her palm.

She lathered her arms and legs with rather more effort
than was strictly necessary, but she still couldn't erase
thoughts of the possible consequences of Reed's actions.
Even though she told herself that if she had never set
eyes on him before this holiday, she would be acting differently, it didn't help. She *had* set eyes on him. She had
slept with him, for God's sake! And she had a daughter
to prove it.

But *he* didn't know that, a small voice inside her
argued. And if she *was* over-reacting to what had
happened, so was he. Why hadn't *he* made light of it?

Why hadn't *he* laughed it off? And why was *he* behaving as if something disastrous had happened?

Helen shook her head. She didn't want to think about Reed's reactions. His behaviour was not her concern. It was her own feelings she had to get into perspective, and she wasn't making a terrifically good job of it.

She finished soaping her body, and then let the spray cleanse her skin. She watched the rivulets of water running from her breasts and thighs, pooling in the tray at her feet, and then disappearing through the grille. She waited until the water ran crystal-clear before turning off the taps. Then, stepping out of the cubicle, she wrapped herself in one of the huge emerald bath-sheets she found stacked on a rack.

Towelling herself dry, the truth, which so far she had avoided facing, refused to be ignored any longer. There was only one explanation for the way she had reacted, and although she might not like it, it had to be confronted. No matter how unreasonable it might seem, Reed's kiss had done more than just initiate a response from her. It had ignited some dormant fuse inside her, and while it was possible that the way she was feeling now had nothing whatsoever to do with what had happened between them ten years ago, the fact remained that what had attracted her to him then attracted her still.

The mirror above the small Vanitory unit reflected the confusion she was feeling. How was it possible that she could feel any attraction towards a man who had taken their previous association so lightly? How could she allow his kiss to mean anything to her, when he didn't even remember her name?

It was a painful revelation, and it was difficult to put on her clothes and prepare to join him again. Once more, she was in the position of wishing she had never set foot on this most beautiful of islands. How simple, in retrospect, her life in England seemed.

Reed had evidently followed her example, and taken a shower. When Helen emerged into the main cabin, she found him in the process of preparing lunch, but although he was wearing dry shorts he had not bothered to replace his shirt.

The polished wood dining table was set with place mats and silver cutlery. The fragile stems of wine glasses reflected in its shining surface, and Helen concentrated on the table to avoid looking at Reed's powerful torso.

'I hope you like smoked salmon,' he said suddenly, revealing that, although he had not actually looked in her direction, he was aware of her presence. And taking her cue from him, Helen hesitated only a moment before seating herself at the table.

'Mmm, I love it,' she replied, as he set an iced dish of butter beside a crusty wholemeal baguette. 'This looks nice,' she added, for good measure, almost as if the idea of sitting in this confined space with him, and eating *anything*, did not sound like anathema to her.

'That's good.'

Reed looked at her then, a long considering look that Helen deflected by refusing to meet his eyes. But she was aware that he shook his head somewhat grimly, before turning away to take a bottle of white wine from the fridge.

'Do—er—do you need any help?' she ventured, after a moment, wondering if he had forgotten to put out the rest of the food, but Reed made another negative gesture.

'I can manage,' he assured her drily, uncorking the bottle and filling her glass, before setting it down on the table. 'Try the wine. I think it's been chilling long enough.'

While Helen sipped her wine, Reed produced a whole smoked salmon, sliced and scattered with capers, on a silver tray. A wooden bowl was next, spilling over with a crisp salad, and tub of soft cheese that looked white and creamy. Evidently, when the master of the house asked for a picnic lunch, nothing was too much trouble, she thought irrelevantly. Certainly, this meal bore no resemblance to any picnic she had ever prepared. But then, she was not in the habit of sharing her food with someone of Reed's unlimited resources.

'Help yourself,' he said now, sliding on to the banquette opposite, and pushing the smoked salmon towards her. He picked up the bottle. 'More wine?'

'Oh—no. Not yet.'

Helen slid her fingers protectively over the rim of her glass. The wine was delicious, and she could feel it releasing at least a little of the tension inside her. But, because of that, it was dangerous, and she had no intention of being caught off guard again.

'As you like.' Reed filled his own glass, and watched her as she made a complete hash of trying to lift a little of the smoked salmon on to her plate. 'Do you want me to do that?'

Helen sighed, and put down the serving fork. 'If you wouldn't mind...'

'I don't mind,' he replied, in a completely neutral voice. 'Give me your plate.'

A few moments later, the plate was set in front of her again, the salmon glistening appetisingly on a bed of salad, with a generous portion of cream cheese for garnish. There was more than she would have given herself, and she couldn't help noticing that he was not half so generous when it came to his own plate. Indeed, he seemed as lacking in appetite as she was herself, and she found herself wishing she could say something to alleviate the situation.

'Will—er—will we be going back after lunch?' she asked at last, unable to think of anything else, and Reed's mouth compressed.

'Immediately after,' he assured her briefly, seeming to find the wine of more interest than the food. 'Don't worry. Despite your anxiety, you're perfectly safe with me.'

Helen took a deep breath. 'I'm not anxious,' she declared, and although the words sounded defensive, it was true. No matter how unlikely it might seem in the circumstances, she did trust him. But whether that trust was based on her knowledge of his love for his son, or from some other source, she couldn't be absolutely certain.

'No?' Reed questioned now, regarding her with some scepticism. 'Forgive me if I find that hard to believe.'

Helen bent her head. 'That's your problem,' she said tautly.

'Yes, it is.' Reed's fingers drummed on the table for a moment. 'Or rather, you are,' he added cryptically.

He paused, and then continued softly, 'Because we have met before, haven't we, Helen? As soon as I touched you, it all fell into place.'

CHAPTER EIGHT

HELEN jumped out of the launch as soon as it nudged the jetty. And, leaving Reed to see to its mooring, she walked quickly up the path to the house. He called her name once, but she pretended not to hear. She needed to get away—not just from him, but from everyone. She needed a little space to marshal her thoughts, to consider what she was going to do. But, most of all, she needed some time to cope with her emotions. She had been fighting tears for far too long, and she needed the relief of shedding them.

But not yet, she thought resignedly, realising Jon was waiting for her on the veranda. Evidently he was feeling much better, and she reflected on the irony that it was she who had the headache now. And he wasn't alone, she saw, running a nervous hand round the back of her neck, which was damp with sweat. A girl, probably someone of Jon's age, Helen estimated, or younger, was seated in the rattan chair next to him, a tin of Coke dangling from her fingers, and one bare leg draped provocatively over the arm of the chair. And, as she was wearing only a silky vest and skimpy satin shorts, little was left to the imagination.

'Where have you been?' Jon exclaimed as Helen got nearer, getting up and going to meet her. With a humorous expression belying the belligerence of his words, he put his arm about her shoulders, and bent to kiss her.

It took the utmost effort for Helen not to turn her face away from his seeking lips. As it was, his mouth only grazed hers, but happily Jon didn't seem to notice. 'I was beginning to think you'd left me,' he remarked, hugging her against him as they walked towards the veranda. 'Do you know what time it is? It's half-past four!'

'I know. I'm sorry.' Helen thought those words were becoming an integral part of her vocabulary. 'Your— your father took me sailing. It took longer to get back than we thought.'

'No kidding?' Jon's response was sardonic, but his smile softened the impact of his words. 'Well, anyway, I haven't exactly been desolate. Susie's been keeping me company, haven't you, Susie?'

The girl shared Jon's smile, but the look she bestowed on Helen was rather less friendly. 'Any time,' she conceded, running scarlet-tipped fingers through her spiky blonde hair. 'We go way back, don't we, Jon?'

'As far as it goes,' Jon agreed easily, forced to let Helen go as they climbed the steps to where Susie was sitting. 'Anyway, sugar, what do you think of my lady? Didn't I tell you I had impeccable taste?'

Helen stepped quickly aside when he would have slipped his arm around her again, cringing at the callow introduction. This was a side of Jon she had never appreciated, and it was galling to think she was noticing it now, and comparing him with his father.

'Hi.'

Susie's greeting was less than enthusiastic, and Helen guessed she was disappointed that their *tête-à-tête* had been interrupted. Helen knew a moment's impatience. She wondered how long Jon had been entertaining her, and whether the headache he had had that morning had been not as debilitating as he had made out. She couldn't help but think that if Jon had not abandoned her to his father's mercies, she would not now be in the position she was in. In consequence, her sympathies were definitely strained.

'So what's up with you, then?' Jon enquired perceptively, when Helen made no attempt to be sociable. 'Oh, I know. You're feeling guilty for leaving me alone for so long.'

'I am not feeling guilty,' retorted Helen between her teeth, although the truth was, she was—if not for the reasons he imagined.

'Well, OK.' Jon's teasing expression disappeared. 'But, in case it's of any interest to you, yes, I am feeling much better.' He paused, and then added acidly, 'I can see you're just dying to know.'

'Oh, I am.'

Helen sighed, wishing she could sound more convincing. But it was difficult to speak objectively when all she could think about was how long it might take Reed to tie up the launch, and follow her up to the house.

'You don't sound it,' declared Jon accusingly, adopting a martyred air. 'Anyway, if it hadn't been for Susie, I'd have spent a pretty miserable afternoon. And I was worried about you, if you must know. You could have fallen overboard—drowned—anything!'

I wish, thought Helen cynically, and then stifled the negative thought. There was no future in feeling sorry for herself now, she knew, and if not for herself, for Alexa, she had to control her fears.

'I'm sorry,' she said again, trying to inject some emotion into her voice. 'Of course I care about how you feel. But I wasn't to know you'd make such a—such a swift recovery.'

'Perhaps not.' Jon shrugged. 'So—where did you go?'

'Where did we go?' echoed Helen blankly, casting a nervous look over her shoulder. And then, realising they were waiting for an answer to the question, she forced herself to concentrate. 'Oh—um—some bay, near St George's.'

'Coral Cove?'

Helen licked her lips. 'That could be it. I don't know. It—er—it was very pretty.'

'Yes, it is.' Jon was looking distinctly less hostile now. 'The land shelves away quickly from the beach, doesn't it? And you can anchor really close to the shore.'

'That's right.'

But Helen was in no mood to stand discussing its merits. She desperately wanted to get away before Reed put in an appearance, and despite her efforts she was amazed Jon couldn't see the duplicity in her face. But then, why would he? she reflected bitterly. He trusted her. And he trusted his father.

'What did you think of the yacht?' Jon asked now, and she had to drag her attention back from the brink.

'Oh—it's beautiful,' she exclaimed, and then, realising there was one way, however humiliating, to get out of this, she added, 'But I'm afraid I discovered that I'm not a very good sailor. I—er—I was seasick.'

'No!'

Jon was instantly sympathetic, the last of his irritability giving way to genuine compassion, but Helen didn't want his pity.

'Yes,' she said, effecting a rueful grimace. 'I suppose that's why you thought I was so unsympathetic. Quite honestly, I still don't feel totally normal.' Which was the truth.

'Oh, baby!' There was no way of avoiding the hug Jon gave her then, and Helen managed not to flinch from his embrace. 'Why didn't you say so straight away? Wait until I speak to the old man. I'll have something to say about his seamanship!'

'Oh, no—please.' Helen felt a wave of perspiration break out on her forehead, and what little colour she had deserted her. 'It wasn't his fault. Honestly.'

And it wasn't. But she could hardly tell Jon the reasons why she had felt so nauseous on the way back. Being seasick had been her body's way of rejecting a situation that was rapidly becoming indefensible. But how long could she hide her feelings from him?

'Well, anyway, after what he's had to say about my navigation in the past, I shall definitely say something,' Jon insisted, grinning. 'I guess he told you I turned the last boat over? Yes, I somehow thought he would.'

Helen managed a faint smile. 'Well, that's your problem,' she murmured, pressing her hand against his chest so he was forced to release her. 'However, if you don't mind, I'd like to go up and have a shower. I'm feeling rather hot and sticky.'

'OK,' Jon acquiesced. 'Where is Dad, by the way? Don't tell me you had to swim home?'

'Of course not.' Helen could legitimately look behind her now, and her heartbeats accelerated at the sight of Reed coming up the path from the dock. 'Um—here he is now. I—I'll leave him to tell you all about it.' She turned to the other girl then, obliged to make some effort

to be polite. 'Er—nice to have met you, Susie. Maybe
I'll see you again some time.'

'I'm sure you will,' promised Susie pleasantly, but the
expression in her eyes belied the innocence of her words.
'I'll look forward to it,' she added, but Helen hurried
into the house with the distinct impression that she and
Susie were not destined to be friends.

However, Helen forgot all about Susie when she
reached the sanctuary of her own apartments. Closing
the door, she leant against the panels and closed her eyes,
welcoming the coolness of the wood against her back.
It was such a relief to be alone at last, and she expelled
a weary sigh before pushing herself away from the door,
and walking across the floor. The carpet was springy
beneath her feet, and, tugging off her boots, she curled
her toes into its soft pile. The compensations of the flesh,
she thought wryly. Surround yourself with enough
physical barriers, and you began to think you were spiri-
tually unassailable. But you weren't. Eventually, something—*or someone*—scaled the defences you had put up,
and tore them down, leaving you weak and defenceless.
As she was now, she acknowledged dully. As she had
been ever since Reed made his startling statement on the
yacht.

She had been totally unprepared for it. But then, is
anyone ever really prepared for the worst? she wondered. You think you are, but when it happens you soon
realise you aren't. Until then, all she had had to cope
with was her own sense of grievance against Reed, which
on reflection did not seem half so terrible as she had
made it. But now, suddenly, she was faced with a whole
new set of circumstances, and the awful expectation that
sooner or later Reed might put two and two together
and realise he was Alexa's father.

Of course, it hadn't happened yet, and perhaps it never
would. But could she take that chance? Certainly, she
had not had time to think of that when Reed had first
made his accusation. Her initial reaction had been dulled
by what had gone before, and she was still fighting the
insidious attraction his kiss had inspired. Indeed, she
had been trying so hard to behave naturally that, even
when he'd said what he had, she didn't immediately

comprehend what he was implying. But Reed had been determined that she should...

'I said—we have met before, haven't we?' he repeated, as she shredded the smoked salmon on her plate. 'Years ago. In London. At an exhibition at the Korda Gallery, if I remember correctly.' He stared at her grimly. 'Was that why you were so anxious to deny the fact that you had worked in an art gallery—however briefly?'

Helen couldn't answer him. For four days she had been living in fear of his remembering who she was, and, now he had, she was speechless.

'I knew there was something familiar about you,' he continued, watching her with dark, assessing eyes. 'But— your hair was brighter then—redder; and you were— well, not so slim.'

Puppy fat, Helen could have told him bitterly, as the memories came flooding back. She had been heavier in those days, her breasts fuller, her hips rounder. Which had made her look older, she admitted. Reed had obviously assumed she was well above the age of consent when he... Of course, she could also have added that having a baby and having to hold down a job as well as look after it refined the body's resources. And she didn't regret losing the weight. She would probably have done so anyway, as she got older. As for her hair—well, she did use a toning shampoo these days, that, over the years, had muted its brilliance.

'I am right, aren't I?' Reed asked now, taking a gulp of his wine, revealing by his actions that he was not as calm as he would like her to believe. 'Say something, for God's sake!'

Helen thought about denying it, but she quickly discarded that notion. She had the feeling that she would arouse more suspicion by refusing to admit the truth than by being at least partially honest.

'All right,' she said. 'We did—know one another once. But, as you say, it was a long time ago.'

'Ten years at least,' agreed Reed, his brows drawing together incredulously. 'My God! And you weren't going to tell me, were you? What kind of a fool do you think I am?'

Helen stared at him. What kind of a fool did *she* think *he* was? He had a nerve.

'Why do you think I should have told you?' she countered, her nails digging into her palms. 'You didn't remember me. You didn't even remember my name!'

'I didn't *know* your name,' Reed retorted harshly.

'You did——'

'No.' Reed's jaw hardened. 'My memory may not be as good as it used to be, but if I'd known your name I'd have remembered it.'

'But you must have.'

'Why must I?' His brow lifted. 'If you remember, our introduction was—unconventional, to say the least.'

And it had been. In spite of herself, Helen couldn't deny the surge of merriment that rose inside her at his words. But it was a hysterical merriment at best, that caught in her throat and nearly choked her. Besides, this was no time to have hysterics. His explanation had made her think, and she didn't want that. She didn't want to consider that she might not even have told him her name. And that if she hadn't . . .

'I don't suppose I thought names were important,' he went on wearily. 'Not then, at any rate. And afterwards, after we—well, you had gone.'

'You expected me to remember yours,' put in Helen defensively, and Reed sighed.

'I suppose that's true,' he admitted. 'But as I opened the exhibition at the gallery, I suppose it was easier for you.' He paused. 'Actually the gallery was owned by a friend of Tori's. That was how I came to be involved.'

'Oh.' Helen was momentarily silenced. So Victoria, too, had played her part. Thank God, she hadn't kept in touch with Bryan Korda. He knew nothing about what had happened to her afterwards.

'Had you forgotten that?' Reed asked now, and Helen shrugged. It was easier to pretend than to answer him. But if she had hoped that was the end of his questions, she was mistaken. Reed was determined to have his pound of flesh.

'So why didn't you say anything?' he demanded. 'I assume you were hoping that I wouldn't remember.'

'There was Jon,' said Helen quickly, moistening her lips. 'I—are you going to tell him now?'

Reed's long fingers massaged the stem of his wine glass. Then he lifted his head and looked at her again. 'Do you expect me to?'

'I don't know. I don't know what you're going to do, do I?' Helen was feeling slightly sick. 'I suppose you think I shouldn't have come.'

'Where?' Reed's lips twisted. 'With me today? Or to Bermuda?'

'Why—to Bermuda, of course.'

'But you didn't know, did you?' he pointed out drily. 'Tori told me about the mix-up over the surname.' He paused. 'Would you have come if you'd known Jon's name was Wyatt?'

Helen couldn't look at him. 'I—probably.'

'There are you, then.' Reed made a sound of frustration. 'So, life serves up these little difficulties from time to time. We just have to deal with them.'

Helen hesitated. 'H-how?'

Reed sighed. 'How do you want to deal with it?'

'I've told you—I don't know.'

'No.' Reed took another mouthful of wine. 'No, you don't, do you? That's why we're having this conversation, I suppose.'

'I'm sorry.'

Helen spoke tensely, but she wasn't really sorry, and he knew it. She could tell from the way he was looking at her, and in spite of herself she felt a shaft of apprehension penetrate her stomach. Dear God, what would she do if he touched her now? He could. It might amuse him to do so. And she didn't really know if she had the will to resist him.

'So,' he said, 'let me get this straight. The real reason you didn't tell me who you were was because of Jon?'

'Yes.' It was an easy answer.

'What if I say I don't believe you?'

Helen caught her breath. 'It's true.'

'Is it?'

'Yes. In any case——'

She broke off awkwardly, thinking better of what she had been about to say, but Reed wouldn't let her get

away with that. 'In any case—what?' he prompted
evenly. 'Go on. I'm listening.'

Helen heaved a sigh. 'You—you were married.'

'*Were* being the operative word.' He hesitated. 'I hope
you're not thinking what I think you're thinking.' He
regarded her quizzically, and when she didn't elucidate
he went on, 'I didn't have a wife to explain my actions
to, if that's your opinion of events. Diana and I had split
up months before I attended that exhibition. As I'm sure
Jon's told you, she left me for an American football
player. Someone who—in her words—didn't immediately think of a computer when she mentioned *bed*!'

Helen swallowed. 'So you say.'

'So I know.' Reed groaned. 'Why would I lie about
it? It can easily be proved.'

'Well, it's nothing to do with me.'

'Isn't it?' Reed looked sceptical. 'I rather thought you
thought it was.' He rested his elbow on the table, and
cupped his chin in his hand. 'So, what is the reason for
the way you're looking at me? If it's not that, it has to
be something else.'

'You're imagining things.'

'Am I?' He picked up his glass again, and looked at
her over the rim. 'What if I say *I* think it has to do with
what happened that night?' He paused. 'Do you want
me to apologise? It's a little late, but I'm quite prepared
to do it, if it will do any good. You shouldn't have walked
out on me. I was quite sober in the morning.'

'You—bastard!'

Helen would have got up then, but he wouldn't let
her, his hand imprisoning hers on the table. 'I knew it,'
he said grimly, as she gazed at him with hate-filled eyes.
'I knew there had to be a reason.' He shook his head.
'But just tell me—how was I supposed to know, hmm?'
He broke off as she had done earlier, but, unlike her,
he didn't need any prompting to continue when she didn't
answer him. 'You should have told me,' he said,
thwarting her efforts to get free of him without too much
difficulty. 'I realise you won't believe this now, but I
don't make a habit of seducing virgins, however willing
they might appear.'

'You're right,' said Helen harshly. 'I don't believe you.'

'Why not?' He gazed at her consideringly. 'You must have known I was attracted to you. For heaven's sake, I still am! That's what all this is about, isn't it? If I hadn't touched you just now——'

'I don't want to talk about it.'

'Well, damn you, I do.' He ground out the words. 'Look—if you and Jon are going to have any kind of a future together, you and I have got to get this settled.'

'Get what settled?'

'This whole situation,' said Reed heavily, releasing her arm now. And, although she could have left the table then, she didn't. Instead, she stayed where she was, rubbing her wrist to restore the circulation.

Reed poured himself more wine, and she noticed, almost inconsequentially, that his hand was not quite steady, clattering the neck of the bottle against the rim of the glass. It made him seem more vulnerable somehow, and although she didn't want to feel any compassion for him she couldn't help the feelings that rose inside her. And, as much to stifle them as anything, she said, 'You—actually expect me to stay here?'

'On the island? Yes. What else can you do?' Reed's mouth compressed. 'If you haven't told Jon about us yet, you can hardly do so now.'

Helen's hands clenched together in her lap. 'I—could.'

'I don't think so.' Reed looked down into his glass. 'Not unless you want to sever your—relationship completely.'

Helen bit her lip. 'We don't have that kind of—relationship.'

'So what kind of relationship do you have?' Reed enquired flatly. 'I'd be interested to know.'

'It's nothing to do with you.'

'No. So you said before.'

Helen frowned. 'When?'

'This morning.' Reed's lips curled. 'You practically bit my head off for suggesting you might know if Jon was still in bed.'

'Oh, yes.' Helen had forgotten that.

'However, it does surprise me,' went on Reed levelly. 'I mean—there have been other men in your life, haven't there?'

For a moment, she didn't understand him, and her face suffused with indignant colour. But then, the realisation of what he meant, and Alexa's part in this, sobered her. She couldn't arouse his suspicions now, by resenting what he saw as simple logic.

'Yes,' she said now, looking down at her hands. 'There was—someone else.'

'Just *one* someone?' he enquired sceptically, and she knew a sudden desire to smash her fist into his sardonic face.

'Oh, go to hell!' she choked unwisely, scrubbing her knuckles across her cheeks, and she was frustrated to hear the betraying tremor in her voice.

'No doubt I will,' he countered, lifting his hand to massage the muscles at the back of his neck. 'But, for now, I suggest we try and make some effort to be civil with one another.'

Helen shook her head. 'Why should we?' she demanded, disturbingly aware that his action had exposed the growth of hair that nestled in the hollow of his armpit. 'What good will that do?' she added, without really thinking what she was saying, anguished by the wave of heat that was threatening to consume her.

'It might just persuade my son that you don't hate my guts!' muttered Reed, aware of her eyes upon him. 'You're not a convincing actress, Helen. I was already having doubts about you.'

'So what?'

She refused to let him see how his words disturbed her, but Reed took her answer differently.

'So,' he said savagely, 'it may be ten years since we meant anything to one another, but——'

'We *never* meant anything to one another!'

'—but, believe it or not, there are some things about you I just know. Call it a sixth sense, extra-sensory perception, anything you like. The fact remains, I did make some impression on your life, or you wouldn't be acting as if I'd raped you! All right. I know what I did was wrong, but you weren't exactly fighting me off.'

Helen gasped. 'You flatter yourself.'

'Do I?'

He was surveying her rather wearily now, and she knew that she had to distract his attention, before he saw something in her eyes she would rather he didn't see.

'And you're bloody arrogant,' she said, saying the first thing that came into her head. 'I suppose it doesn't occur to you to think that I might have wanted to forget that particular incident in my life, does it? Oh, no. Even after ten years, you still think you're unforgettable!'

'That's not what I meant, and you know it,' Reed exclaimed indignantly. 'My God, I've never considered myself any great catch, believe me! And, as far as the past is concerned, we both know now that any prolonged association between us would have been totally impracticable.'

'Why?'

The question should never have been voiced, but once again her tongue was running ahead of her brain, with disastrous consequences.

'Why?' Reed echoed the word wryly. 'Well—I should have thought that was fairly obvious.'

Helen stiffened. 'Because we are from different backgrounds?' she asked scornfully, but Reed only shook his head.

'No,' he said, leaning towards her. 'Don't be naïve. You heard what Luther Styles said the other night. I'm Jon's father, aren't I? I knew I was too old for you then, and I should have had more sense. You must have thought so, too. Or you wouldn't have walked out on me, would you?'

Helen's teeth tore into her lower lip. She had 'walked out' on him, as he put it, for reasons she couldn't begin to explain to him now. For one thing she had had her parents to think about. Even without the obvious connotations of what had happened, at sixteen she had been half afraid to face what she had done.

'At least I know why you've been treating me like the devil incarnate,' he said suddenly, emptying his glass with one defiant flourish. He tilted his head back and looked at her. 'You never forgave me, did you? Will you believe me if I tell you I never forgave myself?'

Helen couldn't take much more. 'Can't we just forget about it?' she exclaimed at last. 'Please—I don't want to think about it any more.'

'All right.' Reed tipped up the wine bottle, found it was empty too, and scowled. 'But I want to ask you one more thing.'

Helen pressed her knees together. 'What?'

He pushed the bottle and glass aside and stretched across the table. Without giving her time to guess what he was about to do, he curved his fingers about her throat, and she gazed at him in horror as his hand slowly tightened.

'I want to know why you walked out on me,' he said, and she thought for a moment that history was about to repeat itself. Only this time, he wasn't drunk, just determined. 'What happened?' he demanded. 'Did I— hurt you?'

'I—I——' She could hardly speak, and as if just realising his own strength his fingers relaxed. 'Yes.' The word was choked. 'Yes, you did,' she lied unsteadily. And then, tearing his hand from her neck, she scrambled off the banquette. 'I want you to take me back now,' she added hoarsely, and leaving the table she crossed the floor, and stumbled up the stairs of the companionway.

CHAPTER NINE

OF COURSE, that was when she had been sick, Helen remembered now, halting by the french doors that led out on to her balcony; not on the journey home, as she had let Jon believe. For what had seemed like hours, she had knelt against the rail of the yacht, emptying her stomach into the translucent waters of the bay. She had gone on retching long after there was nothing left inside her to bring up, and running a hand over her flat midriff now, she felt the ache of muscles that had been badly abused.

And what had Reed said that had been so shattering, after all? Why had she been so upset because her masquerade was over? It wasn't as if he had threatened

to expose her to Jon. On the contrary, he had said he
wanted to put things right between them because of Jon.
Yet that wasn't exactly what she had wanted to hear,
and she didn't know why.

And why had he wanted to know why she had left
him that night? It wasn't as if he had cared, one way or
the other. She had thought—no, not thought—hoped,
expected, *believed*, she would see him again, when she'd
left the hotel in the early hours of the morning. He had
known where she worked, after all. She had told him
about the wine bar, letting him think she was supporting
herself at college. But, six weeks later, when she'd discovered she was pregnant, he was not around. He hadn't
been around since that fateful night, and because of what
had happened her parents had insisted she give up her
part-time job.

Initially, she had never told anyone, not even her
parents, who Alexa's father was. She had let them think
it was someone from the wine bar, who had taken her
out and taken advantage of her. It was easier that way.
To have explained that she had been seduced by a man
nearly seventeen years her senior, a man her father could
have traced, would have been too humiliating. Instead,
she had insisted on having her baby, and they had agreed
to help her.

She had half believed Reed must have been married.
It had been some solace when she was feeling particularly low. It didn't excuse what he had done, but it did
explain why he had never tried to see her again. And,
at that time, she had clutched at any straw.

It was obvious now that he had had no such commitment, so she should have been feeling even more
anger towards him; but somehow she wasn't. In fact,
she felt empty inside, and it wasn't just a physical
condition, she admitted ruefully. It was as if all her life
she had been waiting for this moment, and now that it
had happened it was just an anticlimax.

Of course, there was still Alexa to consider. But at
least her identity was no longer in jeopardy. Reed
evidently assumed that, after their brief affair, there had
been a procession of other men. It was galling to have

him think it—but it afforded her daughter some protection.

She sighed. Fate was a funny thing. Just when you thought you had your life in shape, something happened to distort it. If she hadn't met Jon in that bar in Germany, she wouldn't be here. And if she hadn't worked at the wine bar in Kensington, she would never have got to know Bryan Korda.

She sighed. Of course, to be absolutely fair, she shouldn't have been working in the wine bar. She really hadn't been old enough to work on licensed premises, but if she hadn't been there Clive would not have asked her to help out at the Korda Gallery on the evening of the party. And if she hadn't gone to the party, she wouldn't have met Reed.

It was because Clive, who owned the wine bar, was a friend of her father's that he had agreed to take her on. She had only worked there evenings, of course. During the day, she had attended the local secretarial college.

And, as it happened, the wine bar was next door to the Korda Gallery. Bryan Korda was a regular patron of Clive's, and over the few months she worked there Helen had got to know him quite well. With his encouragement, she'd visited the gallery, and because she became interested in it he had spent a lot of time teaching her about art. In consequence, on the odd occasions when his receptionist was absent due to illness, or holidays, he had asked Helen to fill in for her. She couldn't always do it, naturally. Her college work had always come first. But during her own holidays, and on the occasional evening, she had taken him up on his offer.

That was how she'd come to be there on the fateful evening of the exhibition. Clive had been asked to cater for the event, and, because casual waiters were not that easy to come by, he had had no hesitation in asking Helen if she would mind helping out.

Helen remembered she had been delighted to do it. She had been quite excited at the prospect of attending the party, in whatever capacity, and Bryan Korda had promised she would have plenty of time to enjoy herself. Looking back now, she suspected everyone had thought she was attracted to him, but that had never been a factor in their relationship. Even though he had been no older than Reed, she had never thought of him in that way. Indeed, until Reed came along she hadn't had much interest in men, young or old, even though, working in the wine bar, she had had lots of propositions.

The night of the party, she had left home early to help Clive set up the bar in the gallery. She had worn a new outfit, she remembered: a red polyester shirt that looked like silk to her uncultured eyes, and black velvet trousers that had accentuated the length of her legs. Of course, looking back now, she recognised the fact that the clothes had made her look older than she was, but Clive had approved, and she had felt good.

The drinks had been set up, with Clive's barman in charge, and the buffet tables had been laid with finger-food of all kinds. There had been hors-d'oeuvre of shrimp and caviare, quiches, vol-au-vents filled with spicy meats and chicken, sausage rolls, bacon rolls and lots of rich pies and tartlets. There had been a side of ham, a smoked salmon, she remembered, her stomach curdling a little at the thought, and an enormous bowl of punch, whose fruitful origins had been lavishly spliced with rum.

The guests had started arriving at about half-past six, but it was nearly seven before Reed appeared. Helen had known the minute he had arrived, because Bryan went rushing off to meet him, and her first glimpse of her nemesis had been across the heads of the other guests.

Of course, she had not expected to meet him herself. He had been the guest of honour, and, although Bryan could be charming when they were alone, on occasions like this he tended to panic. Besides, she really had had nothing to do with the exhibition. She was just a kid Bryan found it amusing to cultivate. Not someone who deserved a personal introduction.

All the same, Helen had found her eyes drawn to Reed again and again during the evening. She didn't really know why. Bryan himself was more conventionally handsome than his visitor. But there had been something about Reed that attracted her, and she'd watched the women who warranted his attention with an undeniable feeling of envy.

He had seemed so worldly, so sophisticated, she reflected now. As well as tall, and lean, with clothes that
fitted him in all the right places so that you were left in
no doubt as to the width of his shoulders or the muscular
power of his legs. And, whereas Bryan got all hot and
bothered in situations like this, Reed evidently took it
all in his stride. He was polite and well-mannered, he
smiled frequently, and if he wasn't a connoisseur he
certainly knew enough about art to convince his at-
tentive audience.

Helen sighed. She had been so naïve then, she thought
impatiently. For the first time in her life, she had
encountered a man whose personality had overridden all
her preconceived ideas about sex. After all, he must have
been in his early thirties at that time, with angular
cheekbones, and deeply carved grooves beside his mouth.
Not at all the kind of man she would have expected
herself to be attracted to. And yet from the moment he
walked into the room she had been aware of him, and
she had had to fight the urge to put herself within his
charmed circle.

But she had met him, she remembered ruefully, though
not in the way she would have wished. She had been
circulating among the guests, offering a tray of champagne cocktails, when one of the older women had
backed right into her.

Remembering it now, Helen still cringed at her initial
reaction when the woman had barged into her. She had
had no hope of saving the tray from disaster. The woman
had been tall, and much more heavily built than Helen
was. In addition to which she was teetering on ridiculously high heels, so that she lost her balance, and tried
to grab Helen to save herself. In consequence, they all
went down—Helen, the tray, and the woman.

Of course, it caused an immediate uproar, with people
dodging out of the way of spilling champagne and flying
glass. Bryan rushed across to see what was happening,
and looking up into his infuriated face Helen knew he
was going to blame her for what had happened. It didn't
help to discover that the woman who was presently being
helped, protesting, to her feet was none other than Lady
Elizabeth Benchley, one of the gallery's most generous

patrons. Nor that most of the liquid had fallen on the back of Lady Benchley's gown, which just happened to be a Dior original.

'I'm so sorry,' Bryan was saying, over and over again, as Helen extricated herself from the tray, and scrambled to her feet. 'That girl is so clumsy, you wouldn't believe! What can I say? She should never have been allowed near a tray of drinks!'

'Are you all right?'

It was as Helen was standing staring, red-faced, at Bryan and Lady Benchley that she heard the low attractive voice addressing her, and her breath caught in her throat.

'I—I think so,' she got out, turning jerkily to face him, and Reed touched her waist with a steadying hand.

'You're not cut, are you?' he added, the distinct trace of a smile tugging at the corners of his mobile mouth. 'You both went down very—hard.'

Helen's lips quivered. 'I know,' she choked out, an uncontrollable tide of mirth rising inside her now that she could see that only Lady Benchley's pride had been dented. 'Oh, God! Bryan's going to kill me!'

'I'd be more inclined to kill him first,' remarked Reed drily. 'He appears to be loading you with all the blame.'

Helen sobered as she met Bryan's angry eyes. 'Well— it was my fault,' she murmured unhappily. 'Oh, lord, do you think Lady Benchley will expect me to compensate her for a new dress?'

'She may send the bill for its cleaning to the gallery, but it wasn't your fault,' declared Reed flatly. 'I saw what happened, and she walked right into you.'

Helen swallowed and looked back at him. For a few moments she had forgotten who she was talking to, and now, realising what she had said, she felt the hot colour stain her cheeks once again.

'Um—well, thank you,' she said uncomfortably, aware that Bryan was unlikely to take her word for it. 'I—er— I'd better go and get a brush and dustpan, and clear this mess up.'

'I'll help you,' said Reed, squatting down and beginning to gather the larger pieces of glass on to the

tray, and Helen was gazing at him disbelievingly when
Bryan observed what was happening.

Excusing himself from Lady Benchley, he came across
to them, his expression one of utter condemnation.
'What the hell do you think you're doing?' he demanded
of Helen. And then, to Reed, 'Mr Wyatt, really, there's
no need for you to do this.'

Reed straightened. 'I was just helping your assistant
out.' He pushed his hands into the pockets of his suit
jacket. 'Accidents will happen.'

'This was no accident,' retorted Bryan, turning back
to Helen. 'It was rank carelessness! Hasn't anyone ever
told you that when you're carrying a tray of glasses you
don't go bumping into people?'

'I didn't——'

'Don't you dare deny it! What are you saying? That
Lady Benchley deliberately caused you to knock her
down?'

'No, of course not, she backed into me——'

'Nonsense! You obviously weren't looking where you
were going,' Bryan informed her coldly. 'I should have
known better than to allow you to help out on an
important occasion like this. Well, you can go and get
your coat, because you're fired! Do you understand? I
don't want to see you in this gallery ever again, do you
hear me? And,' he added, putting his lips close to her
ear, 'I shall have something to say to Clive the next time
I see him. Something about the dangers of employing
under-age staff!'

'I think you're being a little hasty, Korda,' Reed inter-
posed at this point, but Helen didn't wait to see if his
intervention did any good. She was hurt, and humiliated, and as she pushed her way through the throng of
people, who had been watching the display with undisguised curiosity, she was sure they all blamed her for
what had happened.

Stan Macdonald, Clive's barman, caught her arm as
she brushed past him to collect her belongings. 'Hey—
what's going on?' he asked, but although his tone was
not accusatory Helen could only shake her head. Her
eyes were burning with the effort of holding back her

tears, and, grabbing her black jacket from the office, she hurried out the door.

In the alleyway that ran between the gallery and the wine bar, she stopped to blow her nose and recover her composure. She couldn't go home in this state, and while she was tempted to go and tell Clive what had happened she was very much afraid he would have little sympathy for her. And when Bryan was through complaining about her, she didn't think she'd have a job at the wine bar either. Clive wouldn't want to risk losing his licence, and the few pounds a week she had earned to supplement the family income would be forfeited.

She sighed, hunching her shoulders against that eventuality. It was so unfair, she thought, pushing the damp tissue she had been using back into her pocket. She had not been to blame. Not entirely, anyway. And, as humiliation gave way to indignation, she thought how unjust Bryan had been. He hadn't seen what happened. He couldn't really judge the situation. It was just that Lady Benchley spent a lot of money in the gallery, and he was afraid of losing her favour.

The only bright spot of the evening had been meeting Reed Wyatt, and she had been too shaken up to really appreciate it. And he had been nice, she remembered wistfully. Much nicer than she had expected, actually. Even though she had considered he was an attractive man earlier in the evening, she had consoled herself with the thought that he couldn't possibly be as distracting as he looked. But he was. He had proved to be the only one who had cared about her feelings, and she shivered a little when she remembered how she had felt when he touched her.

Of course, he had only been polite, she told herself glumly. She shouldn't attribute anything personal to what had, after all, simply been an act of kindness. He had probably felt sorry for her, she thought gloomily. She had made an absolute fool of herself.

Sniffing, she glanced quickly about her, to make sure no one had observed her bout of self-pity, before starting off towards the main road. It was still fairly light, the warm summer evening only reluctantly giving way to night. It was early, too. Barely nine o'clock. She had told her parents not to expect her before eleven o'clock at the earliest. Bryan had promised to get her a minicab, as Clive usually took her home.

Realising she would have to make her own arrangements this evening, Helen decided not to call a cab. If she was to lose her job, she couldn't afford to spend money on cabs when it wasn't absolutely necessary. The gallery was just off Kensington High Street, not far from Kensington Gardens. She could walk to the nearby Underground station, and take the Tube home to Chiswick.

Pushing her hands into her pockets, she started to walk, ignoring the occasional whistles and cat-calls that came her way. Her father wouldn't be especially pleased about her travelling on the Tube on her own at this time of the evening, but it couldn't be helped. She was sixteen and a half, after all. And, as Clive had always maintained, she looked eighteen at least.

She had gone about a hundred and fifty yards when she realised a car was slowing its pace to match hers, and she automatically moved away from the kerb. There were plenty of people about, and she wasn't exactly scared, but she had always been taught to be cautious, and kidnapping did go on.

However, the car—a low green Mercedes—stopped, and a man got out. 'Can I give you a lift?' he asked, his voice unmistakable, and Helen gazed disbelievingly at Reed Wyatt.

'A lift?' she echoed, swallowing her astonishment. 'Wh-where?'

'Wherever you like,' replied Reed humorously, a smile playing about his lips. 'Home. To a restaurant. You choose.'

Helen stared at him. 'A restaurant?' she repeated, her mind latching on to that almost incredible suggestion.

'I thought you might be hungry,' he said. 'I guess you didn't get a lot of time to eat back there.' He nodded back over his shoulder. 'Humble pie wasn't on the menu.'

'Wasn't it?' Helen couldn't prevent the corners of her mouth from tilting upwards. Then, in an effort to normalise the situation, she added, 'Well—thank you for your support anyway. But there was really no need for you to feel sorry for me. You shouldn't have left the party. I can make my own way home.'

Reed, who had been resting his arm on the car door, now slammed it shut and came towards her. 'I'm not doing this because I feel sorry for you,' he said, and although he wasn't touching her Helen felt as if the air between them were vibrating with energy. 'I'd like to take you for supper. Will you let me?'

Helen took a shaky breath. 'You're parked on double yellow lines,' she said, not answering him. 'You're not supposed to park on double yellow lines.'

'I know.' But he didn't sound interested. 'Well? Will you have supper with me?'

Helen moistened her lips. 'Where?'

'Anywhere. Wherever *you* like.'

Helen hesitated. 'I—I've got splashes of champagne on my trousers.'

'So?'

'So, are you sure you want to do this?'

'Yes, I'm sure.'

He was looking down at her with eyes that were so much darker and more intent than she had imagined them to be. And he was asking her to have supper with him, she thought incredulously. It was like a dream come true. Only it wasn't a dream, and she wasn't altogether sure she could handle it. After all, her experience with men was so limited, and it was obvious he thought she was older then she really was. She wondered what he would say if she told him she was only sixteen. She thought she knew the answer.

'Is it such a difficult decision?' he asked now, touching her cheek with the knuckles of one hand. 'I thought we were friends.'

Friends! Helen breathed a little unsteadily. What did he mean by that? And she had thought she had exaggerated that encounter over the broken glass!

'You can trust me, you know,' he added softly. 'I'm not a rapist, or a sadist, or someone who takes advantage of innocent young women, and you did give me the impression that you liked me.'

'I did?' Helen gulped.

'Yes.' Reed pushed his hands into his pockets, as if by leaving them free he might be tempted to touch her again. 'You've been watching me all evening. Or was that just my imagination?'

Helen caught her breath. 'How do you know that?'

'How do you think?' he countered. 'I've been watching you, too.'

Helen shook her head. 'I—don't believe you.'

'Why not? Compared to most of those old tabbies in there, you were like a breath of spring.' He smiled. 'That hair—it's like a flame.'

Helen put up a nervous hand to touch her hair, and then withdrew it again. 'I don't know what to say.'

'Say yes,' he urged her huskily. 'Before I get a parking ticket.'

Helen's lips twitched. 'I—all right,' she said, before she could mentally talk herself out of it. It was rash, and unwise, and all the other epithets she had ever been warned against, but it was too late now. She had committed herself, and nervous excitement bubbled inside her as he led her to the car.

The car itself was sleek and luxurious, smelling of leather and the indefinable essence of Reed's habitation. It was a heady mixture of aftershave, soap, and Scotch whisky, combined with the clean male scent of his body. He settled Helen in the passenger seat, and then walked around the car to get in beside her, giving her a lazy smile before starting the engine.

'So,' he said, pulling out into the traffic of Kensington High Street, 'what's it to be? The Ritz? Or Colonel Sanders?'

Helen gave him a jerky look. 'Not—not the Ritz,' she declared firmly, not at all convinced he wasn't teasing her. 'Just—somewhere ordinary.'

'OK.' Reed grinned at her. 'Somewhere ordinary it is.'

In the event he took her to a Japanese restaurant, in the basement of a hotel in Park Lane. It wasn't what Helen would have called ordinary. The hotel itself was very well known, and although the Japanese restaurant did not demand a formal standard of dress, it was never-theless very different from any of the eating places she was accustomed to. The lighting was diffused, and subdued, and they sat in a cushioned booth that gave them total privacy.

With Reed's assistance, Helen ordered *teppanyaki* steak and lobster, with a clear vegetable broth to begin with, and a sharp lemon sorbet for dessert. She drank sake—which Reed told her was rice wine—for the first time in her life, and made a creditable job of using her chopsticks. Reed himself, she noticed, ate very little. But he did have several *sakazukis*—or cups—of the potent rice wine, and every time she looked at him she found him looking at her.

Because of this, and because she was nervous, Helen talked more than she should have done. But she couldn't help anticipating what her mother and father would say if she told them she had accepted an invitation from a man she knew nothing about, and in consequence she made up a whole new identity for herself to fit her surroundings.

Not that she had really lied, she consoled herself now. But she had allowed him to think she had a place of her own—albeit a bed-sitter—and that she was paying for herself to attend secretarial college, by working evenings at the wine bar.

The waiter brought lemon tea at the end of the meal, and, glancing at her watch, Helen was relieved to see it was only half-past ten. Her parents were not likely to worry about her much before midnight. They trusted Clive to see that she got home safely.

Permitting herself a covert look in Reed's direction, Helen couldn't help feeling some amazement that she was here at all. She could imagine how Lady Benchley would feel if she knew that the *waitress* was dining with the guest of honour. And Bryan, too. She doubted he would believe it.

All the same, she wished Reed would tell her something about himself. He was fairly reticent about his own background, and, although she had guessed from his accent that he was an American, he had not told her what his occupation was, or where he lived.

'Did you enjoy it?'

His question startled her, and she realised with some confusion that for the past few minutes she had been staring at him quite openly.

'Oh—oh, yes, it was lovely,' she conceded hurriedly. 'It—er—it was very kind of you to invite me. Thank you very much.'

Reed's lips parted. 'Now you've made me wish I hadn't asked,' he remarked drily. 'You don't have to thank me like a polite child; I've enjoyed it, too.'

Helen flushed. 'I'm not a child,' she protested, and Reed inclined his head.

'No,' he said. 'Perhaps not.' His eyes drifted down to the rounded swell of her bosom; and, intercepting his gaze, Helen was embarrassed to discover that her breasts were clearly evident beneath the silky material of her shirt. 'You just sounded like one for a moment,' he added, and she forced herself to meet his amused gaze. 'It's my advanced years. I have that effect on young women.'

She was sure he knew exactly what effect he had on young women, but she didn't know how to answer him. She knew he was teasing her, but she had no experience of how to deal with it. Or him. If it had been his intention to put her at her ease, he hadn't succeeded. On the contrary, now that the meal was over, she was intensely aware of her own immaturity, and how desperately she wanted to keep him interested in her.

'Don't look so worried,' he murmured now, and she thought how frustrating it was to be so transparent.

'I'm not worried,' she insisted, but she was, and he knew it.

'I meant what I said, you know,' he told her gently, watching her troubled expression with lazily sensual eyes. 'I have enjoyed this evening. Particularly the latter part.' He smiled. 'You did me a favour, you know, by giving me an excuse to leave.'

Helen wet her dry lips with a nervous tongue, unaware of the provocation in doing so. 'I can't believe that,' she said, folding her napkin into a rather uneven oblong, and he lifted his immaculately clad shoulders in a dismissing gesture.

'Why not?' With his eyes on her mouth, he shifted deliberately towards her. His weight depressed the cushion only a couple of inches from her hip, his dark-trousered thigh a bare hand's breadth from hers. 'I'd be a fool if I didn't find the company of a beautiful woman more exciting than that of a group of boring old fogies.'

His breath wafted over her, only lightly charged with alcohol, but Helen couldn't prevent the shiver of anticipation that slid down her spine as he continued to look at her. It trembled on her tongue to say she wasn't a beautiful woman, but she knew, instinctively, that that was not the thing to say. Besides, did it really matter whether she was beautiful or not? He had said she was, and even if he was only being gallant she shouldn't contradict him.

'How—how long are you planning staying in London?' she asked instead—anything to distract his attention from the fact that her knees were quaking, and he frowned.

'I'm not sure. A few days. A week, maybe.' He was non-committal, and her heart palpitated when he lifted one of her hands from the table and cradled it between both of his. 'Such white skin,' he said, lightly stroking her knuckles with his thumb. 'Some of the women I know would pay a fortune to have skin as fair as this.'

Helen quivered. 'It—it's not such an advantage,' she ventured weakly. 'I—burn very easily.'

'Yes.' Reed looked at her face now, and Helen could see her own reflection in the strangely heated depths of his grey eyes. 'I can see that.'

'Oh——' She put up a nervous hand to her cheek, feeling its hectic colour without needing to see what it looked like. It was the bane of her life that she blushed so easily, and right now, she was sure, her face must be shining like a beacon.

'Don't look like that.' Reed lifted one hand, and brushed his thumb against her cheek. 'It's quite refreshing to meet someone who hasn't learned to hide their feelings. Am I embarrassing you? Is that why you're so intense?'

Helen moved her face helplessly from side to side. 'You're—not embarrassing me,' she denied, although in truth she thought he was. Though perhaps not for the reasons he imagined. Just being near him like this was enough to turn her limbs to fire.

Reed withdrew his fingers from her face with evident reluctance, brushing her mouth as he did so. She wasn't sure if his touch was deliberate or not, but her lips parted almost automatically, and when he resumed his examination of her hand again she could still taste his skin on her tongue.

'Relax,' he said, turning her hand over to expose her palm, and Helen drew an uneven breath. 'I'm only holding your hand,' he added softly. 'Considering what I'd like to do, I'm being very public-spirited.'

Helen felt like saying he wasn't just holding her hand. He was doing more, so much more, than that. But, once again, she kept her opinion to herself. After all, how could she tell him that when he touched her she felt the repercussions from the top of her head to the soles of her feet ...?

'Can I get you anything else, sir?'

The Japanese waiter's polite enquiry was an unwelcome intrusion, and Helen wished he would have chosen some other moment to interrupt them. Reed was presently employed in tracing her lifeline with the pads of his fingers, and her body felt as if it were melting and dissolving beneath that sensuous caress.

'What?' Reed's response was resigned, but he did not sound as irritated by the waiter's intervention as she was. 'No. No, I don't think so,' he continued, looking to Helen for her confirmation, and she shook her head. But, as he had, at the same time, pressed her palm down on to his muscled thigh, Helen was in no state to make any coherent judgement.

'If we could have the check,' Reed suggested smoothly, almost as if he were indifferent to the touch of her hand on his leg. He lifted his own hand slightly, as if testing to see whether she would withdraw hers given the chance, and when she didn't he gave her a mind-bending smile. 'Thank you.'

'Thank you, sir.'

The waiter departed, and Helen had the feeling that in those few, hardly private, moments their relationship had altered substantially. Not that she had taken advantage of the situation. Despite the fact that she would have liked to flex her fingers around the taut muscles of his thigh, she hadn't moved. Indeed, she was finding it incredibly difficult to believe she was actually touching him so intimately, and when he looked at her again she couldn't withstand his intent appraisal. Using the excuse of reaching for her bag to remove her hand, she gave him what she hoped was a confident smile as she put a little more space between them.

'So that's it, is it?' he murmured, lounging on the cushioned bench beside her, his eyes dark and intent. 'I guess I have to take you home.'

Helen swallowed. Visions of them drawing up outside her parents' house in Chiswick, in the big Mercedes, filled her with alarm. For one thing, she had told him she had her own place; for another, her father was bound to hear the car, and look out of the window.

'Of course, you could invite me in for coffee,' he appended, lazily. 'In fact, that might be a good idea. Black coffee, I mean. For me, if not for you.'

Helen shook her head. 'I—I couldn't do that.'

'OK.'

His eyes narrowed a little and, realising how rude that had sounded, Helen struggled to find a convincing explanation. 'I mean—I don't live alone.' That sounded bad, so she added quickly, 'That is—I share—with a girlfriend.'

'Ah.' She wasn't sure whether he was convinced or not, but at least that guarded look had left his face. 'So— that won't do.'

'No.' Helen felt terrible. 'I'm sorry.'

'No sweat.' He shrugged, and reached in his pocket for his wallet as the waiter reappeared with the bill. He extracted a credit card, and a handful of notes. 'OK?'

'Yes, sir.'

As the delighted waiter pocketed his tip, and took the credit card away for notification, Reed drummed his fingers on the table. His indulgent mood seemed to have disappeared, and Helen imagined he was thinking what a bore the evening had turned out to be. And it was all her fault.

She sighed. It would have been nice to have had a place of her own to invite him to, she thought wistfully. But until she was eighteen her father was unlikely to permit it. Besides, until she had a proper job she couldn't afford to support herself. What she earned at the wine bar wouldn't even pay for her clothes.

Conversely, there was no way she could invite Reed to her parents' house. She could just imagine their reaction if she brought a man home who was more their age-group than hers. She'd never be able to convince them that she hadn't encouraged him. And they'd be bound to think the worst, because he wasn't like them.

She sighed again. It had been such a wonderful evening. She had never enjoyed herself so much with anyone, and he had been so nice, and considerate. He had treated her as an equal, instead of patronising her. And when he held her hand, her limbs had turned to water.

She looked at his profile—the narrow cheekbones, and the thin-lipped mouth. His lashes were long, longer than hers, she acknowledged ruefully, and paler at the tips, like the bleached silver resilience of his hair. His hair was longer than average, too, alternately brushing over or tucking beneath his collar. It made her want to touch it, to slide her fingers through its silky strands, and scrape her nails against his scalp. But most of all she wanted him to touch her again, and if they left the restaurant now the evening would be over.

He turned his head then and looked at her, and Helen abruptly lost her breath. She didn't know if it was extra-sensory perception or what, but something had attracted his attention, and she couldn't seem to get any air into her lungs. Her eyes were ensnared by his, and whatever he saw in their depths made his eyes burn with sudden fire.

'We could have coffee here, in the hotel,' he ventured, after a pregnant moment, and Helen's mouth felt parched.

'Could we?' she got out through stiff lips. 'Um—all right.'

If Reed was surprised by her instant capitulation, he didn't show it. But he did hesitate a moment before saying softly, 'You're sure?'

'Why not?' Helen gave a nervous shrug of her shoulders. She had committed herself now, and she wasn't about to reveal her immaturity by changing her mind.

Reed watched her for a few more seconds, and then made a gesture of assent. 'Good,' he murmured, and then the waiter came back with the slip for him to sign, and Helen gave a sigh of relief.

CHAPTER TEN

HER relief had not lasted long, Helen reflected now, leaving the window to sink down wearily on to the side of the bed. If she had known then what she knew now, she would never have accepted Reed's invitation.

Or would she? If she was perfectly truthful, she would have to admit there was an element of doubt. It was all very well thinking about what she should have done, but would she have done it? She had been so young, she thought ruefully, but it was hardly an excuse. She had known the risks she was running, and yet she had still gone ahead with it. Still accompanied Reed to his suite, on the unlikely pretext of sharing a pot of coffee.

She sighed. Of course, when she accepted his offer of coffee, she hadn't known exactly what he meant. She hadn't known he was a guest at the hotel, or that after ten o'clock the only place they could have coffee was in his room. She had assumed there was some lounge, or a coffee shop, maybe, where they could continue their conversation. But the coffee shop had been closed, and the crowded bar was not an option.

Even so, she acknowledged honestly, she could have refused to go upstairs with him. Reed would not have caused a scene. That was not his way. She could have made some excuse and left the hotel. There had been plenty of taxis waiting outside. She had seen them when

they came in, before the valet had taken Reed's Mercedes
for parking.

But she had done none of those things. And why? she
asked herself now. Because she had had too much pride?
Because she hadn't wanted him to think she was too
young, or too silly? No. Helen closed her eyes, and tipped
her head to rest on her shoulder. She hadn't left the hotel
because she hadn't wanted to leave Reed. It was crazy,
considering she had only known him for a few short
hours, but she had been totally infatuated with him.

Looking back, Helen realised she had not really
understood the dangers of what she was doing. In spite
of what had happened in the restaurant, her experiences
with men had not led her to believe there was any
situation she couldn't handle. Oh, she had been naïve,
there was no doubt about that. But then, she had never
met anyone like Reed Wyatt before.

Of course, he might argue that he hadn't been exactly
in control of his actions either. After all, he had been
drinking fairly continually all evening, and a combination of champagne, Scotch, and sake was hardly a
rational choice. Indeed, she remembered, he had swayed
a little when he first left the booth, and his arm about
her shoulders had been as much for his sake as for hers.
Could he have driven her home in that condition? she
wondered. Somehow, she doubted it.

Even so, riding the lift to the twelfth floor had been
a daunting experience. It was after eleven o'clock, and
she spent the time calculating how long it might take her
to drink a cup of coffee and get home. The result was
not favourable, but it was too late to think of that now.

Reed's suite of rooms provided a brief diversion. The
spacious lamplit apartments, furnished with Edwardian
elegance, were very impressive. And, although the huge
bed, visible through an open doorway, was hardly in
period, the huge sitting-room, with its separate dining
area, was unrestrainedly luxurious.

'Take off your jacket,' Reed advised, taking off his
own jacket and loosening his tie, and Helen, who had
only put her jacket on in the lift, reluctantly complied.

The coffee arrived as she was folding her jacket, and
placing it neatly on a high-backed chair by the door.

Evidently the service in the hotel was excellent, and Helen stood awkwardly to one side as the waiter carried the tray into the room and set it down on a low mahogany table. Reed, who had been helping himself to another drink from the tray of decanters set on a bow-fronted bureau, thanked the man handsomely, and the waiter went away with a smug smile on his face. Helen wondered what he was thinking, and didn't like the supposition. She was not unaware of what interpretation he must have put on the situation, and she felt her colour deepen.

'Aren't you going to to sit down?' Reed suggested mildly, indicating the velvet-covered sofa, and Helen nodded. But she seated herself in one of a pair of matching armchairs, and let him think what he liked of it.

A half-amused expression on his face, Reed finished the Scotch in the cut-glass tumbler he had poured himself, and then crossed the room. Seating himself on the sofa, he spread his legs, resting his forearms along his thighs. 'So,' he said, indicating the tray in front of him. 'Don't you want to do this?'

'Oh.' Helen coloured anew. It hadn't occurred to her that the tray was closest to the sofa, or that she might be expected to serve the coffee. She had been so intent on carrying this off, without making a fool of herself, that she hadn't considered the practicalities of the situation. 'Oh—all right.'

Reed shifted obligingly to one side, his arms along the back of the sofa on either side of him, straining the buttons of his grey silk shirt. His skin looked very dark between the buttonholes, Helen noticed, before she dragged her eyes away from his body, and concentrated on her task.

'Er—cream and sugar?' she ventured, perched on the edge of the sofa with at least two feet between them. 'Or would you like it—black?'

'How do you think I'd like it?' Reed asked huskily, and although the double entendre was not lost on Helen she chose to ignore it.

'I don't know, do I?' she responded nervously, and Reed made a careless gesture.

'Guess.'

'Well—black, I suppose,' she conceded unwillingly, and Reed pulled a wry face.

'Do you think I'm drunk?'

'I—why—no.' Helen was getting more agitated by the minute. She finished filling his cup and pushed it along the polished surface towards him. 'Perhaps you'd like to help yourself,' she added, putting the cream jug and sugar basin beside his cup.

Reed forbore to make another obvious comment, and Helen tried to apply herself to pouring herself some coffee. But her hands shook abominably, and she almost jumped out of her skin when Reed leant forward and removed the offending utensils from her hands.

'I'm not drunk,' he told her softly, imprisoning her hands in his. 'At least, not enough to blind myself to certain conclusions. This is the first time you've done this sort of thing, isn't it? I should have realised sooner. I guess the alcohol has dulled my perceptions a little.'

Helen shook her head. 'It doesn't matter——'

'It does matter.' His lips twisted. 'I should take you home right now. And I will, just as soon as the caffeine clears my head.'

Helen had never felt so juvenile. In spite of all her efforts to appear confident and mature, she had failed. He was probably wishing he had chosen someone else to take home from the party. Not a foolish teenager, who didn't know her own mind.

'Hey,' he said now, and she realised he was still holding her hands, 'don't look so down. It's not the end of the world. We've had a very pleasant evening, haven't we? At least, I have. I don't know about you.'

'Oh, I have. Of course I have,' exclaimed Helen hurriedly, gazing up at him with troubled eyes. 'And I don't have to go home. Not yet. Not unless you're tired of my company.'

Reed expelled his breath rather noisily. 'That isn't exactly what I was saying,' he said, avoiding her gaze, and looking down at her hands crushed between his. 'As a matter of fact, it's my decision to take you home, not yours. I shouldn't have brought you here. It was not a good idea.'

Helen swallowed. 'I see——'

She tried to draw her hands away from him then, but his hands tightened. 'You don't see,' he said thickly, lifting his head to look at her for a moment, before averting his eyes again. 'You don't see at all. That's the trouble.'

'But——'

'Ssh,' he sighed, and then, almost as if it was against his will, he lifted her hands to his face, and pressed his lips to her knuckles.

She shuddered then, the touch of his mouth against her skin sending a hot rush of fire through her veins. She had never experienced such a shattering sensation, and when he turned her hand over and touched her palm with his tongue she trembled all over.

She guessed he had felt the betraying response of her body, because he released her then, reaching for his cup of coffee, and swallowing half of it at a gulp. Then, after giving her a brief regretful glance, he got abruptly to his feet.

'Have you finished?'

His almost curt enquiry was hardly encouraging, but Helen now knew why he was determined to take her home. It wasn't because he found her naïve and immature. It was because he was attracted to her. And that knowledge gave her the courage to look up at him and say, 'No. No, I haven't.'

He came down beside her again with a rush, but whether that was because he was angry with her, or because he simply lost his balance, she was never sure. All she was sure of was that he was much nearer to her now, and his lazily sensual indulgence had given way to a raw impatience.

'It's late,' he said, and his voice was low and abrasive. 'Let's not make this any more embarrassing than it already is.'

Helen put down her cup, taking care to see it didn't clatter in the saucer. 'All right,' she said, not quite confident enough to argue with him. 'I'm ready.'

But now it was Reed who didn't move. Closing his eyes for a moment, he raked his fingers through his hair as if he was in pain. And, watching the play of emotions across his face, Helen felt a totally unrealistic sense of responsibility.

'Are—are you all right?' she ventured, touching his sleeve, and Reed opened his eyes to find her looking at him with undisguised anxiety.

'Am I all right?' he echoed half ruefully, and then, as if her innocent enquiry had driven him over some brink of his own making, he grasped her arms just below her shoulders and jerked her towards him.

His hands slid down to her waist as his mouth found hers, his fingers hard and possessive as they moved against the sheer material of her shirt. But although Helen was aware of their arousing touch, it was the heated pressure of his lips that filled her senses, the hungry stroking of his tongue that drove her lips to part.

A momentary panic gripped her as he thrust his tongue into her mouth, but it didn't last. His fingers were stroking her midriff, his thumbs rubbing ever so gently against the undersides of her breasts, and her body refused to comprehend what her brain was telling her. In some remote corner of her consciousness, she was aware that what they were doing was dangerous, if not totally wrong, but she simply refused to acknowledge it. The way Reed was making her feel was so wild and sweet and irresistible that all her bones were melting, and her skin burned like a flame.

'Oh, God,' she heard him moan against her neck, his mouth leaving her lips to nuzzle at the heated hollow beneath her ear. His teeth brushed against her flesh, his tongue finding the little curves and canyons of her ear, and Helen trembled uncontrollably when his hands sought the swollen fullness of her breasts.

Her heart was pounding, the blood singing in her ears with a muted resonance. It filled her head, deafening her to the urgent warning of her conscience. So long as he was holding her, caressing her, causing the innocent reactions of her body to respond to his touch, she had no mind of her own, and acting purely on instinct she slid her fingers into his hair.

He had drawn back a little then, she remembered, acknowledging her own part in her downfall. If she had shown him she was unwilling to go any further, if she had struggled with him, or merely asked him to release her, she knew now he would have let her go. So—he had a conscience, she reflected somewhat bitterly. But it hadn't been strong enough to make him take control of the situation; it hadn't been strong enough to stop him.

And at the time Helen had been too bemused by all the new and disturbing sensations she was feeling to think of herself. His hair had felt so smooth and vital to her touch; his scalp, and the warm contours of his ears, an unfamiliar intimacy. Her hands had moved against his neck, beneath the silky length of his hair, and she had felt the effect it had upon him.

The moment for withdrawal had passed. Even though Reed had made some hoarse protest against her mouth, he was as much at the mercy of his body's needs as she was. And, looking back now, she realised how much of an influence the amount of alcohol he had drunk had had.

Not that she was excusing him, she thought impatiently. He must have known how innocent she was. Heavens, she hadn't even known, before that night, that there was a point beyond which she had no control.

With his teeth tugging insistently at her lower lip, his tongue playing sensuously with hers, he had torn the tie from around his neck and dragged the two sides of his shirt apart. Then, taking one of her hands he'd brought it to his chest, and she'd felt the coarse brush of his body hair against her palm.

After that, things had become a little blurred. She remembered Reed loosening the buttons of her shirt and exposing her functional cotton bra. She remembered her own regret that she hadn't been wearing something more glamorous, but Reed hadn't been interested in underwear. With infinite patience, he had urged her to loosen the single clip that secured her bra, and then his eager fingers had taken its place.

Even now, Helen could remember the spurt of pleasure she had felt when he eased her back against the cushions of the sofa. The sensation, which had emanated from her stomach, and spread down into her thighs, had expanded when Reed touched her nipples with his lips. With his tongue laving the tight areola, he had suckled gently at each rosy peak, his teeth lightly grazing the taut, sensitised flesh.

Somehow—the details of it were confused now—he had removed the remainder of her clothes, and, although it had not been cold in the hotel room, wherever his tongue touched she felt the coolness of air against her overheated skin.

She didn't know exactly when he had carried her into the bedroom. She did remember noticing that the bed had been turned down by the efficient staff at the hotel, but Reed had paid no attention to the neatly folded sheets. Depositing Helen on the bed, he came down quickly beside her, and only when she felt the hair on his chest, teasing her swollen breasts, did she realise that he was now as naked as she was.

However, it was when he moved over her, when his weight crushed her down into the soft mattress, that she knew a moment's pause. The totally unfamiliar pressure of a flat, muscled stomach was startling enough, but when he eased one of his legs between her thighs she felt a mindless panic. His tumescent masculinity, throbbing against her leg, was unbearably daunting. And yet it was exciting, too, and she didn't know how to handle it.

But her panic hadn't lasted, she conceded drily. As if sensing her tremulous uncertainty, Reed had found her mouth again with his lips, his tongue urging her to participate in its possession. Slowly, but inevitably, her fears had subsided beneath its hot persuasion, and when she had learned her lesson well and entwined her tongue with his, his reaction had driven all hesitation from her mind.

Of course, Helen remembered bitterly, there had been one other—minor—complication, but Reed had not let that faze him. His discovery that she was a virgin had caused him to utter a savage expletive, but it had been too late then. Looking back, she supposed it was unreasonable to imagine that he might have been able to stop at that critical moment. Nevertheless, it was easier now to blame him for what he had done.

Not that he had done much more than penetrate the untried folds of her flesh on that occasion, she acknowledged. Her tightness, and his own urgent desire, had accomplished his needs in less than thirty seconds. With a helpless groan at his own lack of control, he had drawn back from her, spilling himself needlessly on the white linen sheet.

She supposed she could have left him then. Indeed, she *should* have left him then. Apart from the fact that technically she was no longer a virgin, a circumstance that was hardly original in a girl of her age even then, she doubted she had conceived. It was always possible, of course. Nothing was certain. But somehow she didn't think so. It had all been too quick. But she didn't leave.

Initially, it would have been difficult to do so. Reed was slumped half across her, and aside from that she felt curiously weak and exhausted. So exhausted, in fact, that she closed her eyes, and when she opened them again she knew she must have been asleep. Her body felt cool, cooler than it had done before, and although she felt chilled and clammy she was quite alert.

She thought Reed must have been asleep, too, because when she tried to move out from under him he groaned protestingly. But, like her, he awakened, blinking sleepy eyes in the lamplight, and gazed at her half unseeingly, before burying his face between her breasts.

She felt his stirring arousal instantly, and this time she was determined not to give in to him. But, somehow, when his sleepy mouth found hers, and his hand slid down between her legs, the demands of the situation no longer seemed so distinct. Whereas before she had been stiff and awkward, now she was totally relaxed, and his questing fingers made a nonsense of her resistance. Almost without her volition, her legs splayed to allow his probing exploration, and she moaned words against his lips that she had never used before.

This time, when he eased himself inside her, there was none of the tension she had felt before. The sharp jabbing pain that had left her feeling weak and helpless didn't happen. All she felt was a warm fulfilment, and an aching need to accommodate his demands.

But it was her own demands that eventually sent her trembling over the brink of total surrender. This time, it was her satisfaction he sought before his own. His initially gentle possession, and the persuasive brush of

his lips, had inspired an urgent need inside her, and it
was she, Helen remembered now, who had begged him
to go on.

And he had, Helen conceded, with an involuntary
shiver of recollection. He had driven them both to the
edge of insanity, time and time again, before her feelings
had splintered into a dizzying arc of pleasure. And, if
he had thought of withdrawing from her then, she
wouldn't have let him, her legs and arms wrapped arøund
him in a positive frenzy of delight . . .

Of course, the accusations had come later. It had been
two in the morning when Helen left the hotel, and by then
she was wrapped in an aura of self-recrimination.

Perhaps she had slept again, she wasn't sure, but what
she was sure of was that Reed hadn't stirred the second
time, when she had scrambled out from under him. He
had been sound asleep, she recalled, one of his legs
imprisoning hers within the intimacy of his thighs. And,
although she had had to shift it, and him, to slide off
the bed, he had only burrowed against the pillows and
slept on.

She had dressed in the exquisitely appointed sitting-
room, rescuing her clothes from where Reed had dropped
them earlier. That had been the start of her doubts and
confusion, she remembered. Everything had looked so
different to her then.

Picking up her panties from the floor, she had felt a
little sick, and degraded, and what had previously been
a sense of joy became a source of shame. There were
smears on her legs, but she didn't stop to wash herself.
She was half afraid he might wake up, and she didn't
want that to happen. She needed time to adjust herself
to her feelings, before she saw him again.

Only she didn't see him again, Helen reflected now.
And, until today, she had blamed him for everything
that came after. Ironically enough, her parents had not
found out what had happened. Not then. For once, her
father had been asleep when the taxi had deposited her
at the front door, and if her mother had heard her come
in she had refrained from mentioning it. If her mother
had been awake, she had probably thought to save her

daughter the hassle of having to explain where she had been to her father. And later on, when Helen had discovered she was pregnant, no one but she had remembered the tumultuous events of that night.

CHAPTER ELEVEN

To HELEN'S relief, Reed did not join them for supper that evening. When Jon asked where his father was, Victoria irritably declared that he had gone into town, and as she was in no mood to humour her nephew the atmosphere at the table was decidedly chilly.

Not that Helen felt very hungry. Even though she had had next to nothing all day, her appetite was virtually non-existent, and she was glad that Jon put it down to her earlier sickness. He probably assumed she was just a bad sailor, she thought ruefully. Which was a pity really, because until that scene with Reed she had enjoyed the day.

Enjoyed the day? Her choice of terminology momentarily staggered her. How could she have enjoyed anything with Reed Wyatt? But the fact was, she had, and that was half the reason she was feeling as she did.

At least Susie—whoever she was—had gone home, she thought gratefully. Holding her own against that young woman, who was determined to stake her place in Jon's affections, was not something she felt capable of handling tonight. Susie had been too shrewd, too knowing, almost, and until she had herself in control again Helen could do without the aggravation.

Jon, however, was another matter. There was no avoiding him, and in spite of all her efforts she couldn't go on treating him as she had been before. Reed was there, between them, as he had been from the first moments of their arrival. And what then had been a cause of some alarm was now a fully fledged feeling of raw panic.

Not that she really feared that Reed might tell Jon about their association. Somehow, that was not an issue. Reed would do nothing to hurt his son; she knew that.

What was truly troubling her was her own part in what had happened.

And she didn't just mean the events of ten years ago, she acknowledged unhappily. She couldn't forget how she had reacted that afternoon. All the time she was taking her shower, she had wondered what she would have done if he had kissed her again. There was no point in pretending she had been indifferent to the hard possession of his mouth...

'Shall we go into town after supper, too?'

Jon's question jarred her into an awareness of her surroundings, and Helen struggled to keep the betraying colour out of her face. But, just for a moment, she had been imagining how it would feel to take a shower with Reed, and her palms were still clammy from the inevitable conclusion.

'Um——' She tried to think sanely and sensibly, but it was practically impossible with the moist proof of her arousal damp between her thighs. 'Um—no,' she got out at last. 'No, I don't think so. If you don't mind, I am rather tired, and I thought I might have an early night.'

'OK.' But Jon was regarding her with curious eyes, and she wondered exactly what he was thinking. He couldn't possibly suspect that there was anything between her and his father, could he? For God's sake, she had done nothing but respond to Reed's kiss.

'I should have thought last night's visit to town would have satisfied your desire for entertainment for the time being,' Victoria observed sharply, and for once Helen was glad of her caustic intervention. At least it gave Jon something else to think about, and she made an effort to swallow a piece of fillet steak.

'You should be thanking me,' Jon responded carelessly, apparently indifferent to his aunt's feelings. 'You wanted publicity for the gallery, didn't you? Well, with my assistance, you got it.'

'Not that kind of publicity, thank you,' retorted Victoria, ringing the bell for the maid to come and clear the table. 'Though I dare say *you* get the publicity you deserve.'

That stung, and Jon took an angry breath. 'Don't you criticise me,' he snarled. 'Just because you think I spoiled

your little soirée! What's the matter? Didn't Luther make
the grade? I heard you'd been chasing after him, like a
bitch in—— '

'*Jon!*'

'*How dare you?*'

Helen and Victoria spoke simultaneously, but Jon paid
little heed to either of them.

'And while we're on the subject,' he added, as his
aunt's face turned purple, 'what makes you think you
have the right to stop me from attending the opening
anyway? You may think it's *your* gallery, but it was *my*
father who financed it, and I'm his son.'

'I sometimes wonder,' declared Victoria unforgivably,
and Helen, who was not used to this kind of family
feuding, wished she could just disappear.

'Well, I am,' said Jon coldly, his lips curling
contemptuously. 'And this is *my* house. What's more,
it'll belong to me one day. Never to you!' And, tossing
down his napkin, he pushed back his chair and walked
out of the room.

'More's the pity,' muttered Victoria to his retreating
back, but the words were barely audible, even to Helen.
As far as Jon was concerned, she was never going to
win an argument, and she had evidently decided to cut
her losses while she could.

However, Helen guessed she was not going to forgive
her so easily for being a witness to her humiliation, and
the arrival of the maid to clear delayed her opportunity
to leave. Instead, she was forced to sit there until the
dinner plates were removed, and a pudding offered. And,
although she refused anything else, Victoria didn't.

There was silence for a while after the maid had left
the room to get Victoria's *crème brûlée*, and Helen was
just wondering if she could excuse herself anyway, when
the other woman spoke again.

'You're very pale,' she remarked critically, and Helen
felt like a fly on a pin. 'Are you sure there's nothing
wrong with you? I understand you were sick this
afternoon.'

The soft option, thought Helen wearily, realising
Victoria assumed she could say anything she liked to her
and get away with it. And why not? she reflected bitterly.

So far, she had done what she could to avoid any un-
pleasantness. But what did it matter? Whatever happened
tonight, in less than two weeks the Wyatts would all be
history.

'I'm still not pregnant, if that's what you're implying,'
she said at last. 'And, for your information, pregnancy
doesn't usually cause *afternoon* sickness.'

'Don't you patronise me!' Victoria didn't like any retaliation. 'I know all about pregnancy, Miss Caldwell.
My sister-in-law saw to that.'

Helen sighed. 'I'm sorry.' She had no real wish to argue
with Reed's sister. 'Anyway, this afternoon——' she
crossed her fingers within the folds of her napkin
'—this afternoon, I was seasick. I'm afraid I'm not a
very good sailor.'

'Ah.' For the first time, Victoria regarded her with a
little sympathy. 'I'm not very keen on boats myself. Not
small ones, at least.' She pulled a wry face, and briefly
Helen saw a trace of Reed in her sudden humour. 'I did
take a cruise once, to the Caribbean, and that was very
nice. But yachts and sailing dinghies—well, they're
something else.'

'I agree.' Helen forced a smile to touch her lips, and
for a few minutes they shared a mutual reminiscence.

And then, as if realising who she was talking to,
Victoria's mood changed again. 'Reed took you out,
didn't he?' she said, and it was almost an accusation.
'Where was Jon?'

'Oh——' Helen had been expecting this, but it still
wasn't any easier to deal with. 'Well, Jon had a headache,
a migraine, I think, and—and Reed was kind enough
to—to offer.'

'I see.' Victoria's nostrils had flared a little at the
mention of her nephew, but Helen's use of her brother's
Christian name was evidently more disturbing. 'He's a
very kind man, my brother. And generous too. Sometimes too generous for his own good.'

Helen wasn't sure what she meant by this, and she was
tempted to ask if the gallery, which had been acquired
with Reed's money, came into this category, but she
didn't.

'Of course,' went on Victoria, with somewhat less aggression, 'I'm sure I don't have to tell you not to get the wrong impression about Reed. I mean, since he and Diana split up, there have been women who've practically thrown themselves at him, and it all gets so—embarrassing.'

Helen stiffened. 'What are you suggesting?' she exclaimed. She had determined not to let this woman upset her, but this was too much.

'Nothing. I'm not saying anything,' Victoria assured her firmly. 'My goodness, you're Jon's—friend.' There was just the faintest pause before the word 'friend' was articulated, and it infuriated Helen. 'I was merely making conversation, that's all. For heaven's sake,' she cast her eyes towards the ceiling, 'why is everyone so jumpy tonight?'

Helen could have said she had only herself to blame if other people took exception to her words. Victoria's line in small talk would have tried the patience of a saint. But, once again, she didn't. If Victoria chose to fret about her relationship with Reed, why should she disillusion her? It might not do her any good, but it wouldn't do her any harm.

The maid returned with the *crème brûlée*, and, deciding that self-preservation was more important than good manners in this instance, Helen made her excuses and left the dining-room. She didn't know where Jon was, and she didn't particularly care. She just wanted to be alone.

She slept intermittently, her desire for oblivion thwarted by a series of bad dreams. The most frightening of these was one where Reed took Alexa away from her, and she awoke in a sweat, her nightie sticking to her. He wouldn't do that—he *couldn't* do that—could he? But the truth was, she didn't know. And Reed had the resources to do whatever he wanted.

Of course, there were other dreams to distract her, though not in any practical way. Dreams where she and Reed were alone together, which in many ways were just as frightening. She didn't want to think of Reed touching her, and kissing her, and making love to her, but she couldn't seem to help it. And she was up at six-o'clock, leaning over the balcony rail, wondering how she was going to get through the next nine days.

But, for once, Reed made it easy for her. He wasn't there when she went down for breakfast, and Jon, who was, informed her carelessly that his father had left the island.

'He's taken the early morning shuttle to Atlanta,' he added, silencing Helen's immediate fears that somehow Reed had found her out, and was on his way to London. 'Some directors' meeting, so Aunt Vee says.' He flicked an indifferent glance towards the other occupant of the table, and Helen was relieved that at least they were being civil to one another. 'He'll be back tomorrow, or the day after,' Jon appended, ladling maple syrup on to his pancakes. 'Now sit down, for goodness' sake. I haven't seen you since supper.'

'You mean, she didn't go into town with you?' exclaimed Victoria, staring at him in surprise, and Helen subsided into her chair, hoping this was not the start of another argument.

'No,' said Jon now, speaking with a mouthful of sticky pancake. He swallowed and licked his lips before filling his mouth again. 'I went on my own. Got any objections?'

'You were very late back,' observed his aunt coolly, purposely averting her eyes. 'Anyway,' she had evidently decided to avoid a confrontation, 'it's nothing to do with me.' She lifted her shoulders dismissingly. 'So, what are you two going to do today?'

'I don't know.' Jon looked to Helen for inspiration. 'What would you like to do, sweetheart? Go out on the bike again? Or sunbathe?'

'Well, in my opinion, as—Helen,' Victoria obviously still found it difficult to use the other woman's name, 'um—as Helen wasn't very well yesterday, perhaps she ought to stay out of the sun today,' she murmured. She smiled at the young woman seated opposite her. 'Actually, I don't think our climate agrees with her.'

You hope! thought Helen cynically, realising nothing had changed. For a moment she had been deceived into thinking that Victoria cared about her. But it wasn't true. She was just using her to score points over Jon.

'Actually, I love the climate,' she retorted, before Jon could think of a suitably caustic response. 'And I'd like to go out on the bike. We could go into Hamilton, if you like, Jon. Didn't you tell me there was a glass-bottomed boat we could take a trip on?'

Jon's brow lifted. 'I thought you didn't like boats?' he queried. 'At least, that was my impression yesterday afternoon.' He gave her a teasing grin. 'Didn't you say something about being seasick?'

'That was different——' Helen was beginning hastily, when Victoria intervened again.

'I think your father said something to upset her,' she declared, proving she was not beaten yet, and Helen thought she could guess what the other woman was thinking. But Victoria's suspicion that she might have made a pass at Reed and been repulsed couldn't have been further from the truth, and it was infuriating when, for once, Jon chose to believe what his aunt was saying.

'Is that true?' he demanded, pushing the remainder of his breakfast aside, and staring at her. 'Did Dad say something to upset you? God, not another attempt to blacken my character!'

'Of course not.' Helen cast Victoria a frustrated look. 'It was nothing like that. I told you. I wasn't very well——'

'Are you sure?''

'Yes, I'm sure.' Helen sighed. 'Jon, your—your father was—charming.' The word nearly stuck in her throat, and she thought how ironic it was that she was having to defend Reed to his son. She hesitated a moment, and then added rather recklessly, 'Your aunt's afraid I might have misunderstood your father's kindness, that's all. Apparently, some women have got the wrong idea.'

'The wrong idea?'

Jon was looking blank, and, meeting Victoria's smug gaze, Helen guessed she had put her foot in it once again. 'Yes,' she said wearily, struggling to find the right words to extricate herself. 'Because he offered to entertain me while you were getting over your headache.'

Jon frowned. 'You mean—he came on to you!'

He looked flabbergasted, but no more so than his aunt, though Helen couldn't take the time to enjoy it. 'No,' she said heavily. 'Aren't you listening? Your aunt thinks I might have—embarrassed him, or something.'

Jon's lip curled. 'You're not serious!' he exclaimed, addressing Victoria now, and Helen hoped she had not said too much. 'You can't honestly think that Helen might be interested in Dad! Lord!' He shook his head disparagingly. 'He's far too old.'

Victoria said nothing, much to Helen's relief, and Jon rolled his eyes towards the ceiling. 'You're crazy, do you know that?' he declared at last. 'You still see every attractive woman as a potential threat. Well, though it pains me to say so, Vee, I don't think you need to worry about Dad finding someone else any more. He's not going to boot you out, so you can relax. He may still admire a beautiful woman.' He stroked the back of Helen's hand with possessive fingers. 'But I'd say your tenure was pretty much secure.'

'Your father has never booted me out,' retorted Victoria, but just her indignation was affected. And Helen could only feel relief that the crucial point was passed. 'In any case, I'm going to the gallery,' she told them, and, getting up from the table, she tottered out of the room on her ridiculous high heels.

Helen breathed more easily after she had gone, especially as Jon chose not to continue with that particular line of discussion. However, when he took the opportunity of their being alone together to come round the table and perch on the edge of her chair, she was less enthusiastic.

'Mmm, you smell delicious,' he said, nuzzling her hair with insistent lips, and although Helen would have preferred to dislodge him she didn't know how to do so without causing another argument.

Even so, there were ways to dampen his ardour, and instead of participating she deliberately buttered herself another piece of toast. 'Well, I'm hungry,' she declared, when Jon protested, and although her appetite had never been smaller she proceeded to eat it.

'So am I,' retorted Jon, rather ruefully. 'But only for you. So, when are you going to admit it? We were meant to be together.'

Helen made no response, and the appearance of the maid precluded any more serious conversation. But Jon's youth had never seemed more pronounced. Sooner or later, she was going to have to tell him that they didn't have a future—not together, at least, she thought unhappily. If Reed's reappearance in her life had done nothing else for her, it had certainly defined her feelings for his son.

Perhaps she should tell him the truth, she reflected. Oh, not the whole truth; not about Alexa; but maybe she should explain that she and his father had once— *what*? What could she say? If she admitted they had once been lovers—— *Lovers!* The word stuck in her throat. They had slept together, that was all. Love hadn't come into it. Nevertheless, if she admitted they had once known each other in that way, would Jon understand? Probably not, she decided bleakly. Indeed, he might even make all the right connections—or in her case, all the wrong ones. He knew what she was like. She didn't— sleep around. And if he put the dates together...

In consequence, she said nothing, and, during the next few days, she was relieved of the necessity of making any decision. With Reed away, she could almost pretend that she and Jon were simply on holiday, without the spectre of the past overshadowing the present. It was cowardly, she knew, and she hated deceiving Jon, who had always been so considerate of her, but what else could she do? And, apart from the problem of evading any emotional entanglements, they were good days. They swam a lot, and played tennis on the grass court at the back of the house. They even went out on the glass-bottomed boat, and Helen glimpsed a little of the island's history in the rusting wrecks that lay offshore.

It was the nights that were harder. Now that the images of the past had reasserted themselves, it was difficult not to play that scene with Reed over and over again in her mind. The trouble was, the more she thought about it, the more she blamed herself for what had happened. It had been easy to load all the responsibility on to Reed when the chances of her ever seeing him again had been so remote. But now, having met him again, having seen for herself that he was not the monster she had imagined, she found it infinitely more difficult to ignore her own guilt.

Reed came back on Wednesday evening, a day later than Victoria had predicted, and it was Thursday morning before Helen was obliged to see him. She thought she and Jon had passed his car as they were being chauffeured into town on Wednesday evening, but she couldn't be sure. The fact was, as soon as she had learned that Reed was on his way home, she had persuaded Jon to take her dancing, and they had spent the evening at a disco at one of the larger hotels.

Consequently, she went down to breakfast on Thursday morning feeling a little like a prisoner going to the block. She had no idea how she was going to handle seeing him again, and it was obvious that Victoria would be watching her every move.

As it happened, however, Victoria was the only person at the breakfast table, and Helen took her seat with some relief. At least she would be sitting down when Reed put in an appearance. It was going to be a lot easier to greet him from the comparative safety of her chair.

'Where's Jon?' asked Victoria, and Helen wished she could ask where Reed was with the same confidence. 'I'd have thought he'd be down to see his father, as he's been away. Particularly after going out last night.'

'Well—I'm afraid I was mostly to blame for that,' said Helen, helping herself to some strong black coffee. 'I wanted to go dancing, and I didn't think his father— would mind.'

She finished with a little rush, as the catch in her throat almost threatened to betray her, but Victoria was unaware of her discomfort. Evidently the fact that Reed was home was more important, and she merely clicked her tongue impatiently, as if to say young people could never be trusted.

'Anyway,' she observed, 'Jon should have known better. I know Reed always acts as if it's not important, but it must be galling for him to know that the only time he sees his son is when he wants something.'

Helen drew a careful breath. 'I don't think I——'

'What?' Victoria stared at her. 'Don't you think it's anything to do with you, is that it? Didn't Jon tell you it's not his own money he's spending? You surely didn't think he earned enough to support himself in the life-style to which he's become accustomed, did you? For goodness' sake, Reed even paid for your air fares—and for everything else Jon's bought since he's been here.'

Helen swallowed. 'I'm sorry. I didn't know that.'

'No. Well, that's typical of Jon. He spends every penny he earns, and then sponges off his father.'

To Helen's relief, the appearance of the maid pre-cluded any response she might have felt bound to make, but all the same it was disturbing to think that Reed had actually paid for her to come out here. Staying here, she felt she owed him enough already, and although the situation was out of her control she wished Jon had told her he was short of cash.

She ordered toast, when the maid asked her what she would like to eat, and it was almost an anticlimax when Reed came into the room as the maid was departing. 'Just coffee,' he said, in answer to her smiling enquiry, and then greeted Helen and his sister with an all-encompassing, 'Good morning.'

Helen answered him politely, pouring herself some orange juice to fill the pregnant silence. She guessed she and Victoria were both remembering what Victoria had said, and added to this was her own uneasiness about what had happened on the yacht.

She had expected Reed to be dressed for the office, but a covert glance in his direction was all she needed to revise her opinion. His blue collared shirt had short sleeves, and his shorts were denim cut-offs. Definitely not the kind of attire he would wear to go to business, and she realised she had been too optimistic. However, a second glance informed her that he didn't look at all well, and she wondered if his business trip had been more arduous than he had anticipated.

'Aren't you going in to the bank?' exclaimed Victoria, inadvertently asking the question Helen would have liked to ask. 'I thought there was a board meeting this morning. I thought that was why you came back last night, instead of waiting for this morning's flight.'

'There is, and it was,' said Reed, somewhat tiredly, taking his seat at the end of the table. He picked up the copy of the previous day's *Financial Times* that was lying by his plate, and glanced at the headlines. 'But you're right: I'm not going in to the bank. Not this morning, at least. Now—could I have some coffee?'

As Victoria was pouring coffee into one of the fragile, gold-rimmed cups, Helen permitted herself another look in Reed's direction. For once, he looked his age, she thought, and it was disconcerting to discover she cared enough to be concerned.

However, it was even more disconcerting when he lifted his head and caught her gaze upon him. Until then, she had succeeded in avoiding eye contact, and her surreptitious observation of his movements had gone unnoticed. But now he had intercepted her studied appraisal, and his eyes darkened disturbingly as they bored into hers.

'Are you all right?'

It took Helen a moment to realise Reed was talking to her, and when she did her face betrayed her sudden consternation. 'I—I beg your pardon?'

'I said, are you all right?' Reed repeated evenly. 'You got over your—er—indisposition?'

'Oh.' Helen swallowed. 'Yes. Yes, I'm fine now, thank you.' She paused, and then, realising something more was required of her, she added politely, 'Did you have a good trip?'

Reed's mouth drew in. 'Passably,' he conceded. And then, just as dutifully, 'What have you and Jon been doing while I've been away? I expect you've seen most of the island now, haven't you?'

'Most,' agreed Helen, smiling rather tensely at the maid who brought her toast. 'The—er—the weather's been wonderful.'

'I thought you'd found it a little too hot for comfort,' put in Victoria abruptly, apparently deciding she had been silent long enough. 'After all, you're not very brown, are you? A little red, perhaps——'

'Her skin's too fair to tan,' Reed remarked, before Helen could think of a civil response, and both women were taken aback. Then, turning to his sister, he continued, 'By the way, Styles was at the airport last night, when I landed. He was apparently on his way to

New York. I didn't know you'd arranged some Press coverage for him in the States.'

Now it was Victoria's turn to go red. 'I haven't,' she snapped, regarding her brother with accusing eyes. 'And you know it.' She took a deep breath. 'How do you know where he was going, anyway? I can't believe he volunteered the information.'

'No. I asked him,' replied Reed pleasantly. 'I took a leaf out of your book, Tori. I've noticed you don't hesitate to speak your mind, when you consider the situation warrants it.'

Victoria grunted. 'So, why didn't you mention it last night?'

'I didn't think of it.' Reed shrugged. 'Believe it or not, I do have more important things on my mind than Luther Styles.'

Victoria gave another snort that sounded like 'humph', but she didn't contradict him. And Reed's timely intervention had diverted the conversation from Helen, for which she was grateful. It gave her the opportunity to finish her breakfast in comparative anonymity, and she made sure she did nothing to draw attention to herself again.

CHAPTER TWELVE

JON came into the morning-room as Helen was leaving the table, and it was embarrassing when he tried to kiss her in front of his father. However, as Victoria was close on her heels—evidently preferring to be alone, to brood over what Reed had told her—she had an excuse to step past him. Forcing a smile, she told him she would see him later, and left him alone with his father, hoping her apparent insouciance in doing so would not prove indiscreet.

Victoria disappeared into the library and, left to her own devices, Helen went out of the house and down to the jetty. Even at this hour of the morning, the sun was hot on her back, and she was glad she had chosen to wear an outfit that afforded her shoulders some

protection. Despite the fact that the jumpsuit's legs were
cut off at mid-thigh, the cotton top was conventional,
with wide, elbow-length sleeves. However, remembering
that Jon had bought the suit the day before in Hamilton,
Helen felt less at ease. After what Victoria had told her,
she couldn't help wondering whether Reed's money had
paid for it. And Jon's comment, that its warm, peachy
colour exactly matched her skin, seemed rather hollow
if that was true.

The motor launch was moored at the jetty, and she
nudged it impatiently with the toe of her boot. It bobbed
on the water, but the picture didn't please her. It
reminded her too vividly of her nervousness the morning
Reed took her out on the yacht, and right now thinking
of Reed was the last thing she wanted to do. Nevertheless, she wished she had refused his offer. He might
never have remembered who she was if she hadn't spent
a whole day in his company.

Pushing thoughts like these to the back of her mind,
she started off along the dock. The sun had bleached
the stone, and it was a brilliant white beneath her feet.
Everything was clean and bright in Bermuda, she thought
moodily. Except herself, that was—and the thoughts she
couldn't stifle.

Beyond the jetty, rocks formed a natural barrier to
the sea's incessant erosion. Trees and shrubs grew close
to the water's edge, too, seemingly indifferent to the
shallowness of the soil, and clumps of flowering cacti
made an exotic splash of colour. In fact, there was colour
everywhere she looked, she reflected ruefully, and she
wished she were able to enjoy it.

Alexa would have loved it here, she knew, realising
her daughter was never likely to visit Bermuda now. Not
with her mother at any rate, Helen amended. What she
did when she was older was not something Helen could
realistically predict.

Not liking the direction her thoughts were taking,
Helen pushed her hands into her pockets and hunched
her shoulders. But she couldn't deny the fact that one
day Alexa was going to become curious about her father.
Right now, it didn't seem important, but how long would
that last?

She had picked her way to the water's edge, and was perched on a rock, gazing out at the Sound, when she sensed she was no longer alone. It wasn't any sound he had made, but rather the extra-sensory perception he had spoken of that caused her to turn her head, and when she saw Reed she got quickly to her feet.

'Um—where's Jon?' she asked at once, looking beyond him expectantly, almost as if she thought Jon were hiding in the trees. But it appeared from the careless lift of his shoulders that Reed was alone, and her pulse raced in concert with the hammering of her heart.

'I guess he's finishing his breakfast,' Reed declared at last, turning his palms towards her in a gesture of obeisance. 'Does it matter? I wanted to speak to you. That's not *verboten*, is it?'

'I—no.' Helen licked her lips. 'No, I suppose not.'

'Oh, your generosity overwhelms me!' Reed's tone was blatantly sardonic, but he didn't look at her as he stepped across the rocks towards her. 'Mmm, this is a pleasant spot, isn't it?' he added. 'I sometimes wish I had more time to enjoy it.'

Helen tried to regulate the intake of air to her lungs, but with him standing barely an arm's length away, it wasn't easy. If it wouldn't have appeared rude, or childish, or both, she would have liked to keep a safe distance between them. But with the sea behind her, and her only route back blocked by his lean, muscular figure, she felt out of her depth, and helpless.

Realising the most sensible course was to behave naturally, she shook her head now and glanced about her. 'Um—surely you don't have to work all the time,' she said rather breathily, as if that were the only topic on her mind. 'My—my boss says, you have to learn to delegate.'

'Oh, I do delegate.' Reed turned his head to look at her, and she wished she had kept her mouth shut. 'But I spend a lot of time travelling to the various branches of the bank. And I guess I use my work as compensation.'

As compensation!

Helen swallowed. 'I see.' It was safer not to make the obvious rejoinder. Their situation was unreal enough as it was.

Reed's expression altered then, and, watching the way his teeth came to draw his lower lip between them, Helen was not reassured. It seemed obvious that he was not deceived by her attempt at evasion, and she looked down at her feet to avoid his knowing eyes.

'Are you in love with Jon?'

Helen caught her breath. The question was so unexpected that for a moment she could only stare at him. Then, gathering her wits, she said unsteadily, 'That's none of your business.'

'I know it's not.' Reed scuffed the toe of his shoe against the rocks. 'But I'd like to know anyway.'

'Why?'

Helen needed some time to regain her composure, but unless she could defuse this situation there didn't seem much prospect of that.

'Why do you think?' he asked now, and she couldn't prevent her disbelieving gaze from seeking his yet again.

'I—don't know,' she said, rubbing her moist palms against her thighs. 'Because—because you're his father, I suppose.'

'Ah, yes.' Reed's lips twisted. 'What other reason could there be?' he observed, but it was not a question. 'Perhaps you think I'm having second thoughts, about approving of your relationship.'

Helen hesitated. 'Are you?'

Reed looked at her wryly for a moment, and then ran long brown fingers through his hair. 'Perhaps,' he conceded. 'I've thought about it a lot.'

Helen moved her head quickly from side to side. 'Well—so have I, as it happens,' she admitted honestly. 'And you don't have to worry. I know what I have to do.'

'Do you?' Reed regarded her firmly now. 'I wish to hell I did. I wish my situation were as simple as yours.'

Helen swallowed. 'As simple as mine,' she echoed. 'What makes you think——?'

'I did go back,' he said abruptly, and Helen's jaw sagged as he drew a harsh breath. 'To the wine bar,' he added, as if she needed any elucidation. 'I went back. But you weren't there.'

Helen gulped. 'You're not serious!' She could feel a wave of hysteria rising inside her. 'Oh, God! Do you expect me to believe you? You didn't go back to the wine bar, and I despise you for pretending you did.'

'I'm not pretending.'

'Oh, please——'

Helen turned away then, her arms pressed across her midriff as if to quell the sense of nausea she was feeling. That he should tell such bare-faced lies, she thought sickly. That he would even think he could make her believe he had cared enough to come back.

He was lying. He had to be lying. Despite Bryan Korda's threats about reporting her, she had continued to work for Clive for almost six weeks after the night she had spent with Reed. And he had never come back. Dear God, hadn't she looked for him in every face that came into the bar? Hadn't she cried herself to sleep for weeks, when he hadn't appeared? Eventually, of course, she had had to accept that she had been a fool. That a man like him took his pleasure where he found it, with no thought for the consequences. But that hadn't stopped her wanting to see him again, and she had gone through hell in those weeks, before she'd lost all hope.

Then, when she'd found out she was going to have his baby, her puerile fantasies had given way to raw panic. She'd been young, and she'd been unmarried, and the feelings she had been nurturing for Reed had no longer seemed so romantic. That was when her parents had proved to be such a tower of strength. And, even though they had been hurt by her refusal to tell them who the baby's father was, they had helped and supported her through those difficult days.

Of course, years later, she had told them the truth. When Alexa had reached school age, and Helen had been old enough to forbid her father to do anything about it. And then it had all seemed like such a hackneyed story. The pathetic confession of someone who should have known better. But they had never reproached her for it, even though they must have wondered where they, themselves, as parents, had gone wrong...

'Helen——'

His use of her name caused a tiny draught of air to fan the nape of her neck, and she realised that, while she had been remembering the past, he had closed the space between them. He was standing right behind her now, and even as she became aware of it his hands curved lightly over the shrinking flesh of her upper arms.

'Please——'

It seemed to be the only word she could articulate, and, although she would have liked to use some stronger expletive to get him to release her, her brain seemed frozen.

'Relax,' he said softly. 'For God's sake, don't be afraid of me! I only want to talk to you. To set the record straight.'

'There is no record to set straight,' said Helen stiffly, moving her arms to evade his hands, and with a weary sigh he let her go. But he didn't move away.

'I did go back to the wine bar, but——' as she began to protest again '—we won't go into that now. Nevertheless, it's relevant to what I'm saying. However unlikely that may seem.'

Helen closed her eyes. 'I don't want to talk about this—— '

'Well, I do.' She heard his harsh intake of breath. 'Lord, what did you expect? You can't believe something like this can happen, without there being repercussions. Since—well, since we spoke on the yacht, I've thought of nothing else.'

'Really?'

Somehow, despite her agitation, Helen managed to put some sarcasm into her tone, and as if her attitude had angered him Reed shifted impatiently.

'Yes, really,' he muttered, and she could sense the tension in his taut body. 'And, whether you believe me or not, you're going to listen to my side of the story.'

Helen's hands clenched at her sides. Damn him, she thought, she didn't want to listen to anything he had to say. He was too damn plausible, that was the trouble. Even after all these years, there was still a part of her that wanted to believe him. And that was what frightened her most.

But she couldn't let him know that, and adopting an indifferent stance she lifted one slim shoulder. 'Well,' she said, gazing out across the Sound, as if anything he had to say were of little interest to her, 'you have had three days to think of an explanation.'

'That's not true!' Reed swore then, and it was obvious from the words he used that he had no trouble in thinking of expletives. 'You just don't want to understand, do you? My God, did you honestly expect me to remember every detail of what happened ten years ago in the space of a few minutes?'

'I—don't—care,' said Helen carefully, but Reed was not prepared to believe her now.

'Don't you?' he snapped, and when his hands gripped her arms again and jerked her back against him, she was left in no doubt that this time he was not going to be ignored. 'Well, that's too bad. Because you are going to hear what I have to say.'

Helen thought of struggling with him, but she had had experience of his strength, and she had no intention of making this situation any more humiliating than it already was. Instead, she bore the discomfort of his fingers digging into her soft flesh, and tried to ignore the pressure of his pelvis against her buttocks.

'I—think you'd better let me go,' she said, with as much conviction as she could muster. Her hand brushed his thigh, and she jerked it away automatically. 'I mean it,' she added evenly. 'This is—silly. Someone—someone might see us.'

Reed's breathing was heavy in her ear. 'Who?' he countered harshly. 'Jon?' He paused. 'Does that bother you?'

Helen took a trembling breath. 'It—it should—bother you. And—and there's Victoria.'

Reed bent his head then, and as he did so his hair brushed the side of her neck. With her hair drawn into its usual braid, she had no protection from him, and the feel of his hair against her skin was unbearably disturbing. 'What—what if I say I don't care?' he enquired, and she couldn't be sure, but she thought his lips touched the delicate contours of her ear.

'You do care,' she protested, but it was a desperate response at best. The longer he held her, the less she wanted him to let her go, and it was almost impossible to prevent her head from tipping towards his tempting mouth.

'Shut up, and listen,' he ordered grimly, though his hands on her arms were no longer hurting her. 'When I went back to England, you were *not* still working in that wine bar.'

Helen shivered. 'Wh-when you went *back* to England,' she echoed painfully. 'You mean, you had a conscience about me?'

'A conscience about you?' For a moment, Reed sounded as if he didn't understand her, but then comprehension seemed to dawn. 'No,' he told her abrasively. 'At least, not in the way you mean. I didn't go back because I'd had second thoughts. I went back because I wanted to tell you why I'd gone away.'

'I—don't—want to hear,' she moaned, twisting her head back, and then wishing she hadn't when she encountered the unyielding expanse of his chest. And, because his head was still bent towards her, her soft cheek grazed the rougher skin of his jawline. 'Please, I want you to let me go. I don't want to hear any more lies.'

'They're not lies, damn you. It's the truth,' grated Reed savagely. 'The morning after—the morning after we were—together, my lawyer called me from Bermuda.' He took a steadying breath, and then continued, 'You know now that Diana and I were separated. Well, he called to tell me that Diana had come over in my absence, and taken Jon back to the States.'

Helen blinked. 'Jon?'

'Yes, Jon.' Reed breathed unevenly. 'And, believe it or not, at that time my son's happiness meant more to me than anything else.'

Helen moistened her lips. 'But—if he went with her——'

'He was eleven years old,' said Reed harshly. 'He didn't have a lot of choice.'

Helen absorbed what he had said. 'I see.'

'Do you?' Reed twisted her round to face him then, and she was alarmed at the greyness of his expression. 'Do you really? Or are you just saying that?'

Helen swallowed. 'If it's true——'

'It is.' Reed's mouth thinned. 'It took me almost two months to get him back again.'

Helen nodded. 'All right.'

Reed expelled his breath wearily. 'You believe me?'

Helen nodded again. 'If you say so.'

'If I say so?' Reed stared at her, his eyes dark with frustration. 'Helen, as God's my witness, it's the truth. At least tell me you believe me!'

Helen didn't know what to believe. As she had half expected, his story had been perfectly plausible, but she was afraid to consider its implications. If Reed was telling the truth, if he had gone back to Bermuda to fight his ex-wife for his son, where did that leave her? And how could she blame him now for not being there when she needed him?

'Helen!'

He shook her gently now, his hands sliding from her shoulders to her throat. But not aggressively, like that day on the yacht. This time, his touch was sensitive, sensuous, his thumbs probing the hollows behind her ears, his eyes narrow and intent.

'Now, tell me,' he said huskily, 'are you in love with my son?'

Helen found herself shaking her head almost involuntarily.

'I'm glad.' His lips twisted, almost with a trace of self-mockery. 'I know what I did was wrong, but I don't know if I could bear to live with the knowledge that you were Jon's wife.'

Helen's throat felt tight. 'You—won't—have—to.'

'No.' Reed's eyes dropped to her mouth. 'Only with what might have been, hmm? I'm sorry I hurt you. That wasn't how it was meant to be.'

Helen's control snapped. 'You didn't hurt me,' she choked out, putting up her hands to wrench his hands from her neck, only it didn't work that way. Instead her hands closed round his wrists and clung, and when she turned tear-filled eyes up to his face Reed's own restraint crumbled.

'You said——' he began, in a strangled voice, and then could go no further.

'I lied,' she told him, knowing he deserved the truth. And, aware she had gone too far to back off now, she added, 'People do that to defend themselves. Why do you think I didn't believe you?'

'Oh, God!'

Reed's groan was anguished as he tipped her face up to his. His hands threaded into her hair, loosening her braid, and causing the fiery curls to catch the sun. Then, with a feeling of inevitability, she saw him bend his head towards her, and his lips found hers in a tentative caress.

Helen's limbs melted, and her hands clutched his waist in a desperate effort to support herself. His shirt parted from his shorts as she dug her nails into the cloth, and the warm skin of his midriff was like silk beneath her fingers.

Reed sucked in his breath then, as if he found the sensation of her hands on his flesh as disturbing as she did. And when her arms slipped round his waist, and her palms spread against the moist hollow of his spine, he made a ragged sound of protest.

But he didn't let her go. And his lips, which moments before had been tasting her lips with infinite gentleness, hardened perceptibly as she burrowed closer. She was against him now, her breasts crushed against his chest, her stomach and thighs intensely conscious of the solid muscles supporting her.

His tongue thrust between her teeth, brooking no denial, and her lips parted instinctively. Hot, and wet, and sensual, it took possession of her mouth as surely as he had once taken possession of her body, and she was no more capable of resisting him now than she had been then.

His hands moved from her hair to her arms, sliding beneath the wide sleeves of the jumpsuit and massaging the yielding flesh. Every inch of her body seemed sensitised to his touch, and when the buttons at the neckline of the suit parted she didn't attempt to prevent them. But, because she wasn't wearing a bra on this occasion, her breasts were unprotected, and Reed's hands found their swollen peaks with evident satisfaction.

He was kissing her unrestrainedly now, his mouth hungry and disruptive, and burningly intent. He was kissing her as if doing so had been all he had thought about for the last ten years, and Helen could feel her senses slipping far beyond her control. She could feel his arousal too, a hard tumescent pressure against her stomach that his thin clothing could barely contain. And she knew a mindless need to touch him that was carrying her over the brink . . .

She never knew what alerted her to the fact that they were no longer alone. It was one of those odd coincidences that she should open her eyes just as Jon was striding back along the path, away from them. He didn't realise she had seen him. The way he was moving it was a miracle that she had. Or perhaps a *miracle* was not the way to describe it. A disaster seemed closer to the truth.

With a little moan she dragged herself away from Reed then, and it was only because he was still dazed by his emotions that he let her. He protested, of course, and he would have jerked her back into his arms, but somehow she evaded him, and pulled the bodice of her suit across her breasts.

'Jon,' she said, in a little choked voice, the sensitive tips of her breasts feeling sore against the soft fabric. 'Jon—was here,' she added, as Reed stared at her uncomprehendingly. 'He—he saw us. But he didn't say anything. He—went back up to the house.'

'*Hell!*'

Reed's response was succinct and instantaneous, and Helen's retreat from reality was halted. As he closed his eyes, and raked his scalp with hard, abrasive fingers, she made a shuddering return to her senses. What had she done? she asked herself unbelievingly. How had she allowed herself to participate in what had been, for him, merely a means of demonstrating his domination? He had wanted to prove a point, and he had succeeded. And because of that, she had to explain to Jon something she had hoped never to have to explain.

'I'll talk to him,' said Reed abruptly, but Helen didn't want that. If Reed told his son they had once been lovers, heaven knew what interpretation Jon might make. She had Alexa to consider, and for Alexa's sake she had to be careful.

'No,' she said now, buttoning her suit and turning away, but Reed was not allowing that.

'No?' he echoed harshly. 'Why the hell not? He has to know sooner or later. And I'm the one to tell him.'

'No,' said Helen again, stepping round him carefully, so that Reed was left in no doubt that she didn't want him to touch her. 'I—I'll speak to Jon. I got us into this mess, and—and I'll get us out of it.'

Reed's mouth tightened. 'Is that how you see this? As—a mess?'

'What else?' said Helen tautly. 'Oh, let's not pretend it meant—anything. To—to either of us. As—as you said on the yacht, we—we are attracted to one another. But that's all it is. A physical attraction.'

CHAPTER THIRTEEN

'BUT why did you really not stay for the whole two weeks, Mum?' Alexa was sitting cross-legged on the end of her mother's bed, while Helen drank the cup of tea Mrs Caldwell had just brought up to her. 'You never did tell us properly,' her daughter persisted. 'Did you and Jon have a row or something? Is that why he hasn't been to see us, since you got back?'

'No, I——'

'Your mother told you what happened,' her grandmother interrupted, picking up a pair of Helen's tights, and draping them over the back of a chair. She cast a thoughtful glance at her daughter, before continuing, 'That friend of his—the drummer—he's in trouble with the police. Jon had to come back to help him. That's why he's gone to Denmark.'

'Oh, Ricky Ellis, yes,' remarked Alexa resignedly, as Helen gave her mother a grateful look. 'But all the same, you'd think he'd have wanted to see *me*. I mean, he said he'd bring me something back. Something really super. And he hasn't.'

'Mercenary article,' said her grandmother affection-ately, ruffling Alexa's blonde curls. 'Now, come along. Off the bed. Before you make your mother spill her tea.'

'I'm not that stupid!' declared Alexa indignantly, but she got down anyway. 'I might as well go and get dressed. We are going shopping, aren't we? You did say that we could.'

'I promise,' said Helen, putting her tea aside, and pulling the pyjama-clad little girl into her arms for an impulsive hug. 'Now, don't forget to wash first, before you put on your clothes. And clean your teeth. I've put your toothbrush in the bathroom.'

'Nana got me a new toothbrush, while you were away,' said Alexa, grimacing, not altogether opposed to being cuddled, but feeling that she had to make a token protest. 'What time are we leaving? You know how hard it is for Grandad to find somewhere to park, if we don't go early.'

'Soon,' agreed Helen, wondering if she had ever had her daughter's energy. 'Just give me a chance to finish my tea, and I promise I'll get up.'

'It is Saturday morning,' put in Mrs Caldwell drily, shooing her granddaughter out of the room. 'Your mother works all week, and she deserves a lie-in at weekends. Just because you're on holiday, that doesn't mean everyone else is.'

'But it is only a week since Mummy came back from Bermuda,' protested Alexa, from the landing, and Helen sighed. 'Are you coming shopping, Nana? Sarah Stubbs says there's a new skateboard at Rosebury's. Do you think Mummy would let me have a skateboard? I wouldn't use it on the street; only in the garden...'

Helen's mother came back into the bedroom as her daughter was finishing her tea, and they shared a wry face over Alexa's chatter. 'I really believe that child is getting more demanding as she gets older,' said Mrs Caldwell ruefully. 'While you were away your father was quite worn out by her blether.'

Helen shook her head. 'I'm sorry.' She paused. 'You know, if she is getting too much for you and Dad, you must say. I'd hate you to feel you have to look after her.'

'And what would you do if we didn't?' exclaimed Mrs Caldwell at once. 'Employ some stranger to look after her, or have her going home to that empty flat after school?'

'I wouldn't do that. Have her go home to the flat, I mean.'

'No, well—we wouldn't let you employ someone else to take care of her. For heaven's sake, she is our grandchild. Our only grandchild, I might add. And, so long as you're working, she's well enough here with us.'

Helen shook her head. 'But if Dad——'

'Your father's not in his dotage yet, young woman. Goodness me, he's only fifty-eight. And, as the little one doesn't have a father of her own to care for her, it's better she has at least one stable masculine influence in her life.'

Helen lifted her head. 'One *stable* masculine influence,' she echoed, ignoring the pain her mother's careless words had evoked. 'What do you mean by that?'

'Well——' Mrs Caldwell did look slightly discomfited now. 'You have to admit, she has no other man to turn to. Not on a permanent basis, anyway.'

'You make it sound as if I'm in the habit of parading a procession of boyfriends through our home,' said Helen tensely. 'There only has been Jon. Before that, there was no one of importance.'

'Does Alexa know that?' enquired Mrs Caldwell, recovering her confidence. 'I know Jon's young, and your father and I have had our doubts about your suitability for one another, but Alexa did like him. She liked him a lot. And now, although you haven't exactly said anything, we can sense that—well, that something's happened.'

Helen put her teacup aside. 'Are you suggesting Jon and I should have stayed together for Alexa's sake?' she asked evenly.

'Then it's true,' said her mother, not answering her. 'You and Jon have split up. I knew all this business about him going to Denmark and not having time to see Alexa was all moonshine. Well, you're going to have to tell her. And soon. It's not fair to keep her hanging on.'

'I know that.' There was an edge to Helen's voice now, and her mother arched speculative brows.

'There's no need to get impatient with me,' she declared, twitching a corner of the bedspread into place. 'It's not my fault if your—holiday—didn't work out. I just wish you'd been honest with us sooner, that's all. We could have done our best to break it to Alexa gently.'

Helen sighed. 'It isn't that simple.'

Her mother straightened. 'It seems simple enough to me.'

'Yes. I expect it does.' Helen rested her elbows on her knees, and dropped her chin into her hands. 'But it isn't.'

Mrs Caldwell frowned, a trace of compassion entering her eyes. 'Why isn't it?' she asked, and smoothing the cover she seated herself on the end of Helen's bed. 'Either you've had a fall-out, or you haven't. Are you going to see him again, or aren't you?'

Helen shook her head. 'I don't know. I don't suppose so.'

'So?'

Helen hesitated, and then, with a nervous glance towards the half-open door, she said, 'There's something you don't know. Something I didn't want to tell you. But—now, well, I suppose I'm going to have to.'

Her mother stared at her. 'It's something to do with Alexa's father, isn't it?'

Helen gasped. 'Who told you?'

'No one told me.' Mrs Caldwell made an expressive gesture. 'Helen, I am your mother. I've sensed, ever since you came back, that something was wrong.'

'I see.' Helen ran her hands round the back of her neck and squeezed. 'I must be pretty transparent, hmm?'

'No. Just human,' replied her mother gently. 'So—what about Alexa's father? Have you seen him again?'

Helen slowly nodded her head. 'He's Jon's father.'

'No!' Mrs Caldwell was stunned. 'But—did you know?'

'Before I left England? Of course not.' Helen looked indignant now. 'Do you think I'd have gone to stay with them, if I'd known he was related to Jon? No. It was a total shock, believe me! I had no idea.'

'And did he know who you were?' enquired her mother, her voice distinctly cooler now, and Helen felt a sense of betrayal for the way she had behaved. To her mother, Reed was still the man who had violated her daughter. It would have probably proved impossible to get her parents to see him in a different light. So it was just as well that situation was not going to arise, she thought hollowly.

'Not initially,' she said at last, and, realising she would have to explain, she quickly outlined the details of what had happened. Of course, she omitted any mention of her association with Reed. That would only have clouded the issue. As it was, her mother was quite prepared to believe that she had severed her relationship with Jon because of his father, and the fact that that might only be a part of the story didn't seem to occur to her.

Which was probably just as well, thought Helen, remembering what had taken place between her and Jon with some misgivings. The amazing thing had been, he had expected her to go on seeing him as if nothing had happened. And it was only when she'd refused that the situation had become untenable.

However, when she had first followed him up to the house, she had been quite prepared for a blazing row. She had been able to think of no other reaction to what he had just seen, and when she eventually tracked him to earth in his room she had already been steeling herself for a confrontation.

And he had been angry. She had known that as soon as she opened the door. But she had soon found his anger was directed more towards himself than her, and when Helen had stumbled out the fact that she and Reed had known one another before, he'd actually seemed to find that amusing.

'So you met in London,' he said, nodding his head, as if that explained a lot of things. 'Well, what do you know? I didn't know he had it in him.'

'It wasn't like that.'

Helen tried to divert him. She couldn't have Jon thinking that she and his father had had an affair. There was Alexa to consider, and, although she knew she was being selfish, she couldn't bear the thought of losing her.

But, as it happened, there was no startling revelation. In fact, Jon was more interested in what was going to happen now, and when Helen insisted that, in spite of what he had seen, there was no question of her and Reed's getting together, Jon was relieved.

'These things happen,' he said, and to her horror and astonishment he actually tried to put his arms around her. Then, making a wry face when she wouldn't let him, he continued blandly, 'Come on, baby, none of us is an angel, are we? Except Aunt Vee, of course,' he added, half maliciously, laughing at his own joke. 'Hey, it's no big deal. Give a little, can't you? I guess the old man got a bit overheated, that's all. You're a good-looking girl, and he's only human. Sure, I was peeved at first, when I saw you two together. I mean, it was quite a blow to my ego, that you might prefer the old man to me. But, if you say there's nothing heavy going on between you, I'm willing to buy that. We've all got our faults.' He paused. 'Even me.'

Helen looked at him then, and, although she believed her expression was anonymous, something of what she was thinking must have shown in her face.

'Well——' he protested, even though she did not want to hear any more. 'I might as well tell you. That night I went into Hamilton on my own, I wasn't exactly a good boy myself.' And although Helen would have silenced him then, he went on doggedly, 'Susie—you remember Susie, don't you?—well, we met up at the disco, and we had a real good time. No strings; no recriminations. Just a good time, that's all. So—who am I to throw accusations? I've got my weaknesses, I admit it. So, what do you say?'

Of course, it hadn't made any difference to what Helen had already decided to do, but it had made it a whole lot easier. And Jon, after realising he was not going to change her mind, had seemed more than willing to book them both an earlier flight back to London. Perhaps he had decided he had had enough of the quiet life for the time being. Or perhaps he had thought he and Reed could both use a period of readjustment. Whatever, he had

made arrangements for them to leave the same evening,
and Helen had left the island without having another
conversation with Reed.

He had been there, of course, when the servants carried
their suitcases out to the hire car, but he hadn't said
much at all. Of course, he had had no way of knowing
what had happened between her and Jon, but she
strongly suspected he was glad to see the back of them...

'And Jon doesn't suspect——'

Mrs Caldwell broke off now, without finishing her
sentence, but Helen knew what she had been trying to
say.

'No,' she said steadily, hoping it was true. But Jon
had never asked how she had met his father, or when,
and she had certainly not volunteered the information.
And their departure from the island had been so precipitate, she was sure he hadn't spoken to his father. Not
that Reed was likely to tell him, she consoled herself
thankfully. It was not something either of them would
want to discuss.

'So,' said her mother suddenly, revealing she was not
as gullible as Helen had thought, 'has he changed much?
Reed Wyatt, I mean. He'll be older, of course. And wiser,
I dare say.' She paused. 'Wasn't he at all curious about
you?'

'Curious?' Helen's heart faltered for a moment, before
regulating its beat. Her face blazed with colour. 'Why
would he be curious about me?'

'Well, didn't Jon tell his father that you had a little
girl?'

Helen nodded. 'Yes.'

'And that didn't intrigue him at all?'

'No.' Helen took a steadying breath. 'Why should it?
I—I let him think there had been someone else.'

Mrs Caldwell's eyes narrowed. 'So he did ask?'

'Not exactly.' Helen realised she had said too much,
and tried to recover herself. 'Um—it was just something—something that was said in passing,' she impro-
vised unhappily. 'Er—don't you think we should be
making a move? If Alexa comes back, and I'm not even
out of bed——'

'How do you tell someone, even in passing, that you've slept with more than one man?' enquired her mother quietly. 'Helen, I may not be very clever, but I wasn't born yesterday.'

'Oh, God!' Helen pushed weary fingers into her hair, and regarded her mother resignedly. 'Would you believe me if I said I didn't want to talk about it?'

'Oh, yes.' Mrs Caldwell nodded. 'I'd believe you. I *do* believe you. I'm sure you don't want to talk about it at all. But we are your parents, Helen. We were the ones who stood by you, when you needed us most. Don't we deserve some consideration? Don't we deserve to know what's going on?'

Helen sighed. 'Nothing's going on.'

'But you're not telling us everything, are you?' persisted her mother. 'You didn't—you didn't do anything—silly, did you?'

'I'm not likely to have another baby, if that's what you're afraid of,' retorted Helen harshly, and then knew a terrible sense of contrition at the pained look on her mother's face. 'Oh—no. No, of course, I didn't do anything—silly, as you put it,' she assured her gently, putting out her hand and squeezing her mother's arm. 'Honestly, Mum, you don't have anything to worry about. My—my association with the Wyatt family is over.'

'Is it?' Clearly, Mrs Caldwell wasn't convinced, but Helen didn't know what else to say to her. She could hardly tell her mother what had really happened. Even now, she could hardly absorb the events of that last morning on the island with any degree of conviction herself. She wanted to forget it; forget everything that had happened, and, if there was a trace of panic in her need to put Reed out of her mind, she couldn't bear to examine it for fear of what she might find.

But, in the days that followed, it became less and less easy to keep those thoughts at bay. Time didn't heal, it merely concentrated the pain, and although exhaustion sent her to sleep the minute she laid her head on the pillow, a couple of hours later she was wide awake and vulnerable.

Of course, she told herself she was crazy to allow this to happen to her, but there wasn't much she could do about it. The cushion of time had been removed, and without its comforting barrier her feelings for Reed returned in sharp perspective. Not that she believed the way she felt now bore any resemblance to the past. In retrospect, those girlish fantasies seemed unreal and immature. Nothing like the shattering wave of emotion that had swept away her inhibitions—and her sanity.

Her only spar in this sea of uncertainty and turmoil was Alexa. Reed's daughter, she thought now, with more satisfaction than sense. At least she had something of him to hold on to, however inglorious that achievement might be. For, having met Reed again, she had had to revise her opinion about him. He had not been the immoral adventurer she had previously thought him. If she believed what he had told her—and she was inclined to do so—he hadn't exactly abandoned her to her fate. He had come back—albeit too late to do anything to help her—and, it could be argued, he deserved to know the truth.

Yet, how much of the truth did he deserve to know? she asked herself bitterly. The truth that he had a daughter, as well as a son? Remembering what he had told her of the legal battle he had had with his first wife, when she had tried to take Jon away from him, how could she face such a prospect with equilibrium? Or perhaps the truth that she herself was in love with him? For she was. She knew that now; had sensed it, in fact, from the first day she arrived in Bermuda.

But neither of these alternatives was an option that was open to her. She couldn't play games with Alexa's future, and the possibility that Reed might use her to gain control of his daughter was not one she cared to consider. She had to accept the fact that Reed was not in love with her, and therefore they had no future together. He had been—*he was*—attracted to her, but that was as far as it went. It wasn't the first time a man had shown interest in her. For heaven's sake, Jon had been interested in her, and other men before him. Just because, on those other occasions, she had felt no answering attraction herself, the situation was no different. For some reason, men found the combination of her fiery hair and pale skin infinitely appealing, and although she knew she wasn't beautiful she apparently possessed something else.

Which didn't make the slightest difference to her present dilemma, except in so far as to say, had Reed not been attracted to her, she might not now be suffering as she was. If he hadn't recognised her, if he hadn't touched her, if he hadn't aroused such strong emotions inside her—if, if, if! But he had recognised her, he had touched her, and the feelings he had aroused would not easily be denied.

Her work suffered, because she found it so difficult to concentrate, and Alan Wright got quite irritated with her. He was used to relying on her completely, and when contracts went astray, and letters went untyped, his usual good humour gave way to frank impatience.

'What is the matter with you?' he demanded, one Friday afternoon about three weeks after Helen's return from holiday. 'For God's sake, if I didn't know better, I'd say you were having marital problems. Alexa's OK, isn't she? I know it's the school holidays, but your parents are looking after her, aren't they?'

'Yes. Yes, of course.'

While Alexa was on holiday, she spent most of her time with her grandparents. During schooltime, things were different. Then, Helen took her daughter to school on her way to work, and either her mother or her father picked her up afterwards. Usually, they took her to the flat, so that she was there when Helen got home. But occasionally they took her to Chiswick, and at weekends Helen often stayed there too.

'So, what is wrong?' Alan protested now. 'Helen, I don't want to hurt your feelings, but I do need an assistant who has some interest in her work.'

Helen shook her head. 'I am interested——'

'—but not enthusiastic,' Alan interrupted drily. 'Ever since you came back from holiday, you've lost that elusive spark. What happened, for pity's sake? What did he do? I guess it has something to do with that pop singer you went on holiday with. I heard you're not seeing him any more.'

Helen stared at him indignantly. 'How did you hear that?'

'From one of the girls in the typing pool.' Alan looked a little embarrassed now, and he ran a rueful hand over his balding scalp. 'Well, that car of his hasn't been around lately, has it?' he defended himself. 'And what with the way you've been working, and every-thing——'

'—you put two and two together and made five?'

Alan sighed. 'Not exactly. Helen, I may be impatient over your work, but I do care about you. If you are having some problems with this bloke, and I can help you with it, you've only to say.'

Helen shook her head now, her momentary indig-nation dispersing. 'It's nothing like that,' she said. And then, because he deserved some explanation, she added, 'We have split up, as you surmised. But it was a mutual agreement. Not something I'm upset over.'

Alan gazed at her helplessly. 'Then what is the matter with you? Helen, you have to admit, you're not your usual efficient self. You gave me the wrong figures to take into that meeting this morning, and I had to spend at least half an hour ad-libbing my way around the estimate.'

'I'm sorry.' Helen bent her head. 'I—I'm just tired, I suppose.'

'But why are you tired? Aren't you sleeping? If not, I suggest you get yourself to the doctor. A young woman of your age—you should have no problems sleeping at all.'

'No.'

Helen acknowledged his appraisal of her condition, and promised she would go and see her doctor if the situation persisted. Then, when he suggested she could finish early, she collected her bag and left the office, grateful for the chance to get out into the afternoon sunshine.

Alan Wright's engineering company was situated near Paddington Station, but Helen caught a bus to Earl's Court, and walked the rest of the way home. Her apartment was situated on the first floor of a converted Victorian mansion, just off Goldhawk Road. It was not a particularly up-market area at the moment, but it was rapidly becoming so. At present, young couples lived in the building, saving hard to buy homes of their own. And, as all the apartments had window boxes, which at this time of the year were overflowing with fuchsias and geraniums, the old building had a distinctly winsome charm.

From Helen's point of view, it was a welcome sight at any time. It was home; and, although she knew she and Alexa were always welcome at her parents' home, it was good to have a place of their own.

Of course, Alexa wasn't there at the moment. She was at her grandparents'. Mrs Caldwell was going to bring her over at teatime. But, Helen thought suddenly, if she took a quick shower and went to collect her, they could spend at least an hour in the park. It would take her mind off what Alan had said, and perhaps help her to pull herself together.

CHAPTER FOURTEEN

THE buzzer went as Helen was taking her shower. Its insistent sound penetrated even the falling spray of water, and Helen sighed impatiently as she clambered out of the bath. She guessed it must be her father, who finished early on Fridays, and must have decided to drive Alexa and her mother over to the flat instead of letting them catch the bus. But he could certainly choose his moments, she thought, grabbing a towel and wrapping it round her. With her hair wet, and dripping on to her shoulders, it wasn't easy to feel grateful.

It was only as she ran across the living-room carpet that she realised it couldn't be her father. He didn't finish that early, and, so far as her parents were concerned, she'd still be at work for hours yet. She guessed it was a door-to-door salesman, ringing all the buzzers to see if anyone was in. That made her feel even less sociable, and by the time she reached the entry phone, which was situated in the tiny hall of the flat, she felt angry and resentful.

'Yes?' she said tersely, picking up the receiver with wet hands.

'Helen?'

The instantly identifiable voice caused her to drop the phone. For an awful moment she thought she must be hallucinating, and that she hadn't heard the buzzer at all, or the achingly familiar tones in her ear. She must be having delusions, she thought sickly; there was no way Reed could be here, in England, standing outside the door. Apart from anything else, he didn't know where she lived.

'Helen?' He said her name again, and the fears that she was losing her mind fled. 'Helen, may I come in? I want to talk to you.'

It really was *him*! Another wave of apprehension swept over her. Why was he here? she wondered. Dear God, had he found out about Alexa?

'Helen, for heaven's sake, will you answer me?'

He sounded angry now; angry and frustrated. As well he might, she thought unsteadily. So long as she didn't speak, he couldn't be sure it was her.

Hardly knowing what she was doing, she replaced the phone on its cradle, and backed away from it. He couldn't get in, she told herself. The door downstairs had a safety lock, and unless he had a key there was no way he could gain entry to the house. So long as she, or someone else, didn't press the release button, the door remained closed. And at this time of day she was probably the only tenant in the building.

Which wasn't totally reassuring, she conceded ruefully. If Reed did get in, there was going to be no one else around to help her. But why should she need help anyway? she asked herself impatiently. For God's sake, she was getting paranoiac.

She wished her apartments overlooked the road at the front of the house, but they didn't. They overlooked the garden. And while that was very nice, from the point of view of not hearing the traffic, it wasn't very satisfying if you wanted to observe the entrance.

The buzzer sounded again. It seemed louder now, but that was only because she was standing right next to it. It rang again and again, until she wanted to put her hands

over her ears to stop the noise. And then it went silent,
which somehow was much worse.

Abandoning the hall, she ran back across the living-
room and through the bedroom into the bathroom.
Unfortunately, the flats were not custom-built, and
consequently the rooms led one from another. Picking
up another towel, she rubbed violently at her hair, and
then, dropping the towel she had wrapped around her,
she pulled on her old towelling bathrobe, which was
hanging on the back of the door.

Crossing the living-room again, she reached the hall,
and paused uncertainly. The entry phone was still silent,
but she had to know if Reed was still outside. And the
only way to find out was to open her door, and step out
on to the landing. The landing window overlooked the
front of the house, and if she craned her neck she would
be able to see if he was standing on the path below.

Not that it would do much good, she acknowledged,
her brows drawn together anxiously, as she unlocked her
front door. If he had gone away, it would probably only
be a temporary departure. He was bound to come back,
and it was up to her to make sure he didn't find her at
home. They could stay at her parents', she thought
tensely. If she explained the situation to her mother, she
was sure she would help her. But would she? a small
voice taunted. Perhaps her mother would take a totally
different view.

She latched the door open, and, securing the belt of
her bathrobe, stepped outside. The rubber-floored
landing was cold to her bare feet, but she scarcely noticed
it. She was totally intent on reaching the window, and
when someone cleared their throat behind her she almost
jumped out of her skin.

'Reed!' she gasped, pressing a disbelieving hand to
her throat, and he straightened from his lounging
position beside her door. Her eyes darted to her open
doorway, as if gauging her chances of reaching it, but
he moved to block the entrance, and she expelled her
breath on a sigh. She should have waited to put her
clothes on, she reflected, aware of her disadvantage. Not
that she rated her chances of running away from him.
Even though he was older, he was probably much fitter.

Not that he looked it, she acknowledged, unable to prevent herself from making an involuntary appraisal of his appearance. He looked as if he'd lost weight; and he looked tired, too, she noticed anxiously. The lines that scored his face accentuated an expression of weary resignation, and she felt a wave of compassion that threatened her common sense.

'Just what the hell do you think you're doing?' Reed asked now, adjusting the black leather jacket he had draped over one shoulder. Its dark pigmentation robbed his face of all colour, and his eyes between their long lashes were sombrely intent. 'Why wouldn't you speak to me? I know you knew who it was.'

Helen moistened her dry lips. 'Perhaps I didn't want to speak to you,' she said, his anger making it easier for her to remain calm. 'Wh-what are you doing here? If you're looking for Jon, I haven't see him——'

'I'm not looking for Jon,' replied Reed, glancing through the door behind him. 'Look, couldn't we go inside? I haven't slept for about thirty-six hours, and I could use a beer, if you have one.'

'No——'

Helen spoke automatically, not trusting herself alone with this man. Already he had aroused her sympathy. What more might he arouse if she allowed him into the flat? She had to think of Alexa. *Alexa*...

'Why have you come?' she asked impulsively. She had to know if he knew the truth. She would have no peace if she let him go without asking. And if he didn't want Jon, what other reason could he have for being here?

Reed sighed, and sagged against the wall. 'So much for British hospitality,' he said, his eyes dark and cynical as they held hers. 'Hell's teeth!' He pushed long fingers into the hair at the back of his neck. 'Why do you think I've come? To see you, of course. What else? To find out if there's any chance of us starting over.'

Helen's lips parted. 'Starting over?' she echoed faintly, while her brain tried to take in what he was saying. Why on earth should he want to see her again, to 'start over' as he put it, unless he knew about Alexa? And if he knew about Alexa why didn't he just say so?

Panic made her careless. There was no time to think about what she could do, what she *should* do. She loved him. Oh, God, how she loved him! But she had to protect herself, and Alexa. She couldn't live with him knowing he had only used her as a means of getting to his daughter.

Before he could divine what she planned to do, she darted past him, squeezing through the doorway of her apartment, and pressing the door shut behind her. But she wasn't quite quick enough. His booted foot blocked the threshold just as the door was closing. And, although she fought to keep him out, his strength was still superior to hers.

'For God's sake!' he swore, as the door slammed back against the wall and Helen stood helplessly before him. 'Are you crazy? Or am I? I actually thought you might be pleased to see me!'

Helen's body froze. She couldn't fight him any more, she thought despairingly. Whatever reason he had had for coming here, she no longer had the will to deny him. And when he looked at her, as he was doing now, she didn't even trust herself to speak.

He looked at her for a long time, and then, as if coming to a decision, he turned back towards the open doorway. 'I see you want me to go,' he said, his lips twisting with some emotion she could only guess at. 'Why did I ever imagine otherwise?' he added, half to himself, and hunching his shoulders he stepped back over the threshold.

'*No*——'

The strangled sound she made was barely recognisable, even to Helen. But she couldn't let him go. No matter how reckless that decision was, she couldn't let him walk away. Not without telling him how she felt.

He didn't turn however. He merely halted in the doorway, as if he was not actually convinced of what he had heard, and Helen, compelled into action, moved towards him. Putting out her hands, she balled them into fists for a moment, before gathering the courage required to touch him. Then, almost tentatively, she put her hands on his hips, and the shudder he gave ran up her wrists and into her arms.

Breathing shallowly, she stepped even closer, and leaning towards him she pressed her lips to the hollow of his spine. The scent of his warm body rose through the thin fabric of his shirt, and her lips moistened the cloth where they touched. But it was intensely satisfying to feel his involuntary response, and gaining confidence from the experience she slid her arms around his waist.

He moved then. As her hands spread against the taut muscles of his midriff, he made a sound low in his throat, and turned towards her. 'God—Helen!' he muttered, slamming the door with one hand and capturing her nape with the other. Then, tilting her face up to his, he found her mouth, and the urgent pressure of his lips destroyed all coherent thought.

They'd kissed before, but not like this; not blindly, passionately, soulfully, so that Helen felt as if she had no will of her own. It was as if she had waited all her life for this moment, and she refused to allow the complications she would have to face for letting this happen to interfere with this brief taste of happiness. The past was dead, and gone, and the future was too uncertain. But right now she was where she wanted to be, and if she had to pay for it later, then so be it.

His hands cupped her face, his thumbs brushing the underside of her lips, and causing them to part. Then, when her mouth opened wide to the sensuous demand of his, his tongue slid into that warm cavern, hot, and wet, and hungrily intent.

Helen clung to him then, because not to do so would have caused her knees to buckle. She burrowed against him, her eager actions loosening his shirt from his trousers at the back, her hands sliding over his smooth skin. His skin was moist beneath her palms, and she wished she could taste him. She wanted to wind herself about him, and never let him go, and, lifting the sole of her foot, she ran it sensuously down his muscled calf.

He caught his breath, his lips moving from hers to find the scented hollow of her shoulder. His hands slid inside the towelling bathrobe, and as they did so she felt the trickling dampness of her hair on her neck. It brought a brief moment of clarity, and Helen was starkly reminded of her appearance, and of what a mess she must look. But then he pushed the offending robe off her shoulders, and a wave of embarrassment took its place.

'Don't,' he said huskily, as her hands automatically moved to cover herself. 'Don't,' he said again, grasping her wrists, and drawing them aside. 'Let me look. I want to. I've thought of little else for the past four weeks.'

Helen moved her head helplessly from side to side. 'I—we—I can't,' she got out jerkily, but Reed wasn't listening to her. With an infinitely sensual flattening of his mouth, his hands had moved to cup her breasts, and when his thumbs grazed the dusky nipples they offered themselves eagerly to his caress.

'Oh, love,' he breathed, not quite coherently, and her heart missed a beat. 'Touch me,' he added, drawing her hands towards him, and although she wanted to look anywhere else her eyes were drawn to the unmistakable arousal of his body.

But, even so, she hesitated. This was all so new to her, and standing here, naked, in the hallway of her home, was still too unnatural to be borne.

'We—we should lock the door,' she said inanely, dipping her legs, as if to bend and pick up her bathrobe, and then thinking better of it. 'Some—someone might call.'

'Oh, yes.' Reed's eyes, dark with desire, seemed unwilling to leave hers, but he turned automatically, and dropped the latch she had set to stay open. Then, when she still made no move to touch him, he unbuttoned his own shirt and tore it off his shoulders, dropping it on the floor beside her bathrobe and his jacket. Stepping over all of them, he lifted her into his arms and walked into the living-room.

'I want you,' he said, and she had no doubt that he meant what he said. And she wanted him too, she thought unsteadily. But how could she tell him that, since he had made love to her, there had been no one else? That for all she had a nine-year-old daughter, she still felt as inexperienced as she had that night ten years ago?

He found the bedroom easily enough. It wasn't difficult. There was only one bedroom, which she shared with Alexa. His lips twisted a little wryly when he saw the two narrow single beds, and for a moment Helen knew a renewed sense of panic. She shouldn't be doing this, she thought restively. If she allowed this to happen now, she would never be able to sleep here again without thinking what she had done, and for a second she struggled in his arms.

But then he laid her on the bed, unknowingly choosing her bed of the two, and she was lost. When he unbuckled the belt of his denims and stepped out of them, before coming down beside her, she no longer had the strength to resist him. His lean body was too desirable, too attractive, too familiar and the brush of his hair-roughened skin against hers was unbelievably voluptuous.

She didn't need him to tell her to touch him now. She couldn't keep her hands off him, and when his mouth found hers again she wound her arms around his waist and slipped her fingers under the waistband of his silk underpants.

His buttocks were taut and smooth, like the rest of him, she thought sensuously, peeling off the pants with unsteady fingers. And he let her. He let her do anything she wanted, and only when his throbbing masculinity sprang into her hands did he utter a groan of protest.

His mouth left hers then, and moved down over her body. He found the fullness of her breasts, and took one engorged nipple between his teeth. He bit it tenderly, taking care not to hurt her, and she moaned helplessly beneath that sensual ravishment. Her hands gripped his shoulders as he moved to tease her other breast, her nails digging into his flesh and unknowingly breaking the skin.

With a smile of satisfaction, Reed moved lower. He laved her navel with his tongue, wetting the tiny cavity fully, before trailing a line of sweet agony down to the cluster of fiery curls that nestled at the juncture of her legs. His caresses brought a drenching surge of dampness to her thighs, and her legs parted instinctively, before she clamped them tightly together again.

She felt as if her body were on fire, and yet she wasn't prepared to give in. The blood was coursing through her veins, and she could hardly hear for its thundering pressure in her ears, but still she trembled. She ached for Reed to take her, but she was still naïvely hesitant, and, as if sensing her withdrawal, he moved back to her mouth.

He was on top of her now, his weight pressing her down into the mattress. His tongue played with her lips, inviting hers to join him, and when she tentatively sent it forward he sucked on its sensitive tip.

She responded then, reacting almost involuntarily, winding her arms around his neck and anchoring his lips to hers. She couldn't get enough of his kisses, of the shamelessly erotic possession of his mouth, but when she wrapped one leg around him, too, Reed pressed down on the pillow beside her head and forced himself away from her.

'Helen, Helen,' he groaned, his eyes glazed and dark with passion, 'I have only so much self-restraint. I'm trying to be patient, but you're not making it easy. Don't do what you're doing, unless you want me to lose control!'

Helen gazed up at him, her lips parted and glistening from his kiss. She found she quite liked the idea that she could make Reed lose control, and her hands slid along his narrow cheekbones, until her fingers were level with his mouth.

'Perhaps—perhaps I want you to lose control,' she whispered, examining the thought, and finding it incredibly appealing. Her eyes darkened, and she parted his lips with tentative fingers, allowing their tips to enter his mouth. 'I think perhaps I want that very much,' she added, barely audibly, and Reed closed his eyes against her artless provocation.

He bent his head, and buried his face between her breasts, and Helen's hands slid naturally into his hair. It was clean, and silky soft, and slightly moist—like his skin, she thought, with some satisfaction—and, giving in to her emotions, she allowed her legs to part.

His thigh was between hers now, the blunt shaft of his manhood nudging her woman's core. And Reed, who was not immune to the intimacy, said, 'Oh—God!' in a strangled voice.

Then, unable to prevent himself, he pressed into that sweet honeycomb. But, as her muscles expanded to let him in, and he sensed how tight she was, he uttered a

disbelieving groan. There was no hiding the fact that it
had been years since any man had touched her there,
and Reed's brows descended as he gazed into her anxious
face.

But then it was too late for questions. Her warm,
yielding flesh was all too desirable, and Reed was already
beyond the point of no return. With a tender urgency,
he brought her to a shattering fulfilment, seconds later
succumbing to his own shuddering climax...

Some minutes afterwards, Helen opened her eyes. As
her temperature subsided, the air felt cool against her
damp flesh, but it wasn't just that which had disturbed
her. She had been drifting, still rapt in the pleasures of
her senses, drugged in the aftermath of Reed's love-
making, and reluctant to admit the waiting world. She
hadn't wanted to open her eyes. She hadn't wanted to
come down to earth. And, most of all, she hadn't wanted
to think about the reasons that had brought Reed to
London, or consider a future based on the mistakes of
the past. She wanted to live in the present. She wanted
to hold this moment close, for as long as he would let
her. To pretend he really loved her, without any strings
attached.

But Reed was not so unwilling to get on with the rest
of his life. She realised his moving had disturbed her,
and although all he had done was rest his elbows at either
side of her head, and push himself a bare few inches
away from her, it was enough. He was looking down at
her now, his eyes narrowed, and his expression one of
searching appraisal. She guessed what was coming before
he spoke, and her lids dropped to hide her eyes from
the expected condemnation in his gaze.

But all he said was, 'I'm sorry,' and her eyes darted
upwards disbelievingly. 'I thought—oh, I don't know
what I thought,' he continued softly, stroking her cheek
with the knuckles of his hand. 'I guess I found it difficult to believe you, when you said there'd only been
one other man in your life. But now I have to.' He bent
his head, and touched her nose with his lips. 'It's been
a long time, hasn't it? I hope it was as good for you as
it was for me.'

Helen drew an unsteady breath. 'Another man?' she said, echoing his words because her brain refused to concentrate. What other man was he talking about? He couldn't mean Jon, unless he hadn't believed her.

'Your daughter. Alexa—is that right? Alexa's father,' prompted Reed, grazing her cheek with the roughening stubble of his beard. 'I know you don't want to talk about it, but I want you to know that I'm sorry I ever doubted you. I didn't mean to hurt you, but when you love someone you don't always say the kindest things.'

'You—love—me?'

Helen could hardly articulate. Her throat felt so tight, and breathing was a problem. It wasn't true. He was only saying that to get to Alexa. He didn't love her. She was only a necessary obstacle.

'Yes, I love you,' Reed repeated now, his murmur of assent silenced in her mouth. His lips moved insistently, possessively, over hers. 'Didn't I tell you before? No? Oh, well.' His mouth curved ruefully. 'You've only yourself to blame. You didn't exactly welcome me with open arms.'

Helen had to get away from him. She couldn't think straight with his thigh wedged comfortably between her legs, and his lips making a nonsense of any resistance. It would be far too easy to give in, while his male beauty was seducing her senses. Right now, she would have promised him anything, just so long as he would make love to her again.

Pressing her palms against his shoulders, she pretended she couldn't breathe—which wasn't that far from the truth. And, although he was obviously reluctant, Reed rolled obediently on to his side. The narrowness of the bed didn't make scrambling off it any easier. In her haste to get away from him, she ended on the floor.

'Hey——'

He rolled across the bed to help her, but she quickly backed away from him. The rough twist of the carpet was abrasive against her bottom and thighs, but it was more dignified than crawling away from him, and the inevitable picture that evoked in her mind.

'Helen!'

He sat up now, shamelessly indifferent to his own nudity, and apparently bewildered by her withdrawal. If she hadn't known better, she would have said he didn't know what was happening, and she had to drag her gaze away from him, before she gave in once again.

The towelling bathrobe was still lying in the hallway of the apartment, but the towel she had used earlier was closer to hand. It was still damp, and it felt clammy as she wrapped it around her, but at least it made her look decent, even if she didn't feel any better.

'What's going on?'

Reed's voice was puzzled, and Helen thought, inconsequently, what a good actor he was. Anyone listening to him would be inclined to believe he was totally in the dark, and she wondered why he kept it up when she had evidently guessed what he was doing.

'We—we have to talk,' she said, choosing the least original opening she could think of. 'How—how did you find out? Did—did Jon guess the truth?'

Reed frowned. 'I don't know exactly what truth you're talking about,' he said, 'but yes. I have talked to Jon. He gave me your address, as a matter of fact. Though when I came first you weren't here.'

Helen tucked the towel more securely beneath her arms, and perched rather awkwardly against the dressing-table. She was intensely aware that the towel barely came to the tops of her thighs, and while it was silly being coy now, when he had seen and touched every part of her body, the situation was such that she couldn't relax.

And, as if sensing this, Reed slid his legs over the side of the bed. But when he would have moved towards her she edged away, and although she guessed he was getting impatient he stayed where he was, and waited for her to continue.

'Why—why did you speak to Jon?' she asked now, and Reed heaved a weary sigh.

'Why do you think?' he demanded. 'Because I needed to know that whatever had been between you two was over. God, when you left the island like that, I didn't know what to think.'

Helen swallowed. 'I told you——'

'I know what you told me,' said Reed, with rather less
control. He picked up the denim trousers he had discarded earlier, and ignoring the fact that he was not
wearing his underpants he thrust his legs into them.
Standing up, he fastened the button at his waist. Then,
with a muscle of his jaw jerking revealingly, he turned
to face her. 'The thing is,' he added unsteadily, '*I* needed
to see you again. I've never felt this way about any
woman before, not even Jon's mother, believe it or not.
And, although it's taken me the better part of three weeks
to get here, you have to remember I'm a little old to risk
this kind of rejection.'

Helen stared at him then. 'It's not—rejection——'

'Isn't it?' Reed returned her stare with grim enquiry.
'It looks like it to me. You know, for a moment——'
He glanced back towards the bed, and then jerked his
gaze away again. 'For a moment there, I really thought
you cared. It shows how wrong you can be, doesn't it?
I actually thought Jon was going to be the only obstacle.'

'Jon?'

'Yes, Jon,' said Reed wearily. 'I thought he was the
only person who might stand between us. But when I
spoke to him—when I told him what had happened ten
years ago—it was strange. He was almost—sympathetic.
He genuinely seemed to—to understand, if that's the
right expression.'

Helen stiffened. 'You told Jon—everything?'

'Yes. Why not?' Reed sighed. 'Don't worry. He'd already told me that you and he were not seeing each other
any more. But naturally he was curious. Why not? It's
not every day your father makes a fool of himself over
a woman half his age.'

'I'm not half your age,' said Helen, getting up from
the dressing-table and pressing the palms of her hands
together. Somehow, none of this conversation was going
the way she had expected, and the knowledge that he
had told Jon about their association didn't make any
sense.

'Well, it feels like it,' said Reed now, running his hands
round the back of his neck, and expelling a heavy breath.
'I just wish you had let me go before—before any of—
this had happened.'

'I—let you go?' Helen breathed uneasily. 'Would—would you have gone?'

'Oh, yes.' Reed dropped his arms and levelled a look at her. 'I'd have gone,' he agreed flatly. 'I'm not a masochist. Do you honestly think I'd have risked this kind of torture?'

Helen blinked. 'But—but what about—Alexa?'

'What about Alexa?' Reed made an impatient gesture. 'I'm not an unreasonable man. I know she's your daughter, and I know she'll probably always have first place in your affections. I could live with that. For God's sake, Helen, don't tell me this has anything to do with your daughter. You're surely not afraid I'd expect you to choose between us?'

Helen was stunned. 'You—don't—know?'

'Don't know what?' Reed lifted his shoulders bewilderedly, and if there had been any doubt left in Helen's mind it was instantly dispelled. He didn't know Alexa was *his* daughter. That wasn't why he was here. He hadn't come to take her away from her mother. And, therefore, if he hadn't, it must mean he really loved her——

Helen's breathing felt suspended. But only for a moment. Even as a dizzying sense of exhilaration swept over her, she felt the first twinges of apprehension. If Reed didn't know, she would have to tell him, and the prospect of doing so filled her with alarm. How would he take it? How would he feel about her, for keeping it a secret all these years? Oh, it was easy to excuse herself, on the grounds that she hadn't known where he was. But she had never tried to find him, had even pretended to Alexa that her father was dead.

Reed was putting on his socks now, evidently deciding that her question had been totally irrelevant. He didn't understand what she was saying. His whole attitude was one of disillusion.

Realising she couldn't allow him to go on thinking she didn't care about him for a moment longer, Helen moistened her lips. 'Don't—don't go,' she said, taking an involuntary step towards him, and when he lifted his head and looked at her she added softly, 'I do love you. I—

I just had to be sure about something, that's all. Will—will you forgive me?'

The pain and indecision was wiped from his face at a stroke, and although there was still a trace of disbelief sheltering behind his lashes his reaction was such that she was left in no doubt as to his answer.

'Do you mean it?' he demanded, tossing the boot he had been holding aside, and reaching her in a few short strides. 'Dear God, Helen, don't ever do anything like that to me again!' His hands cupped her face, and he gazed down at her as if he still couldn't believe what he was hearing. 'I'm never going to let you leave me again. I don't think I could stand another separation.'

Helen let him kiss her, because she couldn't help herself. Her mouth opened beneath his, like a flower to the sun, and when his hands tugged away the towel she was powerless to resist. The last few minutes had been too painful to be borne; for her, as well as for him. She just wanted to forget them. To obliterate them from his memory.

The sound of a key turning in the lock was like a sudden douche of cold water. It had been early when she got home, and what with that, and Reed's arrival, Helen had completely forgotten the time. But now, standing in Reed's arms without a stitch of clothing on her, she realised it was late, too late to do anything but try and rectify the situation. Her mother was never going to believe that nothing had happened, but that was the least of her worries. She was more concerned about Alexa, and what she was going to think. What a way for her to meet her father! But perhaps it was not such a bad way for Reed to meet her.

'It's my mother,' she said now, drawing back from Reed reluctantly, and snatching up the dress she had worn to the office. 'She's brought Alexa,' she added, averting her eyes, and belatedly remembering the revealing heap of clothes in the hallway. Oh, well, she thought resignedly, tugging the dress over her head, and hoping her mother wouldn't notice she had nothing underneath it. It wasn't as if her mother didn't already suspect something. And if Reed meant what he said, then they had to meet sooner or later.

Reed grimaced now, but he obediently bent to pick
up his boot again, and she flashed him an adoring smile
before going out into the living-room. Better to attack
then defend, she thought, keeping the smile glued to her
face as her mother and daughter appeared in the
doorway. What was it she had once thought about being
an actress? Since meeting Reed again, she seemed to be
continually playing a part.

'Whose is this coat?' It was Alexa who spoke, holding
up Reed's leather jacket with a doubtful look on her
face. 'Is it Jon's? Is he here? I thought you said we
wouldn't be seeing him again. Has he come back?'

'No. I——' Helen was more aware of her mother's
face than her daughter's, particularly as Mrs Caldwell
was carrying her bathrobe and Reed's shirt over her arm.
There was no way she was going to bluff her mother,
she thought wryly. She didn't need a crystal ball to know
Mrs Caldwell had guessed the truth.

'You should have warned us you had a visitor, Helen,'
she said now, dropping the garments she had been
holding rather disdainfully over a chair. 'I hope we're
not intruding.'

'Of course not.'

Helen bent to give Alexa a kiss, but as she did so she
sensed, rather than heard, Reed come into the room
behind her. Straightening, she glanced round, noticing
with some relief that he had put on one of her baggy
sweaters. At least he looked presentable, she thought,
still feeling a little light-headed at the realisation that he
actually cared about her. Her appearance meanwhile
probably shouted the truth of what they had been doing
from the rooftops, she thought. And, with her hair still
damp and uncombed, her mother's words were definitely
ironic.

Reed arched a rueful brow in commiseration, and her
heart skipped at the shared intimacy. Already, some of
the strain had left his face, and she knew an exultant
sense of satisfaction.

Then Alexa, who had been watching Reed with some
curiosity, took a tentative step forward. 'I know who
you are,' she exclaimed, to Helen's, and her grand-

mother's, consternation. 'You're Jon's daddy, aren't you? You must be. You look ever so like him!'

The bottom seemed to drop out of Helen's stomach. It had never occurred to her before, but of course it was true. Jon did look like his father. But so did Alexa. The intriguing trace of resemblance had not been to Jon at all.

'God!'

She didn't have to hear the word Reed used, or interpret his sudden sucking in of breath, to know that her daughter had inadvertently betrayed the truth. There was no time now to choose her words, or shape the essence of what she had to say into some acceptable form. With those few telling sentences, Alexa had revealed her parentage, and they all stood like statues as the silence expanded.

But, once again, it was Alexa who spoke. 'What's the matter?' she asked. 'What's wrong?' And when no one made any attempt to answer her her face crumpled anxiously, and her eyes filled with tears. 'What's the matter?' she demanded again, catching her mother's hand, and then her grandmother's, begging to be re-assured. 'Why are you looking like that? I haven't done anything wrong. He does look like Jon. He does! Why are you all so cross?'

'They're not cross with you.' It was Reed who answered her, crossing the floor between them, and squatting on his haunches in front of her so their eyes were on a level. 'It's just that your mother and your grandmother are embarrassed because I'm here. But don't worry.' He straightened and looked down at her. 'I'm going.'

'You are?'

Alexa still looked weepy, and Helen, who had watched their exchange through burning eyes, felt the rush of tears behind them.

'You—you don't have to go,' she burst out tremulously, but the face Reed turned in her direction was cold and accusing.

'Oh, I think I do,' he told her harshly, picking up his shirt and jacket, and walking towards the door. 'Goodbye, Alexa,' he added, with a bitter-sweet smile for the child, and, nodding in Mrs Caldwell's direction, he left the apartment.

CHAPTER FIFTEEN

IT WAS after ten o'clock when the buzzer sounded again.

Somehow, Helen didn't quite know how, she had prepared Alexa's evening meal, sat with her while she ate it, and got her to bed. The little girl usually went at nine o'clock on a Friday, after the silly situation comedy she always found so amusing. But tonight Alexa had offered no objections when her mother put her in the bath at eight o'clock, instead of eight-thirty, and she had given Helen an extra-long hug, as if sensing that, whatever her mother said, something was seriously wrong.

Mrs Caldwell had left shortly after Reed. She and her daughter had had a short but succinct conversation, during which Helen had given her mother a brief résumé of what had happened, both on the island and after. And, although Helen guessed she would have liked to make a comment, her mother seemed to have known that this was no time to make judgements. Indeed, she had been more concerned about Helen's state of mind, and she had phoned later in the evening to assure herself that all was well.

From Helen's point of view, everything that had happened since her mother's and Alexa's arrival had been a disaster. She should have told him, she kept telling herself over and over again. As soon as he had said he loved her, she should have told him about Alexa. Not allowed him to find out from the innocent lips of the child.

Of course, she conceded painfully, there was a school of thought that pointed to the fact that she ought to have informed him sooner. If not ten years sooner, then certainly several weeks. But how could she have come out with something like that? And what if he hadn't believed her?

No, she consoled herself firmly, there was no way she could have told him before today. It had been too long.

Too many things had happened. And, aside from anything else, she had Alexa's feelings to consider. She couldn't treat her daughter like some inanimate object.

All the same, remembering how Reed had reacted to the little girl she felt a stabbing regret. If only things had been different, she thought. Ironically, if Reed hadn't been Alexa's father, he would be here with her now. But, for all her agony, she wasn't sorry for the relationship. It was because she was Reed's child that Alexa was so precious.

It was late when the buzzer sounded. Fourteen minutes past ten, and too late for any casual caller. Of course it could be a wrong number, she thought without conviction, getting to her feet. But if it was Reed, she had no choice but to let him in.

Thankfully she was still dressed, she thought, looking down at her cotton vest and well-worn jeans. Not the kind of outfit she would have chosen to wear, if she had even suspected he might come back. But at least she looked respectable, if a little puffy-cheeked. But what could she expect, when she had spent the last hour and a half, since Alexa went to bed, weeping?

She hurried into the hall, before he could sound the buzzer again. The noise was penetrating, as she knew from experience, and the last thing she wanted to do was wake Alexa now.

'Hello?' she said, picking up the receiver, and this time she had to wait for a response.

'It's me,' he said, after a daunting interlude. 'Are you going to let me in? Or do I bluff one of your neighbours, as I did this afternoon?'

Helen didn't answer. She just pressed the button that released the door downstairs. Then she disconnected the chain from the door and lifted the latch, leaving it ajar, before going back into the living-room.

She had had the television on, not really watching it, but hoping that, if Alexa did wake, she would hear it and not her mother crying. But now she turned it off, pushing her hands into the front pockets of her jeans as she straightened.

She heard him come into the hall of the apartment, and close the door. There was the infinitesimal pause while he crossed the hall to the living-room door. Then he was standing in the open doorway, wearing his shirt and the leather jacket now, and carrying her sweater in his hand.

She didn't know how she had expected him to act. After the way he had looked at her that afternoon, she had been prepared for anger, passion, bitterness and resentment, or any permutation in between. She wasn't afraid of him. She knew enough about him now not to nurture useless emotions of that kind. But the very fact that he had come back said something, and after the way he had left her she had to be on her guard.

He leaned against the frame of the door for a moment, and, although her intention had not been to plead with him, she couldn't help the desperation in her face. She was at the end of her tether. He held all the cards now, both literally and metaphorically, and no one could deny his right to see Alexa, as seldom or as often as he wished.

Her instinct was to stare at him, but she forced herself not to do so. Apart from a single, searching glance, she kept her gaze riveted to the floor at her feet. She didn't know what he was thinking. He was far more expert than she was at keeping his feelings hidden. But at least the frozen look had left his face, and his eyes weren't accusing her any more.

'Aren't you going to ask why I've come?' he suggested at last, his voice low and perfectly controlled. If he did have something to say, he wasn't going to hurry into it, and Helen's nerves tightened as she tried to match his mood.

'Why—why have you come?' she enquired obediently, permitting herself another glance in his direction. She thought she could be casual about it, but the sight of him standing there, so remote and unapproachable, tore her to pieces. Oh, God, she thought despairingly, she needed him so much.

'I wanted to return the sweater,' Reed said, tossing the woollen garment on to a chair. 'Thanks for allowing me to borrow it.'

Helen could have said she hadn't had much choice— but that brought back too many painful memories, so she merely shrugged. 'You—you're welcome,' she replied, wishing she didn't stammer all the time. But with his cool grey gaze upon her, she found it difficult to be calm.

'Am I?' Reed chose to take her words literally. 'I have to say that you surprise me. I get the impression I'm not welcome here at all.'

'That's not true!' The words burst from her, despite her futile attempt to appear detached. 'That's—not—true,' she said again, framing her words carefully this time. 'No one—no one asked you to leave.'

'Like hell!' She tensed, as he straightened away from the door. 'What was I supposed to do? Accept the fact that you'd been lying to me all these weeks with equanimity?'

'I——' Helen's throat felt constricted. 'I haven't been lying to you.'

'No.' Reed's mouth compressed. 'Literally, I suppose, you haven't. I never asked the right questions, so you never gave the right answers.'

'It wasn't like that——'

'What was it like, then?' Reed stared at her bleakly, and for the first time she glimpsed a little of his true feelings. 'Helen, this is my daughter we're talking about, for God's sake! Didn't I deserve to know? Were you ever going to tell me?'

Helen trembled. 'Yes——'

'When?' He ran a hand that shook a little across his jaw, and she noticed he had shaved during his absence. Not very expertly however. There were nicks and scratches all over his face. It made him seem so much more vulnerable, and she wanted to ease his pain.

'I—was going to tell you today,' she said steadily. And when he would have interrupted her she went on, 'I was. It's the truth. But you have to see it from my side. It may be hard to believe, but—I was afraid.'

'Afraid?' Reed stared at her disbelievingly. 'What did you have to be afraid of?'

'You,' said Helen simply, standing her ground. 'I—I thought you might—take her away from me. You still might. I'm sure you can.'

Reed gaped at her. There was no other way to describe his expression. And then, dragging his scattered wits

together with an effort, he shook his head. 'When,' he
said, 'when have I ever done anything to make you think
I'd do a thing like that? God,' he closed his eyes, 'and
I thought what we had was real.'

Helen's jaw quivered. 'It was real. It *is* real,' she whispered, twisting her hands together. 'Oh, God! how can
you doubt it? When you walked out of here this afternoon, I wanted to die!'

Reed opened his eyes. 'You wanted to die,' he said
harshly. 'And I wanted to kill you. I thought I'd never
forgive you. But—as you see—I just couldn't keep away.'

Helen blinked. 'You mean—you didn't just come back
because of—Alexa?'

'Hell!' Reed left the door, and in two strides he had
reached her, his hands gripping her arms above the
elbow, jerking her up on her toes. 'That's some opinion
you've got of me,' he snarled. 'Isn't it? If all I'd wanted
to do was assert my right to see Alexa, I'd have had my
lawyer draw up the papers. That's what I pay him for.
And he leaves making a fool of myself to me!'

'Oh——' Helen couldn't go on. The scalding tears that
had been threatening ever since he came through the door
wouldn't let her. They ran down her cheeks and dripped
on to her vest, leaving dark smudges on the fabric.

'Don't cry!' Reed's anguished response to her distress
only made the tears run even faster, and with a muffled
groan he gathered her into his arms. 'Don't cry,' he said
again, cradling her close, and burying his face in her
hair. 'Dear God, I didn't mean to hurt you. I just get
so mad, when you won't see the truth. The only reason
I came back is *you*! To find out if there's any possibility
of us having a future together.'

Helen sniffed helplessly, aware of the damp patch on
Reed's shirt beneath her cheek. But she couldn't believe
this was really happening. That, after all her fears, their
love might stand a chance.

Sensing she was making an effort to control her tears,
Reed drew back a little from her, and rested his forehead
against hers. 'You know,' he said, capturing one salty
droplet on his tongue and savouring the intimacy, 'I
haven't known a moment's peace since you left the
island. If you do decide to marry me, it will be quite a

novelty to sleep nights again. Or maybe not,' he teased engagingly. 'But I'd sure as hell enjoy finding out.'

Helen lifted misty eyes to his face. 'You're—you're asking me to marry you?'

'Mmm.' Reed scowled suddenly. 'You're not going to cry again, are you?'

Helen gave him a watery smile. 'Just a little, perhaps.'

'Why?' Reed tried to sound careless of her answer, but there was an element of anxiety in his words. 'You're not going to turn me down?'

Helen sniffed, and then shook her head. 'No.'

'No, what?' Reed had to be precise. 'No—you won't marry me, or no, you're not turning me down?'

Helen would have liked to tease him a little now, but the tension in his expression disarmed her completely. 'No,' she said tremulously, cupping his face in her hands. 'No, I'm not turning you down. I love you.' She took a trembling breath. 'So very, very much.'

He pulled her closer then, his mouth finding hers with undisguised relief. The agony of the last few hours was fragmented by his touch, and with the barriers between them tumbling a sweet sense of abandon entered his kiss.

But Helen was ever vigilant of Alexa, in the next room, able to wake at any time and come and see what was going on. And, although she hoped their daughter was going to get used to seeing her mother and father together, the idea of her finding them, perhaps half naked on the couch, was enough to make her protest when Reed's hand slid beneath the hem of her vest.

'OK, OK, I know,' he whispered huskily, closing his eyes to subdue the urgent clamour of his senses. 'We can't do anything here, because Alexa's just next door. I appreciate that. But just give me a minute to absorb it. The spirit's willing, but the flesh is weak.'

Helen's lips parted. 'Yes,' she said ruefully. 'I can feel that.' She pressed herself closer for a moment, just to enjoy the sense of satisfaction it gave her. Then, when he gave her a wounded look, she took pity on him, bestowing a brief but sympathetic kiss on his mouth, before pulling away.

'I'll make some coffee, hmm?' she suggested, hovering in the doorway to the tiny kitchen, and after a brief pause Reed nodded.

'Yes. Let's have some coffee,' he said, throwing his jacket over the back of a chair, and flinging himself down on to the sofa. 'Make mine black,' he added, looking up at her through his lashes. 'And preferably decaffeinated, if you've got it. I don't need any more stimulus in my system.'

When she came back he was stretched out on the sofa, his eyes closed. She thought for a moment that he was asleep, but when she set his mug of coffee on the low table near by he opened his eyes.

'Sit here,' he said, shifting across the cushions so that she could sit beside him. And, when she did so, he reached up and put his hand behind her head, and kissed her, very thoroughly. 'Just to reassure myself that you're real,' he said, letting go of her reluctantly, and flopping back against the cushions. 'Do you have any idea how much I want you—right at this moment?' He picked up her hand, and took each of her fingers in turn into his mouth. Then he bit her little finger hard, and smiled when she gasped in protest. 'It serves you right,' he said unfeelingly. 'You put me through hell!'

'I put you through hell!' echoed Helen, indignantly, but there was a tender curve to her mouth. 'It wasn't all my fault, you know,' she added. 'You let me leave the island without ever telling me how you felt.'

'I thought I made a pretty fair job of it when I found you down at the rocks,' declared Reed drily, but Helen shook her head.

'You never said you cared for me. I—I just thought it was a—a sexual thing.'

'Well, it's that, too,' admitted Reed ruefully. 'But so much more besides. You should ask Vee. I think I've left her in no doubt as to my feelings.'

'Vee—I mean, Victoria?' Helen frowned. 'What do you mean?'

'Well—I have to admit I got pretty drunk, after you and Jon had left for the airport. Stinking drunk, as it happens. I told Vee she was to blame for you leaving, and then I tore down some of those damned paintings of hers, and threw them into the Sound.'

'You didn't!' Helen was horrified.

'Oh, I did.' Reed regarded her unashamedly. 'In fact if she hadn't been so worried about Styles going off to New York without her, I think she'd have called the police, and had me arrested.'

'Could she do that?'

'Well, she could have tried,' said Reed wryly. 'But, instead of that, she told me I was a fool, and a philistine, or words to that effect, and took herself off to New York on the next available flight.'

Helen gasped. 'Has she come back?'

'Oh, yes.' Reed grimaced. 'A couple of days later. With Styles. But—it seems possible that he may decide to move to the States permanently and Vee's already wondering where she should buy a house.'

Helen stared at him. 'She's actually considering leaving Palmer's Sound?'

'Mmm.' Reed shrugged. 'She's no fool, you know. She could already see the writing on the wall.'

Helen moistened her lips. 'Because of me?'

'Because of you.'

'But—how——?'

'Look, I got the biggest shock of my life when Jon said he was taking you back to London. She knew that. I guess she knew it was only a matter of time before I came after you.'

Helen bent her head. 'And—what did Jon say?'

'When? Today? Or then?'

Helen lifted her shoulders. 'Then, I suppose.'

Reed sighed. 'OK,' he said. 'I guess this is as safe a way to spend the night as any.' His features grew a little harder. 'He let me think you were as eager to leave as he was.'

'Well, I was.' Helen had to be honest, however painful it might be. But, conscious of his puzzled expression, she hurried on, 'I thought you'd be glad we were leaving. And—after what had happened, I—wanted to get away.'

'Why?' Reed slid his fingers up into her hair, and wound a handful of its silky radiance round them. 'Surely you knew what I would think, when you left with Jon.'

'Well, yes. That's true.' Helen nodded. 'But—I have some pride, you know. Or I did,' she added ruefully. 'And I thought you—just—wanted me.'

Reed's eyes darkened. 'I do.'

'In a sexual way, I mean.'

'So do I.'

But he was teasing her, and Helen gripped his thigh and squeezed hard. 'Anyway,' she went on, letting him prise her fingers free and retain his hold on them, 'I needed to put some space between us. I knew, if I stayed, it was only a matter of time before—before——'

'Go on,' he prompted huskily.

'You know what I'm trying to say. As I said before, I knew you were attracted to me——'

'—and you were afraid I might try and make love to you?'

'No. I was afraid I might let you,' admitted Helen honestly. 'And—and I had Alexa to consider. I could see no way of ever telling you that.'

'Ah.' Reed nodded now levering himself up on one elbow, and reaching for his coffee. He took a mouthful, savoured it, and then shook his head. 'My daughter! God, I still find it hard to believe.'

Helen trembled. 'But—you do believe it?'

Reed gave her an old-fashioned look, and then, putting his coffee back on the table, he pulled her down on top of him. 'Don't ask me that again,' he told her gently, tracing the outline of her lips with a reproving finger. 'I don't just *believe* she's mine. I know it. I wish I'd made more of an effort to find you ten years ago.'

Helen bit his finger. 'So do I.'

'Mmm.' Reed watched her with an indulgent look on his face. 'Well, I guess I had my pride, too, you know.'

'What do you mean?'

'Well, you had left the hotel without even saying goodbye. I mean, when I got back to London, and found you weren't working at the wine bar, I began to wonder if you'd left because of me.'

Now it was Helen's turn to tease. 'I had.'

'I know that.' Reed gave a humorous grimace. 'But, joking aside, I didn't find it very amusing. I mean, I had been feeling pretty rotten about the whole affair.

Responsible, I guess. I'd wanted to see you again, to prove to you that I hadn't intended what happened to happen. Besides, I really did want to see you again. But——' he sighed '—you weren't around, and I got to thinking it was probably just as well. That you were too young for me anyway. Which was true,' he added, in an aside. 'And, well, I guess I was pretty cynical, at that time.'

'Diana?' asked Helen softly, and he nodded.

'But tell me about you,' he said, his eyes clouding at the recollection. 'How did you manage? I guess you went home to Mama, hmm? That was your mother I met so briefly this afternoon, wasn't it?'

Now Helen sighed, sliding her fingers into the neckline of his shirt, and noting their contrast to his dark flesh almost inconsequentially. 'Well,' she said, not relishing the answer to this particular question. 'I had lied to you, you see. I wasn't living in a bed-sit. I was living at home.'

'I see.' Reed frowned. 'No wonder you looked so sick when I suggested going back for coffee.'

'Do you remember that?' Helen shook her head, and opened another button of his shirt, pressing her lips to the base of his throat. 'Well, I—I was only sixteen.'

'Sixteen!' Reed, who had closed his eyes when she began her tantalising exploration, opened them abruptly. 'My God! Why didn't you tell me?'

'To avoid this kind of reaction,' she told him mildly, opening yet another button, and brushing her lips against the fine hair on his chest. 'I knew you thought I was older, and—I wanted you to go on thinking it. You made me feel—like a woman.' She smiled. 'I liked that.'

'But, sixteen,' groaned Reed disbelievingly. 'My God, I can imagine what your parents thought of me.'

'I didn't tell them who Alexa's father was,' said Helen simply. 'Not until years later, as a matter of fact. I knew my father would try to find you, and—and I didn't want you to know.'

'Why not?'

Reed stared at her blankly now, and Helen averted her eyes from his taut expression. 'I thought—oh, I don't know. I didn't want you to feel—responsible for me. I suppose I was afraid you were married——'

'Oh, God!'

'—and I couldn't have borne knowing that.'

'Oh, Helen!' He shifted then, rolling over and taking her with him, so that their positions were reversed. 'If only I'd known,' he muttered, burying his face in the hollow of her neck. 'I deserved to feel responsible. It was *my* fault. I knew what I was doing, but I went ahead anyway. My only excuse is that it wasn't just the sake that intoxicated me.'

Helen wound her arms around his neck. 'It doesn't matter now.'

'It does matter. Apart from the fact that you've had to bring Alexa up as a single mother, I've lost the first nine years of my daughter's life.'

'Well—we could have another baby,' suggested Helen softly. 'I'm sure Alexa wouldn't mind.'

'Wouldn't she?' Reed lifted his head to look down at her. 'I wonder how she's going to react to the fact that she's going to have *two* parents. I hope she won't be too disappointed that I'm going to be her father, and not Jon.'

'Well...' Helen was rueful. 'It's going to be quite a surprise to her. I—I told her her father was dead.' She flushed. 'It seemed the easiest way.'

'I see.' But Reed didn't sound too distraught. 'Oh, well, I guess that's better than telling her I deserted you.' He grimaced. 'And maybe Jon has done me a favour after all.'

'How?' Helen shivered as Reed's hand slid down her body to cup her bottom, adjusting his body to hers, even though their clothes represented an impenetrable barrier.

'Well,' his voice was not quite steady either, 'he's obviously made a friend of Alexa. She might like the idea of being his sister, if nothing else.'

Helen bit her lip. 'He's going to hate me, isn't he? When he finds out about Alexa.'

'I think he knows already,' said Reed drily, withdrawing his gaze with some reluctance from the taut peaks outlined beneath the cotton vest. 'I told you he gave me your address, didn't I? Well, I've been thinking about what he said, and I think he's guessed the truth.'

'What do you mean?'

'Well—little by little, he has learned the facts, hasn't he? He knew you had had a baby nine years ago. OK, that's not such a unique event on its own. But ally to that the fact that he saw us together; that he knows, as of this afternoon, exactly when we knew one another before. He's not a fool, Helen. And——' his lips tightened '—he must know you don't sleep around.'

'Mmm.' Helen shifted so that he could slide one of his legs between hers. 'Jon and I never had that kind of a relationship. In some ways, it was almost platonic. I hope he won't mind too much.'

'So do I,' said Reed huskily, 'but, right now, it doesn't seem to matter. So long as we're together, that's what counts.'

Helen thought later that it was just as well the door into the bedroom needed oiling. Without its betraying squeak, she and Reed might just have remained unaware that they were no longer alone. As it was, the door creaked, and Reed groaned almost simultaneously, but Helen managed to push him off her and pull down her vest before Alexa reached the sofa.

'I can't sleep, Mummy——' she was beginning, before she realised her mother was not alone.

She frowned then, and Helen, caught in the act of scrambling off the sofa, cast a rueful look down at Reed. It seemed they were fated to spend their time explaining their way out of awkward situations, and he closed his eyes in sympathy, before pushing himself up from the cushions.

'What're you doing?' Alexa asked now, blinking and gazing at Reed with none of her usual good humour. She was evidently not as pleased to see him now as she had been earlier, and her jaw clenched belligerently. In her striped nightshirt, with her blonde curls tousled, she had a decidedly sulky expression, and Helen didn't know what to say to normalise the situation.

'Your Mummy and I have been talking,' Reed intervened abruptly. 'I'm sorry if we disturbed you, but we've known each other for a long, long time, and we had a lot to say.'

Alexa pouted. 'You didn't 'sturb me,' she told him shortly. And then, to her mother, 'Why didn't you tell me he was coming?'

'I didn't know——' began Helen unequivocally, and then shook her head helplessly as Reed caught her eye.

'It's my fault,' he said, attracting Alexa's attention again. 'I didn't tell your mother I was coming back. Don't blame her; blame me. My shoulders are quite a bit broader than hers.'

Alexa regarded him doubtfully for a moment, and then returned her gaze to her mother. 'But when are you coming to bed?' she demanded plaintively. 'It's awfully late.'

'I know.' Helen sighed. 'But—but as—Jon's daddy says, we have had a lot to talk about.'

'A lot of it about you,' put in Reed quietly, and they both looked at him as he got to his feet.

'About me?' Alexa looked puzzled at first, and then, as if remembering their reaction to what she had said that afternoon, she added, 'I didn't do anything wrong. You said so.'

'And it's true,' said Reed gently. He smiled. 'And if you're worried about what happened this afternoon, let me explain. I was just—surprised to see you, that's all. I didn't know you were so—pretty. Or what a big girl you were.'

Alexa looked sceptical. 'I'm not pretty,' she said scornfully. 'Grandad says I'm too much of a tomboy.'

'Well, I think you're pretty,' said Reed firmly. 'And smart, too. You knew I was Jon's daddy, after all.'

'Hmm.' Alexa was looking a little more interested now, but it was soon apparent where her interest lay. 'Am I really pretty?' she asked, with the age-old vanity of the coquette. 'Really?'

'Yes, really,' Reed assured her, ignoring the resigned look her mother was giving him. 'And tomorrow, the three of us are going to go out and buy you the prettiest dress we can find. Then we might all have lunch together at my hotel. Would you like that?'

Alexa hesitated, and looked at her mother. 'Can we?' she asked anxiously, and Helen felt the momentary press of tears. Her daughter was not used to treats of this kind.

Money had never been that freely available, and Alexa knew that as well as she did.

'If you'd like to,' she said now, and she saw the way the little girl's face lit up.

'I'd like to—very much,' said Alexa politely, turning back to Reed with a smile, and Helen could tell from his expression that he was as relieved as she was.

It was going to be all right, she thought, feeling his fingers slide briefly between hers, before he spoke to Alexa again. Not that she imagined that a shopping spree, and lunch at a grand hotel, would solve their problems. They had a much longer way to go than that, and for all her apparent acquiescence Alexa could still prove difficult. But they had all the time in the world to get it right; and they would, she was sure of it . . .

Some months later, Helen came into the bathroom of the house her husband had bought in Eaton Square, and perched on the side of the bath. Reed was soaking in the sunken bath, his silvery blonde hair damp and tousled, his lashes, with their sun-bleached tips, dark against his cheekbones. He looked well, and handsome, thought Helen with satisfaction before he opened his eyes, the months since their wedding putting flesh on his bones and removing much of the strain from his face.

'Mmm, do that again,' he murmured, when she leant across and bestowed a lingering kiss on his lips. 'And again.'

Helen gave a soft laugh. 'No,' she said, as he opened his eyes. 'I want to talk to you.'

'That sounds ominous.' Reed pulled a face. 'I thought you just went to take Alexa to your mother's.'

'I did.'

Reed had bought the house in Eaton Square so that they were able to divide their time between London and Bermuda. It meant Alexa saw plenty of her grandparents, and they, in their turn, had already been out to the island for a long, relaxing holiday. It also meant they saw Jon, too. Oddly enough, he had adjusted to the idea of Helen as his stepmother almost as well as Alexa had to him becoming her brother.

Helen thought it was because she and Reed were so happy together. She was sure that was why her parents had accepted the idea of Reed as their son-in-law without too many reservations. And Reed had considered their feelings a lot. He had shown an amazing amount of patience with them, and with Alexa, who was slowly adapting to the idea that Reed was her new daddy. Of course, the physical aspects of the relationship had yet to be explained to her, but that would come in time, and meanwhile she had accepted him as part of the family. And why not? Helen thought, in her more cynical moments. Alexa's life had changed almost as much as her own had, and there was no doubt she enjoyed all the love and attention.

But now Reed squinted up at her, and said, 'Well? Everything's OK, isn't it?'

'Oh, yes.' Helen smoothed the hair back from his forehead with a caressing finger. 'Are you coming out of here?'

'Why?' Reed caught her hand in soapy fingers, and dipped it into the water. 'Why don't you come in?'

Helen's pulses reacted automatically to his touch, but she pulled away. 'I can't.'

'Why can't you?'

Helen smiled. 'I told you, I want to talk to you.'

'We can talk in here,' said Reed reasonably, but Helen shook her head.

'I've taken baths with you before, remember?' she told him huskily. 'And we don't do a lot of talking.'

'OK.'

Reed shrugged, and before she could get out of his way he got up, dripping water all over her. Then, taking the towel she passed him, he made a moderate job of drying himself, before stepping out of the bath.

'So?' he said.

'You're not dry,' she protested, taking the towel from him and using it on his chest and stomach, but Reed took it from her and tossed it aside.

'I thought you wanted to talk,' he reminded her huskily. 'You're not exactly going the right away about it.'

'Oh——' He could still make her blush, and Helen snatched up his bathrobe and gave it to him. 'Put that on, then, and come into the bedroom,' she exclaimed.

In their bedroom, she turned to face him. 'I'm— pregnant,' she said abruptly. She twisted her hands together. 'Does it matter?'

Reed stared at her. 'Does it matter to you?' he asked, after a moment, his tone guarded.

Helen shook her head. 'Only—only if you're—not happy about it.'

Reed blinked. 'If *I'm* not happy about it?'

'Well——' She spread her hands. 'What's Jon going to say? We've only been married four months.'

'To hell with Jon,' said Reed impatiently, reaching for her, and enfolding her in his embrace. 'My God! I thought you were upset about it, not Jon.'

'As if I would be,' Helen protested, turning her lips against his neck, and he groaned.

'As if *I* would be,' he countered, drawing back to look into her face. 'Don't you know how much I love you yet? So long as you're happy, that's all that matters.'

'Oh—I'm happy,' Helen whispered. She took his hand and pressed it against her flat stomach. 'I like the idea that part of you is growing inside me again. And this time you'll be there to share it with me.'

Reed's mouth took on a sensual curve. 'Yes, I will, won't I?' He paused. 'What about Alexa?'

'Oh, I don't think you need to worry about her,' said Helen softly. 'Just the other day she was asking me how long it took to have a baby. Apparently, one of her schoolfriends in Hamilton had been boasting about the fact that her mother had just had twins. We probably won't be able to equal that, but I don't think she'll mind.'

'She's a great kid, isn't she?' said Reed huskily.

'She's yours,' said Helen simply, and after that there wasn't much more to say.

HARLEQUIN PROUDLY PRESENTS A DAZZLING CONCEPT IN ROMANCE FICTION

 One small town,
twelve terrific love stories

JOIN US FOR A YEAR IN THE FUTURE OF TYLER

Each book set in Tyler is a self-contained love story; together,
the twelve novels stitch the fabric of the community.

LOSE YOUR HEART TO TYLER!

Join us for the second TYLER book, BRIGHT HOPES, by
Pat Warren, available in April.

*Former Olympic track star Pam Casals arrives in Tyler to
coach the high school team. Phys ed instructor Patrick
Kelsey is first resentful, then delighted. And rumors fly about
the dead body discovered at the lodge.*

Following the success of WITH THIS RING,
Harlequin cordially invites you to enjoy the
romance of the wedding season with

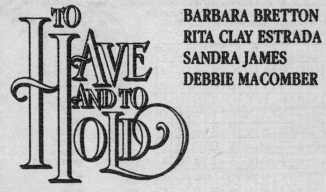

BARBARA BRETTON
RITA CLAY ESTRADA
SANDRA JAMES
DEBBIE MACOMBER

A collection of romantic stories that celebrate the joy,
excitement, and mishaps of planning that special day
by these four award-winning Harlequin authors.

**Available in April at your favorite Harlequin
retail outlets.**

THTH

ZODIAC WORD SEARCH CONTEST

You can win a year's supply of Harlequin romances ABSOLUTELY FREE! All you have to do is complete the word puzzle below and send it to us so we receive it by April 30, 1992. The first 10 properly completed entries chosen by random draw will win a year's supply of Harlequin romances (four books every month, one from each of four of the series Harlequin publishes—worth over $150.00). What could be easier?

S	E	C	S	I	P	R	I	A	M	F
I	U	L	C	A	N	C	E	R	L	I
S	A	I	N	I	M	E	G	N	S	R
C	A	P	R	I	C	O	R	N	U	E
S	E	I	R	A	N	G	I	S	I	O
Z	O	D	W	A	T	E	R	B	R	I
O	G	A	H	M	A	T	O	O	A	P
D	R	R	T	O	U	N	I	R	U	R
I	I	B	R	O	R	O	M	G	Q	O
A	V	I	A	N	U	A	N	C	A	C
C	E	L	E	O	S	T	A	R	S	S

Used with permission of D. J. Verrells.

PISCES   **ARIES**
CANCER   **GEMINI**
SCORPIO   **TAURUS**
AQUARIUS   **LIBRA**
CAPRICORN   **SAGITTARIUS**
LEO   **EARTH**
VIRGO   **STAR**
FIRE   **SIGN**
WATER   **MOON**
ZODIAC   **AIR**

HOW TO ENTER

All the words listed are hidden in the word puzzle grid. You can find them by reading the letters forward, backward, up and down, or diagonally. When you find a word, circle it or put a line through it. Don't forget to fill in your name and address in the space provided, put this page in an envelope, and mail it today to:

Harlequin Word Puzzle Contest
Harlequin Reader Service®
P.O. Box 9071
Buffalo, NY 14269-9071

NAME _____

ADDRESS _____

_____

CITY _____ STATE _____ ZIP CODE _____